The Christmas Locket

Lynette Rees

© Lynette Rees 2019
Contact Lynette:
http://www.lynetterees.com
Blogs:
https://lynetterees.wordpress.com/
http://www.nettiesramblings.blogspot.com
email: lynetterees@mail.com
Facebook author page for latest updates:
http://www.facebook.com/authorlynetterees/

Acknowledgement
to Helen Snow

Many thanks for your invaluable help and support with this book and for your fabulous title suggestion, 'The Christmas Locket'.

Dedication

This book is dedicated to my beautiful daughter, Leyna, a constant light in my life.

Chapter One

Spitalfields, Whitechapel
London 1861

Soft powdery snowflakes fell from the sky settling on her nose and eyelashes, as Bessie Harper trudged along the street. She hoped it wasn't going to stick before she returned home as she was a woman on a mission and didn't intend getting stranded for the night in this abysmal neck of the woods with its harlots and harridans.

'Ding dong merrily on high, in heaven the bells are ringing!' A man and two women jostled past her laughing and singing their hearts out in the street, obviously merry themselves after leaving one of the many pubs in the area.

It was the week before Christmas and Bessie Harper didn't feel too merry herself. As if she didn't have enough to do other than go fetch that great big lummox home before he drank the place dry. She let out a long breath into the frosty night air and sighed very loudly. Her feet were like blocks of ice and her fingers felt like they belonged to someone else so she flexed them to improve her circulation. Her old fella was in the pub again and if he didn't get himself home soon, there'd be hell to pay. But then again, she'd told herself on more than one occasion that she only had herself to blame, getting herself knocked up at such a young age to Albert Harper, a man who should have known better than to take advantage of a fifteen-year-old young slip of a thing.

Albert was already married and childless to a frump of a woman at the time, who he'd told her on more than one occasion was cold towards him. So, when she'd found him paying her plenty of attention at the inn she worked as barmaid, she had felt more than a little sorry for the man. But now as she looked back on it with her more worldly head on, and not the one she had back then as a daydreamer and an optimist, she could see he had well and truly led her on. More fit he had got himself a hot water bottle than to have taken a young girl to his bed when his wife was out working at the washhouse during the day. But warmed his bed she had and very nicely for him too and maybe things would have carried on forever and a day like that, if she hadn't got herself up the spout. Then all hell had broken loose with that revelation as Bessie had been banished from her own home by her strict, authoritarian father, and Albert had left his wife to be with her.

She tutted to herself as she marched purposefully towards the Ten Bells public house. She was just passing Itchy Park at the back of Christ Church when she heard a mewing sound. She hovered outside the wrought iron railings for a moment and peered in the distance. For once the park was empty, and gazing around her beneath the dim shadows created by the gaslights on the street outside, she expected to see a cat there, crying for someone to rescue it from the cold.

'Puss, puss!' she cried. She loved animals and couldn't bear to see one outside on such a perishing night as this, but then she heard something else. A child's cry. Surely not? So, she'd been mistaken, it hadn't been a cat but a young child she'd heard.

Rushing over in the direction of the cries, she noticed a writhing bundle on one of the benches. She knelt down to lift the bundle to see it was indeed a young child of no more than a few months old. A baby? Really? Although the baby was well wrapped in a woollen shawl, its face felt cold to the touch. She lifted the infant in her arms and cuddled it to her breast. 'There, there, now little 'un, you're quite safe with me,' she murmured as she rocked the child gently in her arms. There was plenty of life in the child at least but how long had he or she been left there? It didn't bear thinking about and on such a frosty night as this, if the baby stayed outside much longer, he or she could die from the cold.

Thinking she heard a rustle behind her, she quickly turned her head, but there was no one there.

'Hello!' she shouted out into the darkness, in the hope that some young woman would emerge from the bushes and reveal herself as having had urgent need to spend a penny, but no one came forward as the child's cries got louder and more urgent. This baby needs feeding, Bessie thought to herself.

Deciding to get some warmth, she marched quickly to the nearest place of safety— a chop house. She wasn't going to take the child in that Ten Bells with all its drunkards, harlots and harridans! No, sir.

Echoing footsteps caused her to walk on quickly as a prickle of fear coursed her spine.

Don't be daft Bess, yer scared of yer own footsteps! Not much further to go now and you and the babe will be safe.

The lights were getting closer, a few steps more and they'd be there. She half expected a hand to clamp down on her shoulder to prevent her taking the baby to safety.

Once inside the warmth of the chop house she breathed a sigh of relief and located an empty table and ordered a mug of warm milk and piece of bread and butter. In the light, she could see that the child had previously been well fed as its cheeks were rounded and slightly pink, so he or she had not been left alone for long. Its deep brown eyes were now wide and blinking as it appeared to take in its surroundings, turning its head in the direction of any unfamiliar noises and voices.

'SSSh,' she soothed as she laid the child down on the bench, swiftly breaking pieces of bread into the mug of warm milk and then, sitting the child on her lap, spoon-fed small pieces into the child's mouth. As a waitress passed by and smiled, she paused for a moment and then, returned to the table.

'Everything all right there, ma'am?' she asked. 'What an adorable child. There was one in here just like her earlier.'

'Really?' Bessie raised a thoughtful brow. 'How long ago was this?'

'Not an hour since. Why do you ask?'

'I just found this child freezing on a bench at Itchy Park, all on its own. I've no idea who he or she belongs to. Looks like they was abandoned or somethin'. Can you be sure this is the same child what was in 'ere earlier?'

The waitress drew nearer and placed her wooden tray down on the table. 'Yes, I'm almost positive of it. I recognise the little dark curl on the forehead and those long lashed brown eyes.'

Bessie gazed at the child intently and it was then she noticed for the first time the child was clutching on tightly to something in the palm of its hand. Coaxing the hand gently open, her eyes widened to see an engraved silver locket there.

'Well bless my soul, look at this?' she whispered to waitress for fear of being overheard as there were some rum sorts sitting in the booths surrounding her and if they should see it, they might well nick it for themselves.

'What is it?' The maid squinted her eyes to see.

'It's some sort of locket.'

'Open it,' the waitress urged. 'There might be a clue there. I'll take the baby for you.'

Bessie nodded and she watched as the waitress lifted the child, who now seemed to be sated from the food as it lay comfortably in the young woman's arms, resting its head on the waitress's shoulder. Bessie fingered the pretty locket in her palm. It had a filigree design on the outside and she flicked it open with her fingernail to reveal a lock of hair and a screwed-up piece of paper inside. 'What's this?' she said as much to herself as to the young girl.

''Ere you wanna open that up,' the girl said, now sitting down opposite Bessie on the facing bench with the infant on her lap.

Bessie unrolled the piece of paper and flattened it with her hand on the table, '"Take care of my baby".' She turned the locket over. 'And it's engraved with the name "Adella" on the back,' she said thoughtfully. 'Maybe that's the child's name?'

The waitress vehemently shook her head. 'No, 'tis not,' she said. 'I heard the woman being called "Adella" by someone.'

'By who?' Bessie wanted to know.

'By a man. He looked a bit older than the woman, not old enough to be her father mind. About ten years older, I'd say. I saw him press some coins into her hand.'

'What sort of gent was he?'

'A toff I'd say.'

'And Adella herself?'

'A bit dishevelled looking, but clean and she was wearing good quality clothes.'

Bessie wondered to herself why the man was giving her money. Maybe she'd promised him a good time at Itchy Park so she could put a roof over the heads of herself and her child for the night and some food in their bellies. It was the same for many young women around here and maybe the same thing would have happened to her too if Albert hadn't stood by her. Maybe she had a lot to be thankful for. Had the young woman gone behind a bush with the man leaving this young child on the bench? A shiver of fear tingled down her spine. What if Adella had gone behind a bush at Itchy Park and never came out again and was lying there with her throat cut from ear to ear? Maybe that's why the child was alone.

Wanting to know more, she asked. 'Did the man and woman leave here together?'

The waitress shook her head. 'No, ma'am. I saw him leave and hail a hansom cab outside here. A few minutes later, the woman and baby left 'ere and I don't know what happened after that 'cos I was busy.'

Bessie blew out a breath of relief. Not murdered in Itchy Park then. But what had happened to the woman to make her abandon her child like that?

'What yer going to do now?' the waitress asked as she gently bounced the child on her lap.

'I really don't know.' Bessie chewed her bottom lip. 'I could go to the police I suppose, but then what if the woman only abandoned her child for a short while and intended to go back for him or her? Wouldn't she get into trouble?'

The waitress nodded. 'She might, she might get slung in the slammer or something, or carted off to a mental institution.'

Bessie couldn't bear thinking about that. She'd once had an aunt who'd lost a young baby in child birth and had gone to a mental institution, never to return home again. The last time Bessie had laid eyes on her had been to see her rocking herself back and forth in a chair with her arms wrapped around herself, crying and wailing very loudly so that the sounds had echoed off the walls of the severe institution. She was never to see her again after that, and the family never mentioned her name ever again, either.

'No, you're right, I can't go to the police in case the mother shows up. Tell you what, I'll take the baby home with me for the night. Meanwhile, you let me know if you hear of anything like if the mother calls here to enquire or shows up at Itchy Park, you understand? I live at 15 Queen Street, write it down in case you need to, you got that?'

The girl nodded, mouth agape as she handed the infant back to Bessie.

The trouble was, what would her Albert say, when she returned home? They already had two young sons to feed as it was. But for tonight, she'd let him carry on living it up at the pub. Hopefully, by the time he got home, he'd be too drunk to even notice there was a baby under the same roof.

***

On the way home, Bessie decided to check once again at Itchy Park, but when she returned there was only an old man on the same bench where the baby had been found. 'Seen anyone come in here since you was 'ere?' she asked the man, whose head was slumped forward as he made a loud grunting sound as he stirred. It was then she realised the man was asleep. It was no use asking him as, by the smell of the beer fumes emanating from him, it was evident he was drunk. Tutting to herself, she made her way home, carefully cradling the child who, after that sustenance of milk sop, now appeared to be fast asleep. But Bessie realised the child would need changing as she could feel the warm wetness seeping through her clothing to the crook of her arm. Still, at least she could find out for sure now if this babe was a boy or a girl once she changed the child.

When she returned to their small abode, she thanked her next-door neighbour, Mavis, who had kindly babysat for her. 'I put the boys to bed, Bessie, your Jacob led me a merry dance but Harry was a little angel, as usual. How two lads can differ like chalk and cheese...' It was then she noticed the bundle in Bessie's arms as her eyes widened. 'What have we 'ere, then? You taking in washing or something?' She stepped forward to take a peek as Bessie drew back the woollen blanket for Mavis to get a good look.

'No, it's not a bundle of washing, Mave, it's something much nicer than that!'

Mavis startled as she peered inside the bundle to see the child. 'Oh!'

Bessie shook her head. 'You're not going to believe this—I found the child crying on a bench at Itchy Park!'

'Goodness gracious me! Where was the mother?' Mavis asked, lifting her brows.

'I've no idea. I took him or her out of the cold to that chop house near the Ten Bells and fed it milk sop, it was all I could think of to do. The waitress there reckons she saw a young woman with the baby not an hour since and that she was in the company of this posh gent, what gave her money and made off in a hansom cab.'

'Well love a duck! So, what yer going to do? Take her to the police station?'

Bessie shrugged. 'To be honest, Mavis, I don't know what the heck to do. The mother could be in trouble or something and I don't want to cause no more trouble for her.'

'But you can't go keeping her can you, dearie? Not with your Albert, he wouldn't like it. And what about your new pie business? You've been doing well selling those pies to folk lately, you said so.'

That was true. Bessie had taken to baking at the stove early mornings then hawking her pies from two large wicker baskets around the shops and pubs in the area. She'd started to make a bit of profit too, but had hidden the money from her old man. If he got his hands on it, he'd soon fritter it away. Bessie nodded with tears in her eyes. 'Aye, well, I did think of going to the police station, but I just thought maybe I'd hang on to the little mite for a while longer to see if her mother can be located.'

Mavis smiled. 'Look,' she said, patting Bessie's hand, 'I'll help you out. While you're cooking them pies tomorrow when your Bertie is out at work, I'll take the baby to my place for a while. My Jim will be in work too as he's day shifts this week, so neither will know nowt about it. All you'll have to do is keep the young 'un quiet tonight, while Bert's asleep, then tomorrow we'll plan what to do next.'

Bessie smiled and nodded, feeling a little better she'd confided in her neighbour. 'Thank you, you're a real friend.'

Mavis's violet eyes darkened. 'But it's only on the condition that if the mother can't be found in a few days, then you'll have to take her to police or…'

'Or what?'

'The workhouse!'

'Oh, Mavis, that word sends a shiver down me spine. I wouldn't want that for the little mite.'

'I know darlin' but you might have to, you know it makes sense.' Bessie nodded. 'Now, let's have a look and see if it's a boy or a girl, though I reckon I know looking at those long lashes around the eyes.'

Bessie carefully laid the infant down on the table and opened the expensive looking shawl and undressed the child.

'There, I knew it,' Mavis said. 'A beautiful little girl. We'll have to think of a name for her even if only for a few days.'

Bessie thought of the locket in her pocket and the rhyme. 'We'll call her Lucy,' she said. 'Like that nursery rhyme, Lucy Locket lost her pocket…' that rhyme has been going through me 'ead all evening long…'

Chapter Two

By the time Albert came in through the back door, staggering drunk, Bessie had already washed and changed the child and settled her down to sleep in an old drawer that was lined with blankets by the side of the bed. In the corner of the room slept Jacob and Harry in a shared bed. Bessie breathed a sigh of relief. She knew she was safe now as when he came back this late, Bert usually flung himself down on the old horsehair sofa in the living room and slept there in the clothes he was wearing. She'd already left his old work clothes downstairs for him. To tell the truth, this arrangement they often had suited her as she had no intention of getting herself up the spout yet again, not when she had young sons age two and three years old and she was on the verge of building up her pie business. A couple of the pubs had already told her if she could meet their dinner time demand, then she could have regular business with them. But to do that she needed a bigger oven not just the range over the fire place in the kitchen. She had on occasion even taken some next door to cook, but if she was to be serious about this then she was going to have to cart them off to the bake house down the road and cook them there from now on for a small fee.

Lucy let out a little mewl, so Bessie drew back the bed covers and got up in her bare feet, padding across the linoleum to lift the little mite from the drawer. No way could she risk the infant waking up the boys as if they were up whooping and yelling, then Bert might wake up too. She gently shushed the child back to sleep, rocking her gently in her arms. She'd always wanted a little girl but she couldn't put her body through childbirth again, not for any man. In any case, she had suspicions that Bert had been chatting up the young barmaid at the Ten Bells who wasn't much older than she was when they'd first met. He liked them young that much was obvious. She should have been jealous, but the truth was she didn't much care, she'd fallen out of love with him years since. And sad though it was, the reason she'd got together with him 'living over the brush' as it were, hadn't transpired in the end. She'd lost her precious baby girl when she'd gone through a long-protracted labour and the poor wee mite had been born lifeless. Mave had been with her at the time and handed her limp little body over to her. Wept buckets she had as her precious little one looked so perfect in every way. She suffered a bad bout of depression after that and had swayed Bert's advances for some time, but the same thing happened to her a couple more times over the years so she was beginning to suspect she'd never have a child to call her own. The little mites she'd miscarried had all been girls, but her last two pregnancies were both boys and had been strong and healthy at birth. So no wonder, she thought to herself, that she'd taken to little Lucy like that. Had she ever really been in love with Bert in the first place though? Or was it the fact he'd been an older man who'd paid her a lot of attention that had turned her head in the first place? Still, it mattered not a jot now as she had made her bed and ruddy well had to lie in it!

The next thing she knew, she had drifted off on the bed with Lucy contentedly lying in the crook of her arm, then she startled as in the cold light of dawn she heard the back-door closing. Bert was off to his job at the tanyard. Carefully, she carried the young child downstairs with her not to wake the boys. She left the baby on the sofa whilst she went to the outside privy that they shared with a few other houses in the street. Luckily, no one was in there, then she came back inside to bank up the fire. Next, she warmed some milk for Lucy while she boiled the kettle for herself to have a cup of tea.

Bert's clothing from last night had been left in a heap on the chair. She lifted his shirt and inhaled it. *Lavender*. He'd been in the company of a woman, that was for sure. Once upon a time she would have wept bitter tears over it, but it was becoming so common place to her that she swore she'd become immune. Sometimes she wished he'd fall into one of those vats at the tanyard, but then she realised she'd miss his wage coming in even if he didn't always cough up as much as he should.

She sighed as she poured the hot brew in the awaiting cup and sawed off a piece of bread from the loaf on the table to toast in front of the fire later. First she'd have a cuppa, that would set herself up for the day, she'd feed Lucy and dress her and then it would be time to get the boys up out of bed. They were too young for school but sometimes Mavis took them to the park for her to get on with things, or if it was a bad day, she took them into her own house next door.

***

Even before the boys had risen from their beds, there was a tap on the back door and Mavis walked into the kitchen just as Bessie had finished changing Lucy's makeshift napkin, which she'd made from an old piece of towelling she'd cut up into squares; that way there'd be a few to go around to wash and dry between changes.

'How'd last night go?' Mavis drew out a chair from the table and seated herself.

'Very well. Lucy's such a good gal, a very quiet baby, no trouble at all really.'

Mavis nodded, then raised her brows. 'And Albert?'

'Knows nothing for now. I ain't gonna tell him till I 'ave to in case he makes me get shot of her.' She paused a moment as she slipped the little girl's dress back over her soft, pink skin. 'There's tea in the pot if you fancy a cuppa, should still be hot.'

'Aye, there's nowt like a cuppa first thing in the morning. Fancy one yerself?'

'I've just had one, but you go ahead.'

'Rightio, When I've finished this I'll take little Lucy orf yer 'ands, so you can get the boys ready and send them round to me. Then you can get on with yer baking or summat.' She winked at Bessie and poured herself a cup of tea.

Mavis was her best friend and neighbour in all the world and Bessie loved her Northern accent.

***

Bessie was in the midst of rolling out a round of pastry with her floury hands when there was a knock on the front door.

'Blimey, most folk walk straight in around 'ere, not stand on ceremony,' she muttered to herself. But when she opened the door, it was not a friend or a neighbour stood there on her doorstep, but the local constable, Dick Dawkins. Her heart began to thud so fast she feared it had taken on a life of its own. That flamin' waitress must have reported her for taking the baby home with her. Thank goodness the child was next door.

'C…come to buy a few pies for the boys at the station, 'ave yer?' she asked as her cheeks flamed with fear. 'Well, they're not ready, yet, got to bake 'em first.'

His face clouded over. 'Er, no, nice as they are Mrs Harper, I'm 'ere on official business.'

Bessie's heart somersaulted, 'Yer'd better come in then.'

He removed his tall black hat as he entered the house and followed her into the kitchen.

'Please take a seat, Constable.'

He seated himself at the table and placed his hat in front of him, as she followed suit and sat opposite.

'I don't know how to tell you this, Bessie,' he said, his brown eyes hardly daring to meet with her own, 'it's about your Albert…'

Bessie held the palm of her hand to her chest, 'My Bert?' she felt the blood drain from her face. 'What about him?'

He cleared his throat. 'He's er…'

'Go on, spit it out, man,' she said impatiently.

'He's been caught stealing money from his employers.'

'Caught stealing money? Oh, bloomin' heck! How can that be? He only went into work a couple of hours ago?'

'Aye. I know as I was the one who arrested him first thing this morning. We were lying in wait for him when he arrived at his workplace.'

'I…I don't understand?'

'It's been going on a while. His employers have been keeping an eye and noticing things going missing, which they believe he has sold on to others. Have you noticed him flashing any extra money about lately?' He looked around the room as if to gauge if there were any new items on show, but all there were was a scuffed table and chairs, a horsehair sofa and one or two chipped ornaments she'd had for years.

To be honest with yer, Constable, there ain't been anything new in this house for a long while.'

'I can see that, Bessie, love. So where do you think he's been spending the money, then?'

'Probably at The Ten Bells and on that new girlfriend of his,' she sniffed loudly.

The constable's face flushed red as he shook his head. 'Oh, I see. What's her name, then?'

'Rosie something or other, she's quite young, maybe about seventeen. Lives on the premises as she's related to the landlord, I believe.'

'Well, that'll be my next port of call then. Don't get up,' he said standing and laying a hand on her shoulder, 'you've had a nasty shock.'

She looked at him with tears in her eyes. 'Blast bloody Bert Harper! What'll happen to him now?'

'He'll be up in front of the judge first thing this afternoon.'

When the police constable had left, Bessie sat with head in hands at the kitchen table. What would she do now if Bert ended up getting banged up? She'd known when she'd taken him on that he was more of a sinner than a saint. If he had to leave them all for some time she wouldn't get a wage to feed the family, and of course, now even if he escaped prison, there'd be no wage coming in anyhow. She felt in a fit of despair.

She sobbed her heart out for a few minutes, then pulling herself together she wiped her eyes, blew her nose into her handkerchief and washed her face. If she let this pie business fall apart, there'd be no money of any kind coming into the home, even though she worked hard, she hadn't as yet built up the business, she'd only been at it for a few weeks.

I have to pull up me old bootstraps and keep cracking on. I'll finish what I'm doing 'ere, bake these pies and sell 'em, then I'll go around and see Mavis, she'll know what to do. Always talks sense does that one!

Bessie got back on with things with great determination. She rolled out the pastry, lined the pie dishes, added the filling and baked them in the oven, taking some around to Mavis's house to bake at the same time—though she did not at this point, tell the woman what had happened, there'd be time for that later. If she mentioned anything right now, it would only hinder her progress and goodness knew, she'd probably break down again and it would all be too much for her. Work would keep her busy. It was the best therapy at a time like this.

***

When she arrived with her baskets of pies at The Ten Bells, she noticed Rosie stood behind the bar, chatting to a well-dressed man. How could she compete with a young woman like that? The girl tossed her auburn hair back as she spoke to the man who appeared to be besotted with her as he leaned in close, appearing to tease her as she giggled in a coquettish fashion.

Bessie harrumphed, then summoned the landlord.

'Ah, Mrs Harper. You've brought us some more pies, I see?'

She nodded, though she did not feel as enthusiastic today knowing what she did about her husband, in more ways than one.

'Yes, I've got some beef and potato and chicken and leek.'

He lifted the covering cloth on her basket. 'They smell wonderful. How many can you spare?'

'I can sell you a basket of a mix of both if you like,' she glanced towards the barmaid. 'Send young Rosie over to my house afterwards if you have any orders for tomorrow, after seeing what your customers think of the new chicken and leek ones.'

He smiled broadly. 'Yes, will do, though it won't be until late tonight that I can spare her.'

Bessie nodded, 'Very well then.' Before the landlord asked her any awkward questions about Bert, she left the pub. Beneath it all, she was fuming and it was far more about the predicament her husband had got himself into at his place of work than any dalliance with a young barmaid. She'd given up on Albert Harper years ago.

***

'He's what?' Mavis furrowed her brow as they sat together in the living room of her neighbour's house. Jacob and Harry were playing in the backyard and Lucy was fast asleep on the rug in front of the fire.

'He's gone and got himself into trouble at work and been arrested by the police, he'll be up in front of the judge this afternoon, Constable Dawkins told me.'

'So, are you going to go to the court?'

'I wasn't going to but I think I better had to find out exactly what he's being charged with and whether he gets sent down for it.'

'Eeeh Bessie, love, you ain't half had it bad since I've known you as a young lass. Being pregnant so many times by that soft 'appeth and him being so unreliable and all. He's never supported you properly.'

'You're right there, Mave. But that's not the half of it…' she lowered her voice to barely a whisper though there was only the baby there to hear them, but Jim was due home from his shift soon and could make an appearance.

'What?' Mavis's violet blue eyes showed a great deal of compassion. She was ten years older than Bessie and a great comfort to her over the years. It was Mavis who had helped her when Jacob, her first live child had been born. Mavis who had allowed her to catch up on her sleep during the day whilst she nursed the baby for her, and it was Mavis she'd turned to when she'd tried to visit her mother but been thrown out by her father for "bringing shame to their door". She'd felt rejected then as she knew whilst he was still alive, she could never see her beloved Ma again.

Bessie cleared her throat. 'He's got another woman…'

Mavis's mouth popped open. 'I had him down as many a thing but never as a womaniser.'

'He's not usually, but he seems to have a thing for much younger women of a certain age, that's what happened with him and me, remember? I think when a woman gets to a particular time in life, he doesn't desire them anymore.'

'What makes you say such a thing?'

'Because it's true. He dumped his first wife for me when I was a month shy of my sixteenth birthday.'

Mavis nodded. 'I guess that's true, love. How did you find out anyhow?'

'I've suspected for weeks, but this morning after I found his shirt from last night, it reeked of bloody lavender perfume!'

'Oh! I suppose there might be some sort of explanation for it?'

'No, I know. A woman knows these things. You don't 'ave to worry with your Jim, do you?' Mavis shook her head. 'He's good to you, worships the ground you walk on. But it isn't just the perfume, there's other things. When he's off to the pub in the night, he's smartening himself up, wetting down his hair with a comb and sugared water, he doesn't usually give a fig how he looks!' She paused for a moment as Lucy began to stir. 'I guess the little mite will be ready for something to eat soon…'

***

Bessie glanced around the court room and gulped. In amongst the gaggle of spectators, she spied a couple of sharply dressed young men who were clutching leather bound notebooks and pencils—newspaper men from Fleet Street, no doubt. She felt her heart sink at the thought of everyone finding out their business. At least there was no one in the room she recognised, that was something at least.

Everyone stood as the judge entered with a solemn expression on his face—he didn't look the sort to be lenient with anyone, least of all Bert.

Oh Bertie, why did you have to steal from your employer? Was it to impress that young barmaid?

'Be seated, everybody!' the judge bellowed at them and people took their seats. Bessie noticed that the woman seated to the left of her had even brought along a poke of boiled sweets which she was handing out to a couple of women beside her. It was just another form of entertainment to their sort. It wasn't a member of their family stood before the judge; they'd feel differently if it was.

She glanced at the dock to see two tall police constables flanking her husband as they brought him up to stand at the bar, making him seem quite diminutive to her eyes. He looked tired out with big dark circles beneath his eyes, his mouth set in a grim line. Oh, she did feel sorry for him though. How had he got himself into this position? What if the judge decided to transport him to Australia? Or worse still send him to the gallows? Though, surely nowadays a man wouldn't hang for a simple case of theft, would he? And she hadn't heard of anyone being sent off to Australia for a few years.

There was a collective murmur from the crowd as the judge commenced, 'Albert William Harper, you are being charged that on the morning of Thursday, December the 18th, you were caught in flagrante taking possession of fifteen pounds and five shillings by your employer, Mr Josiah Harrison of Harrison,

Harrison and Fothergill, from the safety deposit tin in the said person's office…How do you plead, guilty or not guilty?' He peered at Albert over his specs.

Albert stood trembling and then gulped. 'Not guilty of course! It's not true, Your Honour. I didn't do nuffink wrong.'

'I have a gentleman here who says you did and I shall be asking him what happened in front of this court room of people.'

Albert's face reddened and Bessie knew without a shadow of a doubt that her husband was guilty as sin as he squirmed in the dock, looking all around at everything and everybody bar the judge and Josiah Harrison.

The judge addressed Albert's employer. 'Mr Harrison, can you tell this court room exactly what happened in the early hours of this morning, please?'

Mr Harrison stood and for the first time, Bessie noticed he had another smartly dressed gentleman beside him, who she did not recognise. Was he a legal representative she wondered?

Josiah was well dressed in a long grey frock coat with velvet lapels and silver cravat at his throat. His look said wealth to Bessie and she knew that his sort would be more interested in protecting their financial assets than to worry about a family that would possibly end up in the workhouse once the head of the house was carted away in handcuffs and put behind bars.

There was a long silence as the court room crowd listened intently to hear what the man had to say; even the women beside Bessie had stopped sucking on their sweets. All eyes were on Bert's employer.

'I arrived this morning, a little earlier for work than usual…' he wiped his moustache with the back of his hand.

'And why was this?' The judge asked.

'Because I wanted to lay a trap. I had for some weeks thought that someone was pilfering from the tin in the office as whenever the clerk counted up the money, the sum didn't balance with the books.'

'I see. And what did that make you think, sir?'

'That someone was stealing from me. At first, I thought Charlie Grace was being a clod and couldn't total up properly as he's a new employee. The last clerk had been particularly good. I was about to bring him into my office to put him on a warning when Mr Grace came to me himself with his suspicions.'

'At that point, did you suspect that Mr Grace was stealing from you?'

'Initially, that thought did enter my head, I'd be a liar if I said otherwise. But I got to thinking that Mr Grace had such a good reference from his former employer, a man I know well, that I realised he couldn't be a bad judge of character. But not only that, it was an instinct. I knew Mr Grace could be trusted.'

'So, what did you do then?'

'I spoke to the other directors of the company and they agreed that I could lay a trap.'

'A trap?'

'Yes, I decided to leave the money tin unlocked on the table and one shilling beside it. It was enough to tempt the suspect because I hid in an adjoining room and watched as he entered.'

'And what happened next?'

'I saw him enter the room in a shifty fashion, Your Honour.'

'Shifty fashion? What do you mean by that?'

'What I mean is, almost as soon as he entered his eyes were darting this way and that to ensure he wasn't being watched. Of course he didn't realise I was observing him as usually the adjoining door was left locked. He was clever though as he didn't take the shilling outside the box as people might think, instead, he opened it and took some money from inside, though not all. But this time he had got greedy as he took most of it. In previous weeks there was only the odd shilling going missing here and there.'

'I see,' said the judge looking extremely stern and solemn. 'Have there been any other witnesses to Mr Harper's behaviour?'

'No, only myself, though Mr Grace did say that one day the suspect knocked on his office door and made an enquiry which Mr Grace had to leave the room for, and it was shortly after that he noticed that the petty cash box was a few farthings shorter than it should have been. I didn't take too much notice at the time as I had initially thought the man was incompetent but as the weeks went on, I changed my mind and realised we had a thief in our midst.'

For the first time the judge smiled and nodded. 'And did you challenge Mr Harper when you caught him in flagrante as it were?'

'No, Your Honour. I decided to get the police involved as soon as possible and two of them arrived later.'

'Who were they, do you have names?'

'Yes, sir. They're in this court room beside me.'
He glanced to his left. 'Police Constable Dawkins and
Inspector Read.'

For the first time, Bessie, noticed Dick Dawkins
beside the man and she felt her heart sink to her
boots. But she did sympathise with him. It couldn't
have been easy telling her what had happened that
morning.

'Can you both stand, please?' the judge ordered.

Both men did as instructed.

'P.C. Dawkins, can you give me your account of
what happened this morning?'

The constable nodded and he opened up his small
notebook to read from it. 'On the morning of 18th
December at twenty-five minutes past six, I was
called to the aforementioned premises, where I was
informed by Mr Harrison that a sum of money had
been taken by one Albert Harper. The suspect was
apprehended in Mr Harrison's office while I waited
for the inspector to arrive…'

'And during that time,' asked the judge, 'did the
suspect say anything to you?'

'He tried to make conversation as I know him and
his family, but to keep things on a professional level,
I did not engage, Your Honour. After that, he kept
protesting his innocence, I think he realised then this
was a serious matter.'

'So, you think previously he was trying to soften
you up?'

'Maybe, Your Honour. That's why I kept a
distance. Then the inspector arrived to question him
but Mr Harper tried to evade the questions, so the
inspector then asked me to search him.'

The judge steepled his fingers on his desk. 'And what did that reveal?'

'All the money that was stolen from the tin, exactly as Mr Harrison had told me, Your Honour.'

Suddenly at that point, Albert shouted from the dock. 'It's a fix, Your Honour! I didn't do nuffink, I've been fitted up. I'm an innocent man!'

'Be quiet!' The judge said. 'Or you shall be held in contempt of court proceedings.'

Albert ran his fingers under the collar of his shirt almost as though he already had a noose around his neck. Then the judge nodded at a man in a black gown who whispered something in his ear.

He turned back to Albert. 'Albert William Harper, the evidence presented by the police and your employer is proof enough for me that you committed a theft from your work place. Men have even been sent to the gallows for less! And some even dispatched to Australia to live out the rest of their lives with other convicts. What you did was a terrible thing to violate the trust of someone who had given you secure employment. Many do not have the privilege of regular work. You have abused the trust of your employer, who is a good and fair boss. You have not shown one iota of loyalty towards him, nor have you shown any remorse, so as a consequence, you are to serve two years at Her Majesty's pleasure in prison with hard labour thrown in. I feel for your family as I understand you have dependents in the form of a wife and two young sons...'

By now Albert was squeezing his flat cap between his hands as if his life depended on it, yet looked slightly hopeful to hear the judge say those words to him. But he was not to be deterred. 'Lead him away!' he bellowed at the two police constables who were flanking him.

For the first time, Albert looked across at Bessie, whose eyes were now brimming with tears and he shook his head at her. Even now he was denying his wrong doing. She heard the woman beside her mutter and say, 'Wish it 'ad gorn on a bit longer, it's one way to spend some time out of the cold!'

If she hadn't felt so desperately sad at this moment, she would have liked to slap the woman across the face, but it was all she could do to manage to put one foot in front of the other and leave the court.

Chapter Three

Bessie didn't know how she made it back home—it was all a blur through glassy eyes and confused thoughts. People's faces seemed looming and large until they faded away into oblivion. Their voices muffled and mumbling, it was as if she were no longer part of the real world. Her feet felt like two lead weights as she took one step at a time toward home. By the time she arrived through Mavis's back door, she was in a severe state of shock by what had occurred at the court house, minutes hence.

Bert? Her Bert going to prison for a crime she didn't even realise until this morning he had committed. Surely this was all a bad dream and she'd wake up in her own bed at any moment?

'What happened? You look in a bad way, Bessie, love,' Mavis said, guiding her towards the direction of the fire place and settling her to sit down in front of it in an arm chair. She touched her friend's hand. 'You're freezing cold, gal. I'll make you a hot toddy and then we can talk when yer've warmed up a little.'

Bessie nodded gratefully. She was so absorbed in her own thoughts that she hadn't even noticed Jacob and Harry playing under the table with their wooden toy trains nor Baby Lucy sitting well propped up with cushions, like the Queen of Sheba, on Mavis's old horsehair sofa. The child's eyes were large with curiosity, but for now they were lost on Bessie as all she could see were Bert's eyes, wide with horror as he was led away from the dock to face something truly horrible.

Mavis handed her the drink. 'I've added hot water and a slice of lemon and a spoonful of sugar,' she soothed.

As Bessie sipped the hot rum toddy, she felt it warm her blood and her mind began to clear. 'It were awful, Mave, worse than I ever thought it would be. The judge didn't mess around none, neither. He's got two years in prison with hard labour.'

'But how can that be?'

'He was caught red handed, weren't he? His employer caught him taking fifteen quid from the money tin on his desk. He was lying in wait hiding behind the door. He'd set a trap for him as he realised money and other things were going missing on a regular basis.'

Mavis pursed her lips and shook her head. 'Well, I never thought Bert capable of being a thief.'

'Aye, well he is, there was enough proof there in that court this afternoon from his employer and the police to put him behind bars.'

'What do you reckon he needed that money for?'

'I have an idea why he might have stolen it and who it was to impress...' Bessie blew on the drink and took another sip. 'I think I'm going to 'ave to pay that girl at the pub a visit...'

'Well take yer time, collect your thoughts first as anything could come out the way you're feeling at the moment, you've had a nasty shock, me darling.' Mave laid a hand of comfort on her friend's shoulder.

Bessie nodded, realising her friend was right, but for now she had other matters on her mind. 'How's young Lucy been behaving?'

'Good as gold, bless her. She had a little nap after you left and I changed her napkin. The boys have been well behaved too, though Jacob kept asking where you'd gone and he said he couldn't wait to see his father when he comes home from work tonight. Reckons he was going to make a fort for him out of some old wood he'd gathered.'

The boys! How was she going to explain to them that their father wouldn't be returning home tonight? It didn't bear thinking about.

***

By the time Bessie got to The Ten Bells she was all of a fluster, she hadn't wanted to leave all the kids with Mave for much longer because in an hour or so Jim would be due home from work. He'd want his grub on the table and some peace and quiet, though to be fair to the man, when on occasion the kids had been left there, he'd not complained about it, but she didn't want to chance her arm. Mave had helped her out most of the day, so she was keen to get this over and done with.

She spotted the auburn-haired barmaid at the bar, leaning over chatting to a handsome young man.

'Excuse me, miss,' she said, trying to catch the young woman's attention but there was no response as she was too occupied with what the man was saying to her as she hung on to his every last word.

Raising her voice, she repeated, 'Excuse me, miss!' This time the barmaid whipped her head around and snapped, 'What do you want?'

Bessie's heart began to thud heavily in her chest, the cheeky young upstart, not only content with luring her husband away from her, she was being rude too.

'Put it this way,' she heard herself reply, 'I don't think your landlord or anyone else would like to hear what I have to say about your relationship with my husband, Albert Harper!'

The girl's face reddened from her neck up. That had taken the wind out of her sails.

'I'm sure I do not know to that which you refer to!' she said in an overly refined voice.

'All right then, miss. I shall explain all here in front of everyone,' Bessie said quite calmly as she rolled up the sleeves of her dress as if preparing for a showdown, now feeling she had the upper hand over the situation.

The landlord by now had heard the altercation and he approached Bessie to find out what was going on. Bessie turned to face him. 'I'm sorry to bring this matter into your pub, sir,' she explained, 'but my husband, Albert Harper, was sentenced to a term in prison today for theft and I think that young lady there,' she pointed in the barmaid's direction, 'might know what was going on as he has been paying her a lot of attention lately.'

The landlord looked at the barmaid whose mouth was open as she shook her head. 'I really don't know what this woman is talking about, I've never seen her before in my life,' she protested as she brought the back of her arm to her forehead as if she might swoon at any moment.

What an actress! Bessie thought. 'You ought to be on the stage, love! You give a good performance; I'll give yer that! And you've seen me before as yer uncle buys his pies for this pub from me!'

The landlord shook his head. 'Your Bert was in here and was paying my barmaid a lot of attention but I thought it was just a bit of flirting going on, but this all sounds so serious. I'll take you through to my back room now and see if we can get to the bottom of all of this, Bessie.'

She nodded gratefully. Then the landlord turned to his wife and said, 'Enid, please keep an eye on the bar while I try to sort this mess out. I'm taking Mrs Harper through to our living quarters.'

Enid nodded, though narrowed her eyes in Bessie's direction. The young barmaid was their niece and Bessie wondered if that was on Enid's side of the family the way she was giving her the evil eye.

The landlord led Bessie out to the back room where he asked her to take a seat and then he brought his niece through and ordered her to sit opposite. He remained standing throughout which gave him the upper hand.

'Now then Rosie, what am I hearing that you had some sort of relationship going on with Bert Harper?'

To Bessie's surprise, Rosie nodded slowly and then began to cry, she was far more humble now than she had been at the bar in front of the customers. He patted her shoulder. 'There, there, Rosie, love. This lady just wants to know what was going on that's all.'

The young woman looked at Bessie through a veil of tears. 'I didn't mean for it to 'appen, 'onest, I didn't. But Bertie, well he sweetened me up like, buying me little gifts here and there. Promised me the world, he did an' all.' Her eyes took on a faraway look as if she were in some other place.

It was then Bessie noticed her fingering something on a chain on her neck. 'What's that?' she demanded to know. 'One of his gifts to you?'

Colour rushed to the girl's cheeks as slowly she nodded.

'Lemme see!' Bessie commanded.

The girl brought out the chain from beneath the bodice of her dress and Bessie could see it was some sort of green pendant with a picture of a daisy on it.

'Bertie bought it for me for me birthday,' she said.

'Aye, and while he was spending money on the likes of you, his kids were going starving back home! Tell you that, did he? No, I bet he ruddy well didn't!' Bessie snapped. It was an untruth really as they were far from starving, but it might well have been the case if she hadn't started baking her pies as he had been leaving her short lately.

The girl's eyes took on a vacant expression. 'I 'ad no idea, missus. He never spoke about any of yer.'

'Well, he won't now,' Bessie said curtly, 'he's been thrown in the slammer for a couple of years with hard labour thrown in!'

Rosie's mouth popped open and snapped shut again as if she couldn't quite believe her ears.

'What else did he buy for you?'

'A couple of nice frocks, a bottle of French perfume, oh and he was going to buy me a gold ring from Haverson's the jewellers on the High Street.'

'Pah! He won't be buying you no ring now, love. You're best forgetting you ever set eyes on Bert Harper!'

Then Bessie stood, brushed down her dress as if she was cleansing herself of her husband's immoral behaviour, nodded her thanks to the landlord and made to leave the room. She paused by the door and turning to face them said, 'I came to say what I had to say, and I expect it came as a shock for you as it has for me, but you don't have no house to run and no kids to feed and clothe neither, you're young and can start again!' Then she opened the door and left through the bar room with her head held high, determined that she would not be sullied by her husband's behaviour. She needed now to pull up her bootstraps and make a success of this new business. Albert William Harper could rot in prison for all she cared for leaving her in the lurch like this!

***

After Bessie had collected the kids, from Mavis's house, she bathed Lucy in an old tin bath and then the boys, then she settled them all down for the evening. Luckily, Mavis had fed them all so now there was little for her to do other than tell the boys what had happened to their father. She had thought of telling them an untruth that he'd gone away to work but then she knew they'd keep pestering her with, 'When's Pa coming home!' She pictured them waiting every evening at the window, looking out for him coming along the street, his tapped boots echoing on the cobbles. No, she couldn't do that to them, she had to tell them a form of truth at least.

So, when they were both tucked up inside their shared bed, she settled herself down on the end and explained to them both. 'Boys, you know your father wasn't here this evening?'

Jacob nodded. 'He promised to build me a fort as well!' He stuck his bottom lip out into a pout.

'I know that darling and if he could be here and build you that fort, I know he would, but he's had to go away.'

'Away?' Jacob immediately sat up and hugged his knees, followed by Harry who also sat up, his eyes wide with puzzlement.

'Yes, he did a naughty thing and now he has gone to jail for it, but he will be back some day.'

Harry suddenly burst into tears and Bessie hugged the young lad trying her best not to show that she was feeling upset for the boys too. It wouldn't do to show any kind of weakness in her book, she needed to remain strong and resolute through this. Mavis had agreed that the best thing she could do now while trying to survive without Bert was to carry on with her pie business as at least it brought in some income, but she realised that she needed to think on a bigger scale if she were to help pull them out of poverty.

When her husband returned from prison did she really want him back anyhow? After what he'd done with that young barmaid, all the while still professing his love for her. Did she know him really at all? But then again, he'd only been up to what he previously got up to years ago when he'd first met her. She'd once been a young barmaid too who had fallen for his overpowering attention and charm.

Jacob, who up until now, had tried to hold back the tears was beginning to break down, Bessie watched as his bottom lip quivered and he looked so lost. 'Come here, lad,' she said, opening out her free arm to cuddle him to her left breast as Harry sought solace on the right. They remained hugging one another for a long time and then Bessie looked down and saw that

Harry was almost asleep and that Jacob had stopped crying.

'Come on, boys, it's time for bed. Get under those covers and I'll blow the candle out. If you need me I'm just across the landing with Lucy.'

Once they'd settled down, Jacob looked up at her through narrowed eyes. 'Has Pa gone away because you brought that bloomin' baby 'ere?' He sniffed.

Bessie didn't have the heart to tell him off for his cuss word, but instead kindly said, 'Oh no, Jacob. Your pa didn't know nothing about young Lucy whatsoever, so you can remove that thought from your mind.'

He nodded. 'I don't know if I like her or not.'

'Is that because she's a girl and not a boy?'

'Maybe, boys are more fun.'

She smiled and she leaned over to plant a kiss on his cheek. Harry was already out like a light and, as she closed the door behind herself, she thought what a terrible and life changing day it had been. It had all started off simply with her husband going to work and then not returning home again.

Chapter Four

The following morning Bessie was up bright and early and Mavis called around to help with the kids whilst she baked. 'Once I'm on me feet I plan to pay you a decent wage for yer help,' she explained to the woman.

Mavis wiped away a strand of hair that had worked loose from her bun and fallen across her face. Bessie experienced a sharp pang of guilt that she was putting on the woman though Mave never complained.

'That's very kind of you but you know I love to help as I never had kids of me own.'

'I know that but it's only fair, I shall pay you child minding fees.'

Mave smiled and nodded almost as though she realised it was no use protesting about it as once Bessie made up her mind about something it was usually fixed fast. 'Any more thoughts about going to the police station about Lucy?'

Bessie frowned. 'I have to admit, Mave, I still feel reluctant to do so but maybe I should when I've finished me work for the day. Perhaps the mother did intend coming back fer her and is now upset.' She chewed on her bottom lip.

'Aye, I think it's the best thing to do, if yer like I'll come with you. My sister will be calling later and I can ask her to watch Jacob and Harry for us.'

Bessie nodded. 'Yes, you're right. I'm getting too attached to the little mite and maybe her mother wants her back.' She gazed vacantly at the wall for a moment wondering how she'd feel if someone had one of her boys. But then again, she told herself no matter how bad things got, she'd never leave them in the first place. What did she know though? Who was she to judge another mother? The young woman obviously had her reasons.

'How are you going to explain the fact you've not gone to the police before now? I suppose you could tell a white lie and say you'd only just discovered her at Itchy Park.'

'Aw no, I wouldn't want to do anything underhanded, I shall tell the truth and explain I've been in a state of shock after what happened to Bert yesterday.'

By heck, Bessie, yer one upstanding lady, that you are. But it is the truth and all, you should have seen yer face when you came back from that courthouse yesterday. It were as white as a sheet and your eyes looked hollow and haunted, didn't look yerself at all.'

Bessie shook her head. It was true as she hadn't felt herself at all yesterday, it was as if the rug had been pulled from beneath her feet and she'd landed upside down where nothing made sense any more. But today, although she still felt a little shaky, for time being at least they still had a roof over their heads and food in their bellies. And if she could help it they would never go without, she'd work her fingers to the bone if she had to. Blast Bertie Harper.

'You're right I was in a state of shock yesterday but today I've got me 'ead screwed back on straight, gal. I've made up me mind, I'm going to make a success of this business.'

'That's the spirit. Now after yer've finished your baking, let's get around to the police station as you could do with one less mouth to feed.'

Bessie looked sadly at Lucy, how would she ever bear to part with the little mite? She was growing quite attached to her.

***

'You found a baby on a bench?' The desk sergeant furrowed his brow, his thick wiry eyebrows almost meeting in the middle. He had a big bulbous nose and thick gingery moustache which Bessie couldn't help staring at.

'Yes, it was bitterly cold and I couldn't find the mother, I even called out in case she was in Itchy Park somewhere and asked at a nearby chop house an' all.'

The sergeant nodded. 'Now when did you say this was?' He licked the nib of his pencil and began to take notes on a piece of paper.

'The night before last, it was.'

He scribbled the information down and then glared at her, stopping mid flow. 'And why did you wait until now to inform us of this?'

Mavis looked as if she was just about to intervene when Bessie laid a hand on her arm. 'It was my fault I'm afraid. I'm Bert Harper's wife, he was put away yesterday for theft from his employer.'

The sergeant narrowed his gaze as if he thought Bessie was a criminal too. 'I remember it,' he said solemnly.

'As you can see, she were in a right state of shock,' Mavis suddenly blurted out.

The sergeant relaxed. 'I understand, madam. I'll just go and check with the inspector to see if there have been any reports of any missing children. How old is this baby?'

Mavis held the sleeping child up to him. 'We reckon she's about ten months old, maybe. She's not even walking as yet.'

He smiled. 'So, a little girl then. I'll be back in a tick.'

Eventually, he returned with the inspector who seemed to dwarf him with his large stature. He was a clean-shaven man with a thin black pencil moustache. 'Mrs Harper,' he said, looking at Mavis as she held the child.

'I'm Mrs Harper,' Bessie said, then she sniffed loudly in frustration.

'We've had no reports of any missing children this past couple of days, nor of any young mothers in distress. I think the best thing you can do is take the child to the workhouse and tell them we are aware of the missing mother and abandoned child and to contact us if they hear anything.'

'Oh no,' Bessie said sharply. 'I can't imagine leaving her in that place. I tell you what I'll do, I'll carry on taking care of her and leave you my name and address if the mother shows up.'

The inspector and sergeant exchanged glances, then the inspector turning back to the women said, 'Very well. You have shown honesty by coming here and from what the sergeant tells me, your husband was the man that was put away yesterday. But I must stress if the mother appears, you will have to give the child up.'

Bessie nodded vigorously. 'I will, yes, of course I will, sir.'

***

Days settled down to a pattern of Bessie baking from home and Mavis helping her out with the child care for which Bessie paid her for. Mavis had insisted she would be more than happy to do so for free but Bessie said she would have needed to employ someone anyhow and that Jim would be willing for his wife to work if there was an extra payment coming into the home. To be truthful, it didn't affect the man much as he was out all day at work, but there was the odd time when Bessie worked longer hours than usual. And it was on those occasions, Bessie appreciated that he'd be waiting for his evening meal after a hard day's graft to find it wasn't on the table as Mavis was busy running around after three young 'uns. Though Jim did admit it was nice to see his wife with the children as she'd been unable to bear her own.

Eventually, as Bessie's round grew larger as word travelled about her delicious pies, she decided now was the time to use the bakehouse down the road and she even employed a young lad to take care of the deliveries for her. By the time Bert would be due out of prison, her business would be flourishing, and she'd had no wish to see him during his time behind bars either.

On the day of his release, she dreaded him showing up at the house, she'd been on pins all day long, but in the event, he was a no show and she found out a couple of days later that he'd shacked up with the young barmaid from the pub. Strangely enough, she was glad of it—it would keep him out of her hair.

No one ever did show up at the police station looking for Baby Lucy, and although a couple of days after their initial visit there, Bessie'd given the police details about the locket, the name engraved on it, the note, and information about what the waitress at the chop house had said about the young woman with the older man, Lucy's mother was yet to be located.

***

Lucy was growing into a fine young child who brought such delight to them all. Bessie reckoned she'd now be almost three years old and decided to make her birthday officially February the 14th, Saint Valentine's Day as she was such a little sweetheart. Now they could celebrate it every year.

The boys loved their little sister to bits, but really Bessie had already decided not to pretend to be the child's mother, instead describing her as a niece. So, as Lucy grew up, she referred to Bessie as her auntie.

It was some five years later that Bessie received the knock on the door that she dreaded. She knew that knock anywhere and to see him stood on the door step, looking clean and presentable after all these years as he clutched his flat cap in his hands, fair near broke her heart. Albert William Harper had finally returned home.

***

'What are you doing here?' Bessie blinked several times. He might have looked older and thinner, but it was unmistakably Bert stood before her. She watched as his eyes filled with tears as she allowed him over the threshold, then he stood in the passageway gazing around, shaking, until she took him in her arms and held him. He was a shadow of his former self, a bag of bones really and it shocked her to the core.

'I don't understand,' she said, holding him at arms' length as she gazed into his eyes. 'What's been going on? Has yer fancy piece thrown you out then?'

'Something like that, Bess,' he sniffed. 'I should never have taken up with her in the first place, she turned me flamin' head.'

'Wasn't I enough for you, then?'

'You were everything to me, I can appreciate that now, but we seemed to be drifting apart.'

'Aye, well, I'll not deny that. But if you think you can just waltz back in yer after all that's happened, and, you didn't even come to see how your boys were, either.'

He stood shamed faced with his head lowered for a while. 'That's 'cos I feared your anger, Bess. Not just fer having a bit on the side but fer the theft and losing me job. I saw the way you looked at me in court that day as if you couldn't stand the sight of me no more.'

'Yes, I remember it well. It's not a day I'll forget in a hurry, I can tell you. Well you can come in for a cup of tea but that's all you'll be getting here. Make no mistake—you don't own this house as I pay the rent to keep a roof over all our heads, and you definitely don't own me!' She stuck her chin out in defiance.

'Aye, I know that, Bessie love.' He smiled for the first time.

And she found herself smiling back at him. 'I can't have you moving in here though.'

He nodded. 'It's me own fault, I deserve this rejection from you. But how have you managed to keep up the rent payments all this time?'

At that moment, the back door burst open and in ran Jacob and Harry, closely followed by Lucy. The three children stopped in their tracks and stared at the man before them.

Bert's eyes began to fill with tears as he knelt down to welcome them. Harry and Lucy were wary, as Harry was too young to remember his father and Lucy didn't know him at all, but Jacob, as soon as recognition dawned, flew into his father's arms. Then his father hugged him and whirled him around and around, there was a lot of laughter as the other two children looked on in bemusement.

'Well, sit yourself down then, Bert,' Bessie said. He nodded, knowing there was a level of acceptance there from his wife as he placed Jacob back on his feet, and he took the armchair by the fire place—the very same armchair that was his before he did a bad thing. Then Jacob sat on his father's lap, next joined by Harry, who seemed to think this 'stranger' seemed of interest to his brother so he should check him out too.

'It's all right, son,' Bert said as he sniffed as if to hold back his tears, 'I'm your Dad.'

Harry looked at his mother for confirmation, she nodded eagerly at him and then he was on his father's lap too. Lucy, who couldn't seem to fathom the situation, ran to Bessie's side clinging to her skirts.

When they'd had tea and a slice each of Bessie's homemade fruit cake, Bert looked at Bessie. 'And who is this young child?' he asked, wiping the crumbs from his lips with his handkerchief. 'Are you babysitting for a neighbour?'

Bessie swallowed. 'Er, no, Bert. I'll explain now.' She turned to the kids. 'Can you all go and play in the yard for a few minutes, please?'

Jacob scowled. It was obvious he didn't wish to leave his father's side now that they'd found one another again.

'It's all right, son,' Bert advised. 'Only for a short while so me and your ma can talk to one another, run along now!' Reluctantly, the boy nodded and he guided the other two children out to the yard.

'Right then Bess, what's been going on?'

Bessie began to feel a bit uncomfortable. 'I, er, found her on a bench in Itchy Park the night before you were sent to prison.' She began to twist a lace handkerchief in her hands, her palms were feeling hot and perspiring profusely.

Bert narrowed his eyes. 'So, if you found a young child, why on earth would you bring her home with you and not take her to the police station?'

'I don't know, Bert. I was worried as it was freezing cold.'

He looked at her for the longest time as if he didn't quite believe her. 'Is that little girl your child by another man?' he glared at her.

'No, of course not. She's now almost eight years old, she'd be too old to be my child.'

He appeared to think about it for a moment as if figuring out how many years ago that would be. 'I suppose you're right, she would be too old.' He relaxed, but somehow Bessie realised he was still suspicious of why she'd taken the child into their home in the first place.

***

Somehow or another Albert wormed his way back into Bessie's affections and had his feet planted firmly under the table once again. All of this would have suited all, except for one thing. Bessie still seemed to think he still had it in his mind that Lucy was Bessie's child by another man and that she'd lied about Lucy's age. Lucy did look quite young for her age, so she could understand his thinking.

'How many times do I have to explain to you, Bertie!' Bessie cried in frustration. 'Lucy could not have been conceived whilst you were in prison— she's too old. I'm telling yer the God's honest truth, I found her on a bench at Itchy Park!'

His features became set in stone, his eyes darkening to the colour of flint stone. He'd nodded, but his words did not match his demeanour, and it wasn't too long before Bessie realised that Albert would not take to the little girl at all. He eventually found himself a casual job working at the dock yard as and when required, and when he came home of an evening, he'd gladly hoist Jacob and Harry up onto his shoulders, while totally ignoring Lucy. She became used to it though, and while he wasn't outwardly nasty to the little mite, he didn't include her either. But the child seemed to accept this and things seemed on an even keel until one day four years later, Albert declared, 'I think it's time now to send Lucy out to work, she's old enough to go into service or something!'

Bessie felt as if all the air had been squeezed out of her lungs. Lucy was like a daughter to her, and whilst it was not unusual for children of her age to work, she couldn't bear the thought of sending her away. 'Bert, I won't hear of it, I tell yer. She can help me with me baking.'

'Yer've already got enough 'elp as it is, my dear. Jacob and Harry are good at what they do and Mave next door an' all. No, we'll get more out of young Lucy if we make her work somewhere else.'

Before she had a chance to answer, he added, 'In fact, yer know the geezer what runs the coaching inn called The Horn and Bugle?'

She nodded slowly, mouth agape, half guessing what was to come next.

'He said he's looking for a young kitchen maid.'

'But Lucy doesn't need to go there to work, Bert. She can remain here with us,' she protested laying a hand on his arm, which he quickly shook off.

Bert's features were set in stone. 'Put it this way, Bess…if you don't send her to work there, then I'm taking your beloved boys away from you and you'll never see them ever again!'

Bessie's heart sank at the thought of losing her lads and of Lucy leaving home for the first time, but to keep the peace, she decided to go along with it for time being. There was no way she could afford to cross Bert right now as he had a history of going missing and doing the dirty on her. The mood he was in, if she defied him, she might lose her sons forever.

Chapter Five

The following day, Lucy found herself being walked to the coaching inn by Bessie. Why did the woman seem so sad? It was a mystery to her.

Earlier, Bessie had gently unwound the tightly curled rags in Lucy's hair and brushed her hair until it shone. She'd picked out the dress she'd made for her too.

'Darlin' I have something to tell you.' Bessie'd said while trying to keep her voice light and breezy, but there was no fooling Lucy, she heard the catch in the woman's voice. 'Today I'm taking you to the coaching inn to meet the landlord and his wife, they're looking for a young girl to wash the pots and clear up in the bar room.'

Confused, Lucy had furrowed her brow and asked, 'Won't I be going to school then anymore, Auntie?'

Slowly, Bessie had shook her head. 'No, dear. When a young girl gets to your age, she's expected to work for her keep.'

Lucy thought she'd noticed Bessie's bottom lip quiver, but she'd carried on brushing her hair.

'As long as I can come home at night to you.' Lucy had smiled nervously.

Bessie sniffed and wiped away a tear with the back of her hand. 'I'm afraid that won't be possible, darlin', you see your employers will expect you to stay there as it's a coaching inn, so you might be required at all times of the night and day to be on call.'

'Why's that?' Lucy just did not understand.

'Because coaches can turn up there at any time, dear. Some will have travelled long distances, often through the night like the mail coach that comes from York.'

Lucy nodded, but she felt a strange lump in her throat and painful tears pricked the back of her eyes ready to spill onto her clean frock. 'Does that mean I'll never see you again, Auntie Bessie?'

'Oh, goodness no, child!' Bessie's hands flew to her face, then she turned Lucy around to face her and took her in her arms. 'You will always be welcome here, Lucy, at any time. You'll get time off from your duties of course and you can visit us here. I'll also pop around now and again to see how you're doing as I supply the inn with their meat pies, anyhow. I'm on good terms with the landlord and his wife.'

Lucy nodded as she fought to hold back the tears. 'I understand,' she said.

'There!' said Bessie proudly, 'You look a picture. We'd best be off.'

At that point, the back door opened suddenly as Albert burst into the room. He had a strange gleam in his eyes that Lucy had never noticed before and she trembled.

'Glad to see you've got the little tyke ready to go then, Bess!' he bellowed. 'Make sure you tell them she's fit and well and can work on her feet for hours on end!'

Bessie pursed her lips in annoyance. 'I'll do no such thing!' Auntie looked most affronted as she crossed one hand over the other. 'If I do that, they might take advantage and work her like a ruddy pack horse! Lucy is only a young lass after all. She needs her rest.'

Bert glowered at the girl. 'You've spoilt her something rotten, Bess. Made a rod for yer own back, no wonder she don't want to leave yer side!'

It was true though, Lucy admitted. She felt safe whenever she was around her aunt, but lately she'd felt creeped out around Bert. It was something to do with the way his eyes widened around her. And he'd sometimes lick his lips as if he were the wicked wolf to her Little Red Riding Hood and wanted to devour her. Bessie hadn't seemed to have noticed this and as Lucy was beginning to develop curves, she now wondered if she'd be safer at the coaching inn after all.

***

After walking for what seemed an age, Lucy found herself being led down an alleyway and into the cobbled yard that stank of mulch and manure.

She shivered as she drew her woollen shawl around her shoulders.

'Be careful you don't step in any of that 'orse mess,' Auntie warned.

Lucy nodded and then she caught the eyes of a young man who was dressed in a pair of rough looking breeches, striped shirt which was worn at the elbows, and a pair of leather boots that looked too large for him. Perched on his head was a flat herring bone tweed cap. He winked at her, causing her to glance away as she blushed profusely. The bleedin' cheek of it, while she was with her Auntie and all. But Aunt Bessie appeared not to notice as she headed to the inn with extreme purpose.

A couple of men emerged out into the yard in their long frock coats and top hats causing Lucy to stare at their posh garb. She listened as they spoke with plummy, refined accents that she just wasn't used to.

'You can close yer mouth now, Lucy!' Auntie scolded. 'You swear you'd never seen a coupla toffs before!'

Lucy steadied herself by taking Auntie's arm before she slipped on a fresh dollop of horse dung. She wrinkled her nose in disgust. How was she ever going to get used to waking up in a place like this?

Her eyes scanned this way and that. To her right she noticed a set of stables with half doors, where she had noticed the young lad had disappeared to, but Auntie was leading her to a door at the back of the inn where she stood stock still for a moment, straightened her hat, sniffed and laid her hand protectively on Lucy's shoulder. Then she rapped on the door with the other hand.

'Whatcha want?' a voice bellowed from within.

***

Lucy blinked several times as a wrinkly old crone with a couple of blackened teeth, stared back at them.

'We're here to speak to the landlord...' Auntie explained. 'I hear he's looking for a young girl to help in the kitchen to wash up pots and help clear up in the bar room...'

The woman narrowed her gaze. 'Maybe he is an' all but who was it told yer about the job?'

Auntie cleared her throat. 'My husband.'

There was a long pause as if both women were sizing one another up and were waiting for the other to break the impasse.

When Lucy could see that neither woman was about to give in, she said, 'It was Albert Harper!'

The woman began to smile and then her brown eyes twinkled. 'Bertie? Well bless me soul, I knows him well. Why didn't you say so in the first place?'

Auntie rolled her eyes then slowly, shook her head from side to side. 'So, can we speak to the landlord then?'

'Aye, I suppose so. I work in the kitchen meself. The girl will need to work long hours mind, she'll be on her feet a while without much of a break. The job's not for slackers.'

'I appreciate that,' Auntie said. 'The girl is a hard worker and no mistaking. And I understand she'll be put up here an' all.'

'Yes, but her bed will be under the sink for a while. But once the girl who is leaving has departed after showing this one 'ere the ropes if she's suitable, then there's a little box room she can sleep in. How's that suit?'

The woman scared the heck out of Lucy but to finally have her own room would be grand, she'd never had her own room in all of her life!

Auntie turned towards her and laying both her hands on her shoulders looked into her eyes. 'How does that sound to you, Lucy?' she asked. 'It won't be 'alf bad to have yer own place and you can come and visit whenever you've a spare moment.'

Lucy felt a lump in her throat and she longed to cling on to her Auntie Bessie and snuggle into her bosom but if she did so, she knew the woman would cave in and then she'd go back home and be at the mercy of Albert Harper. She didn't know what was going on with him lately but he was suddenly taking an interest in her which was well out of character.

The woman sniffed loudly. 'Yer better both come in,' she said. 'Me name's Cassie…'

In a corner of the kitchen, was another young girl in a mobcap who was busy stacking away some saucepans. 'This here is Nellie,' Cassie declared. 'She usually works as a parlour maid for the landlady and his wife, but today she's 'elping me as I'm shorthanded.'

The girl looked at Lucy as if she was sizing her up, and she could have sworn she saw contempt behind her eyes. What had she ever done to her? This was a fine start.

***

Lucy settled well into her new position at the coaching house. The work was demanding but the staff were good to her, especially Cassie who slipped her leftovers from time to time. A nice bit of ham on the bone and a thick crust of bread slathered in salted butter went down a treat. The landlord and his wife, Mr and Mrs Harrington, were personable too, but the person that amused Lucy most was Smithy the young stable lad who'd been looking at her the day Auntie had brought her here. He had a tendency to hang around the kitchen door in the hopes that Cassie would feed him titbits, but Lucy began to notice he also hung around at other times too like when she was washing the dishes.

'That lad has taken a right fancy to you,' Cassie said one afternoon when they were both stood at the long wooden sink. Cassie was washing up the plates, pots and pans which were piled high by the side of her. Lucy, who stood on a soap box so she could reach, was drying them in a large roughened towel.

Lucy face grew hot and she hoped she wasn't blushing.

'Oh, I dunno about that,' she said clambering down from the box and carrying a stack of dry dishes to the cupboard opposite.

'Stuff 'n' nonsense!' Cassie splashed her arms around in the soapy water as she scrubbed furiously away at a stubborn stain on the saucepan.

Lucy stopped what she was doing to stare at the woman who had her back to her.

'Yer can tell that lad likes yer as he has a kind of twinkle in his eyes whenever he speaks to you.'

Lucy smiled broadly as she knew Cassie couldn't see her. She'd never had the affections of a young lad before and it made her feel warm and cosy inside. The nearest she had to the feeling of a warm glow was the love and attention she'd got from her Auntie Bessie. The woman had been kindness herself and brought her up as if one of her own, but now her old man was back on the scene, she was beginning to feel left out. She knew in her heart that it was Bert who had persuaded Bessie to make her go out to work. She weren't afraid of no hard work either but she wanted to live back at home. But then again, now it was beginning to feel less like home to her and she feared when he was around she was in danger if left alone with him. To be fair, he hadn't harmed a hair on her head so far, it was just the looks he was beginning to give her that sent a shiver coursing her spine. She didn't feel like that when Smithy gave her one of his looks as he was around the same age as her but that

Bert was old enough to be her father. It made her skin crawl. Creepy was what it was.

***

A few weeks later, after settling in nicely at the coaching inn, her employers gave Lucy a couple of days leave telling her when she returned, the other girl would have left and she could sleep in her room which was classed as a box room. When Nellie discovered this, she immediately took the hump. 'I don't think it's fair meself!' she snorted with her chin in the air and arms folded. 'Yer've been 'ere all of five minutes. By rights I should have that room as I've been here well over a year and I have to sleep in the bloomin' draughty attic!'

'It's fine by me if you'd like to swap rooms,' Lucy suggested kindly. 'If yer ask them, I'll have yer room instead.'

Nellie gave her a hard stare. 'Don't talk rot!' she snarled. 'They've already made up their bleedin' minds and it's obvious they're favouring you over me!' She lifted the pail of coal she'd been carrying, turned on her heel and walked in the direction of the landlord's living quarters. Oh dear, now she'd gone and made an enemy of the girl and it wasn't even her fault either. Jealousy was an awful thing. But still, it didn't take away how excited she was about having a room she could call her own, she couldn't wait to tell Bessie later when the woman dropped off some of her pies at the inn.

Bessie's eyes had lit up like two glowing embers on the fire when she'd heard the news about the room and Lucy having a few days leave. 'I can't wait, me love,' she'd said as she rested her empty wicker basket on the bar top as the landlady removed the pies and stacked them away.

Lucy turned from where she'd been polishing an empty table. It was quiet in the bar that morning as a couple of coach parties had just departed for Bristol. Only an elderly man and his son sat sipping their pints in the corner, next to a roaring fire. Lucy had heard them say to someone they were on their way to Kent for a funeral.

'I can't wait either!' Lucy grinned and she shook her duster.

'I'll make sure to get things ready for you, but you're going to 'ave to sleep on a pallet on the floor as I've given your old bed to Jacob. He was pestering me for it after you left,' she said brightly.

Lucy's heart sunk like a stone to the bottom of the sea. In her mind, she still had that bed to go back to with its creaky bedsprings and lumpy mattress, but it had been her own bed and she'd become accustomed to it.

'Cheer up!' Bessie lifted her chin with her thumb and fore finger to gaze into Lucy's watery eyes. 'Yer always welcome back home any time, you know that, darlin'!'

Lucy nodded but a shadow had passed over her as a shiver coursed her spine as she realised all this was Bert Harper's doing. And she guessed it was his idea for Jacob to sleep in her bed. He wanted her out that much was evident and a little voice warned he wanted her out for good and all.

Over the following few days until her leave, she became morose and people were noticing. ''Tisn't good to mope about, Lucy,' Cassie chastised. 'If I had a nice Auntie's house to go back to, I'd jump at the chance not have a chump on like you've got, gal!'

Bless Cassie, but she didn't understand. All she saw was Bessie's kind face and Bert free with his money by the bar and chatting to all and sundry. He had one face for the public and another behind closed doors that was for sure.

And since she'd told Nellie about being allocated that box room, the girl now hardly spoke to her. There was a definite freeze in the air.

***

A couple of days later, Lucy found herself outside her old home staring at the front door with uncertainty. She swallowed hard. How she would have loved it if things were how they'd always been without having Bert there. Why, oh why, had her aunt allowed this man back into her life when he'd treated her so dreadfully in the past? Mavis next door had once explained to her that things weren't that simple when she'd asked her the same question when Auntie was busy baking her pies. Mave had gone on to explain that love was funny like that sometimes, *'Even if someone has hurt us we can hold on to the feeling that one day they'll change just for us, but of course that doesn't usually happen and the person doing the hoping will come to a point someday where they realise it! No amount of tender loving care is going to make a bad apple turn out good!'*

Lucy had gone home after that with plenty of food for thought and had watched Bert with a new interest as he turned on the smarm to Bessie, draping his arm around her and giving it all the niceties. But all he was doing really was keeping a roof over his head and pennies in his pocket as he no longer had any work to go to because his previous misdemeanour had gone before him. The only sort of work he was liable to get was from employers who wanted their workers now and again and weren't too fussy about their backstories. And any temporary jobs Bert had been offered up until now, he hadn't even been able to withhold for long anyhow.

With some trepidation she rattled the knocker and stood back on the pavement. The weather was getting colder, so she hoped she wouldn't have to wait too long. Ordinarily, in the past, she would have just walked into the home but now she felt like an outsider and it might be impolite to do so. Now to her, it was a house and no longer a home.

The door suddenly swung open and Bessie stood there with a big smile on her face and her arms open wide. She moved forward to hug Lucy and she was in tears to be held in Bessie's embrace once more. 'How I've missed you, love,' she said breathlessly. 'Now you're going to have a lovely couple of days here...' Lucy nodded. 'Come inside.'

Once inside, Bessie took Lucy's carpet bag of clothes and belongings from her and told her to settle herself at the table where she had a special tea prepared for her of potted meat sandwiches and there were jam tarts and an iced sponge cake. The table did look nice and all with a pristine white, lace-edged table cloth and there was a good fire crackling away in the hearth. It was obvious that Bessie had gone to a lot of trouble for her but all seemed too quiet.

Lucy looked around herself in confusion. 'Where's everyone?' she asked.

'The boys are playing football in the alley. I sent them out so you and I can have a bit of a chat in peace,' she said ominously.

'And Bert?' She'd never once referred to him as Uncle Bert and neither did he want her to.

'He's out looking for work,' Bessie said brightly. But there was no fooling Lucy, she knew the man was more likely to be in the Ten Bells supping a few pints of ale at Bessie's expense—he loved his neck oil.

Lucy released a long breath, she was relieved he wasn't here, she could feel more herself when he wasn't around.

Bessie boiled the kettle on the fire then lifted it to the table to an awaiting earthenware teapot where she poured the steaming liquid onto the tea leaves. While she waited for it to brew, she arranged a couple of sandwiches on a plate and placed them in front of Lucy.

'Sit down, child,' she said. Lucy did as told and then Bessie followed suit. 'There's something specific I wanted to speak to you about...'

What on earth could Auntie have to ask her about? Was she about to ask her to come back home? She hoped that was the case, she liked working at the inn but she'd prefer to live at home and go to work on a daily basis even though it was a long trek.

'What do you wish to talk to me about?' Lucy leaned in closer.

Bessie bit her lip. This seemed as if it was something hard for Auntie to say. 'You know you're developing in to a young lady, Lucy?'

Lucy nodded. Of course, she was, she realised that when she'd begun her monthly courses. What was so wrong about that? 'Yes, Auntie.'

'Er, um…you're developing a few curves here and there and becoming very attractive indeed, well…what I wanted to say is that I want you to be careful working at the inn in case any gentlemen try to take advantage of you. Has anyone approached you in a suggestive manner as yet?'

Lucy shook her head. She didn't quite understand what her Auntie meant by this.

'Sorry, if I'm confusing you, Lucy. What I mean is to be wary if anyone tries it on with you. A gentleman might aim to get you into his affections and if you fall for it, you could end up in the family way, do you understand me? They'll promise you the world they will to get their way with you!'

Bessie turned away to pour two cups of tea as if she was embarrassed to face Lucy.

'I do understand you clearly, Auntie. I wouldn't want to get in the family way, believe me. And no man so far has tried to take advantage of me.' She'd stressed "no man" there but what about "no lad"? When she thought about Smithy and the way he was around her, there was no cooling his ardour but so far, he hadn't done anything improper, only chat her up a little and smile and wink at her from time to time.

'I'll be careful, Auntie,' she reassured.

'You see, Lucy,' Bessie said, handing Lucy one of her best china teacups and saucers, Lucy took the cup of tea and set it down before her, 'it happened to me with your Uncle Bert. I was only a little older than you and I fell for all his patter when I worked as a barmaid. Next thing I knew I was pregnant and shunned by my family and made to leave home. I was a marked young woman. That wouldn't happen with you of course, I'd never shun you whatever happened, but it's not what I want for you. I want you to have a good life, me love.'

Lucy nodded. It was beginning to make sense now. Of course, it was. Auntie wanted what was best for her and Lucy was prepared to keep her hand on her ha'penny at all costs.

'Good, that's settled then. I'll call the boys in to join us soon. They're really looking forward to seeing you.'

***

Ten minutes later Jacob and Harry burst into the room.

'Lucy!' Harry exclaimed excitedly and he ran to hug her. He was becoming quite the young man, though he was only a couple of years older than her, sometimes he seemed young. 'I'm so pleased to see you! I've right missed you that I have!'

Harry was always open and free with his emotions but Jacob just stood awkwardly hovering by the door. 'Hello,' he said gruffly.

She knew his ways though and smiled at him. 'My, my, big brother, your voice is breaking!' She exclaimed which caused him to blush. 'And you're growing a beard and all!'

'He's getting like Dad!' Harry said. 'I caught him borrowing his razor the other day!'

Jacob gave him an angry look then grabbed him into a headlock. 'Shurrup! You little runt!' he said.

Bessie stood and with hands on both hips said, 'Now, now, Jacob, we'll have none of that, young man! Go and get washed up the pair of you and then you can join us for sandwiches and cake.'

Jacob released Harry with a thump to the floor. Harry pulled himself up by using the back of Lucy's chair and rubbed his reddened neck. Jacob left the room in a huff and Lucy whispered to Harry, 'Try not to wind him up, you know what his temper is like.'

Harry nodded. Were those tears in his eyes? Normally, Jacob didn't turn on Harry as Harry was so affable but lately, he'd started answering him back and challenging his authority. Maybe they were like two stags butting antlers. Jacob was developing a terrible temper that seemed to go with his red hair. That's what people seemed to say but was that really fair? What did hair colour have to do with anything?

'Jacob wouldn't have done that if Bert had been here!' Bessie said, almost proudly.

Lucy had noticed that Jacob did listen to Bert though and lately was undermining his mother's authority.

When both boys had left to wash up at the old stone bosh in the kitchen, Bessie said, 'How are you getting on at the inn, anyhow? You seemed to be doing well there the other day when I popped in with those pies.'

'Good, thanks. I quite like it there.'

'And you're sleeping all right?'

'Yes. For the first week or so I had to rough it but now I've got a little room of my own since that other maid left.'

'Great. You need your privacy. I don't feel so bad now then. If you're settled you're probably better off back at the inn.'

Lucy's heart sank. She swallowed a lump in her throat and changed the subject. 'Would you like another cup of tea, Auntie?'

Bessie's eyes twinkled. 'Aye, I don't mind if I do.'

***

There was no sign of Bert that evening and Lucy was glad of it. 'I've made up a pallet for you in the corner of our bedroom, Lucy,' Bessie smiled. 'Don't look so alarmed. I've curtained an area off for you to have your privacy. You can hardly expect to bunk up with the boys and as you know, Jacob now has your room. I can hardly turf him out.' In Bessie's eyes, Jacob could do no wrong and Lucy wondered if maybe the woman was letting him have too much of his own way.

After sitting in front of the fire together with cups of hot chocolate, Lucy stood and yawned. She was dead on her feet. 'I think I'll go up, Auntie,' she said, bowing her head to kiss the woman on her forehead.

'I won't be much longer meself. I just want to finish off a few more rows of me knitting,' she said. 'You go up love, take the candle from the mantelshelf.'

Lucy nodded and then she lifted the candle in its brass holder and made her way up the stairs, the flickering shadow from the candle showed off her silhouette as she climbed the stone stairs.

The curtained off area wasn't too bad. The pallet was on the floor but Bessie had placed a small wooden cupboard beside it where Lucy could leave her things, so she set her candle on top of that.

All was quiet and peaceful in the house which lulled her into a false sense of security. She'd forgotten for a moment that Bert had yet to return home.

Chapter Six

Lucy blew the candle out and for a while lay there in the dark feeling the unfamiliarity of it all. Although she'd lived in the house up until now and it had been all she'd known, she hadn't slept in Bessie and Bert's bedroom apart from when she was a young baby when the woman had taken her in. Finally, she drifted off, and was vaguely aware of hearing Bessie coming to bed with her heavy footsteps and equally heavy breathing.

Then all went quiet and the next thing she knew she heard a stumbling noise and Bessie saying, 'Sssh Bert! Lucy's asleep in the corner!'

'C'mon now, Bessie, you know you want to be nice to me darlin', she's probably asleep by now...'

'Shurrup Bert, go to sleep, you're drunk again!'

There was a loud hiccup and then silence, apart from the creaking of the bed springs as he'd climbed into bed with Bessie. Thankfully, there was no more noise after that, only Bert's odd snore here and there, and the next thing Lucy knew daylight was flooding into the room. She heard Bessie bustling around, as she muttered under her breath at the way Bert had discarded his jacket and boots on the floor for her to pick up. Blinking, Lucy sat up and stretched her arms above her head. Then she pulled herself to her feet and peered out of the curtain, hoping that Bert was still asleep. Thankfully, he still was. She glimpsed Bessie making her way out of the bedroom but did not call her for fear of waking Bert. Quickly, she dressed behind the curtain and padded her way softly out of the room. As she passed by, she looked at the drunken pig lying on his stomach on the bed, unshaven and smelling strongly of alcohol. He even still had his shirt and trousers on which were rumpled to high heaven. Why did Bessie put up with this? She deserved so much better. She was a hard worker and a good person.

As she entered the living room, Bessie looked up from where she was stoking the fire. 'Good morning, lovely girl!' she greeted. 'Sorry if Bert disturbed you last night?'

'Good morning! No worries there, I did hear him coming to bed but went straight back to sleep and slept like a log up until now. It's nice having a good long sleep as I'm up at five o'clock most mornings at the coaching inn. What time is it anyhow?'

'Well you ain't had much of a lie in as it's half past six, me love. I need to get on with me day's baking that's why I'm up.'

'Would you like me to help you today?'

'Would you, sweetheart? Doesn't seem fair to me though on your day off.'

'I can't think of anything else I'd rather do today.' And she meant it and all, just being in Auntie's company was enough for her. 'I'll make us some tea and toast, shall I?'

Bessie nodded eagerly. 'There's a good girl you are to me!'

Lucy went to fill the kettle at the bosh and put it on the hob to boil, usually it was put on the fire but she needed that for the toast. While the kettle was boiling, she gave herself a cat's lick style wash at the bosh and dried her face and hands in the rough towel hanging next to it. Next, she cut two slices off the big bloomer loaf beside her and carried them on a plate to the fire place, where she knelt down and speared them on a toasting fork that was hanging by the side of the fire.

'How's the pie business going, anyhow?' she asked.

'Pretty good to tell you the truth but it's more than I can keep up with, I could do with a little bakehouse of me own!' Bessie laughed.

'That might not be such a bad idea. But can you afford it?'

Bessie drew near and whispered. 'I've squirreled a fair bit away from the money I've made the past few years, 'specially since Bert was in the nick, don't tell him though, he has no idea I've done so well. He sees this as a bit of a hobby for me. I suppose if I could move house and it had a little building with it that could be converted for a big oven, that would help. Couldn't afford to buy a brand new one though, not at the mo, but maybe I could purchase a second hand one.'

'That sounds a really good idea. Jacob and Harry could help run the business, too.'

'Yes, they've already been helping a bit lately with deliveries.'

'What about Bert though?'

'How'd you mean?' Bessie blinked several times.

'Well, he's hardly paying his way, he could help out with some deliveries, surely?'

'Pah!' she scoffed. 'Hardly! He reckons he has a bad back and wouldn't be able to push a handcart around Whitechapel for me.'

Why didn't that surprise her? All Lucy could see was a man who wasn't working for his keep. He was a kept man who was as useless as a wet newspaper on a Wednesday!

'I know what you're thinking, Lucy, 'onest I do, darlin'. But I can hardly turn him away now he's got his feet back under the table. Who would take him in for one thing?'

Lucy said nothing, but returned to her task in hand. She had no intention of burning the bread whilst they were discussing Bert Harper. But she had to admit Bessie's idea about getting her own bakehouse was a good one. There was no room here even to build one, there was just a small back yard which led to an alleyway. If she had the right property that either came with some sort of out building or had enough land to build one, it could work. She wanted the woman to do well as she'd yet to taste a pie as tasty as Bessie's. Which got her thinking, maybe she'd ask her auntie if she could take one back for Smithy when she left.

Even Bessie's tea was nicer here. At the inn it was served weak and watery, but Bessie didn't skimp on her tea leaves, by heck she didn't. Her tea wasn't so dark and tannin thick that you could stand your spoon in it, but it was just the right colour as to how Lucy liked it and all: a rich velvety brown, like the golden suntan she'd acquired during the summer from hop picking with the family. Lucy laid down her toast and lifted her cup from its saucer, cupping her hands around the sweet brew, warming them nicely on a cool morning. Autumn was in the air that was for sure.

'I've had an idea for me baking today, Lucy,' Bessie declared proudly with a gleam in her eyes.

Lucy looked up from her cup to study her auntie's face. 'Oh yes?'

'I think I'll bake some apple tarts for a change to go with me meat pies. See if they'll take any around the pubs. When we finish these, we can get off early to market to purchase the best apples!'

'Oh, that's a smashing idea.' Lucy liked the idea of that. And so, with the boys and Bert still out for the count in their beds, Bessie and Lucy set off for the market place with a basket each over the crooks of their arms.

People had already begun to mill into the market, even at such an early hour. Costermongers had set up their stalls, packed with fresh fruit and vegetables. There were even clothes stalls, bakery goods, a hot potato stall and a meat stall and another containing fish, caught fresh that morning, wet and shiny on thick white slabs.

'C'mon buy your fruit and veggies here!' a stall holder shouted. 'Cheapest price in the whole of Whitechapel. Rich shiny apples just fallen from the tree! Mouth-watering spuds—

you won't find any eyes in these, madam!' he said, addressing an elderly lady who was obviously enjoying the patter, enchanted by the gentleman's witty repartee.

'I need a few pounds of them green cooking apples, my man!' Auntie Bessie said shrewdly. 'Don't want any maggots in them neither.'

The man chuckled, as he picked up a few and juggled with them as his young assistant took Bessie's basket as his boss tossed one to him at a time with a flourish to put in her basket, as he juggled the rest one-handed.

It was quite a show as people drew near from other stalls to watch the spectacle before them. A roar, a cheer from the crowd, and then, wild applause.

Aunt Bessie's blue eyes twinkled vividly. It was good to see her happy, something she definitely was not when Bert was around.

On their way home from Spitalfield's Market, Bessie paused a moment and taking Lucy's hand into her own, said in a soft tone of voice, 'Lucy, you know I want what's best for you, don't you darlin'?'

Lucy nodded. 'Of course I do, Auntie. I can well imagine what that man's been saying to you to make you feel so upset. What makes you say such a thing?'

Bessie chewed on her bottom lip. 'It's just I don't want you to think it was I who was getting rid of you.'

'Auntie, I know who it is behind it all, and to be quite truthful, perhaps it is best I'm away from the house most of the time as I don't feel particularly comfortable around Bert.'

'What makes you say such a thing?' Bessie blinked several times in disbelief.

'Oh, I don't know, it's the way he is with me sometimes.' She could hardly tell her auntie the real reason that he now appeared to be undressing her with his eyes.

'Aw, it's just his way that's all, he doesn't know how to speak to you, darlin'.'

But Lucy knew it was far more than that, he'd always resented her presence. She'd just felt it deep down inside. He made a fuss of his own children, but not of her. At first, she'd thought it was because they were boys and she was a girl, so he didn't know how to relate to her, but it ran deeper than that. She'd once heard him questioning Bessie where she'd come from and Bessie had got all flummoxed and sent her out of the room. Then there were raised voices and the sound of her beloved aunt crying. There'd obviously been resentment on Bert's part. He hadn't wanted her in the home.

They spent the rest of the walk home in silence along the cobbled streets. And it wasn't until they were inside the house and Bessie had put the kettle on to boil that she spoke again. 'Aye, I know, darlin',' she said, settling herself down in the armchair nearest to the fire. 'It's not easy for you as you're no longer a child and now a young lady…' her voice trailed off as she touched the brown earthenware teapot with her hand. 'That's odd…'

'What is?' Lucy quirked a brow of confusion.

'The pot is warm and we've been gone for an hour.'

Lucy had never seen her jump out of her chair so fast in all her life, as she bolted up the stairs. Within a minute or two, she had returned huffing and puffing, her face scarlet red, reminding Lucy of the rosy plump apples at the market.

'What's wrong, Auntie?'

'It's bloomin' Bert. He's left the house, the bleedin' flamer! He was supposed to be watching the boys for me to bake today. But it's not that so much as they're getting to an age now where they can almost take care of themselves.'

'What is it, then?' But Lucy had no need to ask—it was written all over Bessie's face, she feared he'd go on another bender.

'The boys are still fast asleep while the rotter has crept out behind me back.'

'Never mind, Auntie, at least you've got me to help with the baking and the lads can have a kick of their football down the alley.'

'Aye, you're right!' she declared clucking her teeth and then rolling up her sleeves as if she meant business. If there was one thing you could say about Bessie, it was that she was a hard worker—there was no stopping her once she started.

They spent the morning baking. While Bessie measured out the flour into the awaiting mixing bowl, Lucy got the boys up from bed and gave them a bowl of oatmeal each and a cup of milk, then ordered them to get washed and dressed and go to play outside, whilst she got stuck into the work with Bessie. They could do this. Bessie's business was growing nicely and she didn't want to let the woman down right now as her auntie needed her. Lucy had heard the customers at the coaching inn ask for the mouth-watering pies and many made a point of staying there just for those pies. They were so popular that customers took them in their coaches, wrapped up in muslin for their long journey ahead.

As Bessie vigorously rolled out the pastry on the floured counter, she sighed heavily.

'What's the matter, Auntie?' Lucy said as she tied an apron around herself to protect her dress.

'I've just been wondering if it's worth all this hassle.'

Lucy could hardly believe her ears. 'Of course it's worth it, Auntie. You are doing so well.'

'Aye, maybe, gal…' she sniffed and turned back to her task in hand.

***

Quite soon the succulent aroma of baked apple and cinnamon permeated the air, giving Lucy a warm, cosy feeling inside. 'I think your apple pies are going to prove popular, Auntie,' she said as she watched Bessie bend down to take a baking tray out of the oven.

'Well, I'm just giving these a go to see how well they sell,' Bessie said, placing the hot tray down in the middle of the large pine table. She was using a thick towel to carry the trays not to burn her fingers.

'They'll go down a storm at the coaching inn,' Lucy smiled, knowing full well she was right about that.

'Aye, I suppose they might as there are some customers of a refined nature what stay overnight at that place. That sort would appreciate them. But you can't beat me meat ones. That's what the working, and drinking men for that matter, yearn for. Fodder for their bellies to soak up all that ale they sup! I'm not entirely sure the apple pies will be all that popular to be 'onest with you though!'

Lucy knew in her heart that her aunt sometimes doubted herself and she guessed Bert had more than a little to do with that. He seemed to chip away at her auntie's confidence with his put downs and jibes. Why did she put up with it?

'Ma!' Jacob stood by the back door with a ball made from a pig's bladder under his arm. 'Got anything for us to eat, Ma? We're bloomin' starvin'!'

Harry was stood in the shadow of his elder brother. 'Be off with you, both!' Bessie said sharply. 'Lucy hasn't long since given yer a bowl of oatmeal each!'

'I know,' Jacob scowled. 'But we're still hungry.' Lucy looked at her aunt for guidance. 'Go on, gal, butter them a slice of bread each to take away with them, and a slice of cheese. Wrap the food up in that piece of muslin there!' She pointed to a spare piece left over from where she'd wrapped up some pies. 'And boys, if Lucy does that, can you promise to stay out another couple of hours till we finish off the rest of these pies?'

Jacob and Harry both nodded eagerly. Bessie smiled at them. Jacob had a way of getting around his mother and the boy took every advantage of it. Though to be fair, Lucy had noticed Jacob often tried to defend his mother against his father's hurtful jibes but he was no match for his father who could get his head in an armlock within seconds. But Jacob was growing and becoming bigger and stronger day by day.

When the boys had left with their impromptu snack, Lucy got to work cleaning up the counters and washing the used pie tins so Bessie could bake more.

'Ideally,' Bessie said, 'I could do with a big oven like I was telling you about.'

Lucy nodded. She realised her aunt was right and to expand her business she'd need to employ staff too, but what chance did she have when Bert was piddling his wife's wages away at the various pubs in the area on a nightly and sometimes daily basis too?

When the final trays of pies were in the oven, Bessie poured them a glass of milk each and they sat at the kitchen table.

Lucy took a sip of her milk, then set her glass down again.

'You look thoughtful there, Lucy,' Bessie said gently. 'A penny for them, gal?'

'I was just thinking, I wonder where me mother is laid to rest?'

Bessie's face reddened. Lucy realised there was a secret she was keeping from her—she wasn't telling her the full story about the circumstances of her birth, she was sure of it. All Bessie had said so far was that her mother, who was Bessie's sister, had died in child birth. Initially, she hadn't questioned this, but lately she realised how different she looked to the rest of the family. Surely, if she was related, she'd have the same strawberry blonde hair as her aunt, or even red hair like Jacob, not the dark locks and dark brown eyes she had? She'd always felt like an outsider no matter how her aunt had included her and that became most apparent when Bert arrived on the scene, before that she hadn't questioned anything. She'd been too young to understand what it all meant.

Was her aunt crying or were her eyes watering? 'Auntie, are you all right? I didn't mean to upset you?'

Bessie shook her head and set down her glass of milk. 'No, you haven't upset me, darlin', it's me what's upset you by not telling you the full truth about where you came from.'

Lucy took a sharp intake of breath; Auntie was about to tell all...

Chapter Seven

Bessie patted the back of Lucy's hand. 'I'm sorry, darlin', I should have told you this sooner…' She swallowed a lump in her throat and dabbed at her eyes with a clean cotton handkerchief.

'I'm listening, Auntie…' Lucy said.

'Well, it were like this,' Bessie sniffed. 'It was near to Christmas and a perishing night it were an' all. It was dark and very cold, there was snow on the ground and a few flakes had just started to fall again when I was out looking for your Uncle Bert around the pubs.'

'Where was he?' Lucy asked.

'Dunno, I never found him in the end, but the search led me to Itchy Park as I was on me way to The Ten Bells. I heard a little mewling sound, at first I thought it might have been a cat or a kitten and I couldn't even 'ave beared to think of a poor little beast being out on a night like that, never mind a baby. But a baby there was on a bench all wrapped up in a white blanket.' She rose from the table and brought something from the cupboard in the corner. Lucy could see it was a brown paper package which Auntie then set down on the table and undid the string to show her what was inside.

Lucy gasped as Auntie opened the brown paper. It was the blanket that Auntie had spoken of. Even though slightly yellowed, Lucy could tell it was well knitted and had probably cost a fine penny. She couldn't believe what she was hearing from Auntie. 'That was me, wasn't it? I was that baby?' She blinked several times in disbelief.

'Yes, it was, me darlin'.'

'Was there anyone with me?'

Auntie slowly shook her head and sat down again. 'I waited a while and cuddled you in, you were wrapped in that knitted blanket, but if you'd been left there much longer, I'd have no doubt you'd have died.' As she spoke her eyes filled with fresh tears at the memory of it all. She shook her head. 'How anyone could have left you like that to the mercy of the elements never mind to the mercy of the low life what hangs around that place…'

'What happened next?' Lucy asked in barely a whisper.

'Well I searched Itchy park high and low, behind the bushes and all in case your mother was there. You know, I figured maybe she'd taken short or had gone there with someone.'

Lucy furrowed her brow. 'Why would she do that?'

'Never you mind, I'll tell you when you're older. Well, there was no one to be found, so I took you to a nearby chop house and gave you some warm milk sop to feed you up. The waitress reckoned she'd seen a young lady with a baby earlier who was in the company of a well-dressed gent, some kind of nob by the seem of it. Must have looked right out of place in that joint with the rum sorts what hang around that place. She left with you that night but never returned. So, I figured she must have left you in the park right afterwards. And when we were looking at you, I noticed you were clinging on tightly to something in the palm of yer hand.'

'What was it?'

'I'll show you now,' Bessie said as she rose again to leave the table.

Lucy could hear her aunt's footsteps ascending the stairs and she returned within minutes dangling something silver and shiny on a fine chain from her fingers. 'What's that?'

'It's a locket, Lucy. In fact, that's why I named you Lucy as I didn't know your name, after that nursery rhyme, *Lucy Locket lost her pocket*...Here take it!'

Lucy took the locket from her aunt and studied it in the palm of her hand, running her fingers over the delicate engraved pattern. 'It's beautiful,' she said.

'It looks like it cost a pretty penny to me to be honest with you. That's a quality piece that's what that is! I'm no expert but...'

'But what?' Lucy was leaning forward in her chair with avid interest.

'But there are a couple of things inside the locket. Open it up.'

Lucy studied it for a moment, then flicked the locket open with her fingernail. She was astonished to see a lock of fine hair inside and a rolled-up piece of paper.

'I believe the hair is yours as it matched your hair that night, all fine and wispy. And if you unroll the piece of paper there's a message on it. Go on.'

Lucy did as told, gasping as she did so. 'Take care of my baby,' she said slowly. She flipped the locket over to see the name "Adella" finely engraved on its back. 'Is that my mother's name, do you think?' She gazed at her aunt's face as she searched for the answer. What she saw there was a warmth and compassion for the whole predicament.

Bessie paused a moment as if searching for the right words. 'Definitely. The waitress heard that toff call the young woman by that name.'

'Adella is such a lovely name. What did she look like, Auntie?'

'I only wish I knew. I never saw her meself and the waitress didn't give too much detail. I should have thought at the time to ask more questions, but I was so concerned about getting you back home into the warmth. I suppose I assumed that you'd been…'

'Been what?'

'Abandoned…'

Abandoned?

Lucy swallowed a lump in her throat that she hadn't realised had formed there. 'So, my mother didn't want me?' Her eyes brimmed with tears.

Bessie shrugged her shoulders. 'We can't make that assumption. There might well have been a good reason why she left you the way she did. And at least she left you somewhere where you would be found.'

'But you know the sorts that hang around Itchy Park! Anyone could have taken me!' Her chin jutted out in indignation.'

Bessie leaned forward and touched Lucy's hand. 'Don't take on so, darlin', we might never find the answer to that one. I'm sure she did what she felt was best at the time, we can't possibly know what she was going through and according the waitress, she was quite young.'

Lucy shook her head in disbelief. 'And what made you lie to me?' she removed her hand from Auntie's touch as if it was burning her.

Bessie's cheeks flamed with embarrassment. 'I...I...don't know. I suppose I thought it would be for the best if you believed I was your real auntie and that your mother had died in childbirth.'

'That's unbelievable.' Lucy felt unable to take any more of this. What her aunt had revealed had opened a huge wound in her heart and to make matters worse, knowing her mother was possibly still alive and out there somewhere and not knowing where, created a whole new sense of misery for her.

'Speak to me, Lucy,' Auntie said.

But Lucy remained silent as she fought back tears. As Auntie stood to check on the pies baking in the oven, she quietly slipped out through the back door.

***

Back at The Horn and Bugle, Smithy was leaning up against the wall near the stables. 'What's the matter, Princess?' he asked softly. She liked it when he called her that as it made her feel really special.

Wiping away a tear away with the back of her hand, she looked him in the eye. 'I've just discovered I was abandoned at birth and my real mother might still be alive.'

He stared at her for a moment as if trying to digest the information she'd just imparted. 'But that's good, ain't it?'

'What do you mean?'

'Well even though you were left behind, you know that your mother might still be around and you might even find her. Before you thought she was dead, so there was no chance of meeting her.'

'I suppose so.' Why did it still hurt? This pain that wouldn't go away, it was like an empty ache inside her heart.

Because you were abandoned that's why! Left to the elements that night and all alone in the world—no child should have to suffer that.

Smithy was quiet for a few moments and then he said, 'You never know, gal, maybe your mother will even call into the coaching inn on her way some place, some day. She'll look so much like you that you'll know without a shadow of a doubt who she really is.'

Lucy nodded, but she thought Smithy's idea was a daft one. What were the chances of that? 'I just want to belong to someone, Smithy…' Her voice began to crack with emotion. 'I don't really know who I am any more. I mean, I thought I did know. Just yesterday I was Bessie's niece and now I find out I'm no relation to her whatsoever!'

Smithy stepped forward and draped a reassuring arm around her. 'Well, I'll tell you summfink, whether you find your mother or not, yer'll always have me and if you want to from now on, you can be my girl!'

She smiled through her unshed tears. 'I think I'd like that,' she started to sob, and within moments she was in his arms feeling safer than she'd felt in a long while.

'So, are you back at the inn now? I thought you were staying at yer auntie's house for a few days?'

'I was, but I don't think I'll return there now.'

He angled his head in a curious fashion, then rubbed his chin. 'But won't she be worried about you?'

'No doubt she will, but she lied to me and I don't like that at all!'

Smithy raised his brows. 'Sounds to me like yer auntie was trying not to hurt you...'

Lucy shook her head. It didn't make any sense to her why Bessie had felt the need to lie to her like that, it was such a betrayal of trust.

***

Over the next couple of days, Lucy spent as much time as she could with Smithy. She couldn't bring herself to return to Bessie's house and now she wondered if she could live without the woman in her life. After all, she hadn't asked the woman to take her in, she'd had no control over the situation, she'd been a helpless baby abandoned to the elements.

It was nice thinking of herself as Smithy's girl though and she thought about the two of them maybe getting married someday. They'd have their own little house and a nice garden too, not an old brick backyard, and they most definitely would not live in this stinky area of London.

Smithy, himself, seemed only too happy to take on the role of being her protector. The only thing she didn't like was his association with a man at the inn called, *Mr Casper*, or just *Casper* to his friends and close associates. The man was forever calling Smithy to his quarters and Lucy wondered what was going on there. She had a feeling that something was amiss and one day, she saw Smithy leave there with a big smile on his face. As he approached, she heard him rattling some coins in his pocket. 'I'm flush today, gal!' he announced. 'I can take yer out for some jellied eels and maybe we could see a magic lantern show or somefink!'

Lucy narrowed her eyes. 'What's going on? Where'd you get the extra money from?' She knew he wasn't paid all that well as a stable boy at the inn. His job was just to support the ostlers, they did the real hard graft.

'Never you mind!' he tapped the side of his nose with a dirty looking index finger.

'Well I do mind, I want to know!' She yelled, thrusting out her chin in annoyance.

He cocked her a cheeky grin. 'Look, gal, all that happens is I do a bit of business with old Casper. He gets me to look for stuff that rich folk leave behind at the coaching inn and he gives me a good price for it. It's all little things these rich people don't even notice they've left behind as they have so much!'

Lucy harrumphed. She guessed this was half the truth as she had once glimpsed the inside of Casper's quarters and it was like an Aladdin's cave in there. There was something shifty about the bloke that she just did not like. She'd once heard Bert refer to Casper as being a "fence", though she didn't really understand what that meant at the time, but now she had a ruddy good idea what it was. He was selling the stuff on to others and getting good prices for it too.

'All right then,' she said as she had nothing better to do as she still officially had a couple more days off work. She'd worry about where he really got the money from later. For now all she wanted to do was to have some fun and forget all her troubles.

'That's the spirit, Princess!' Smithy patted her amicably on the back. 'Just give me another hour and I'll have finished here. There's a coach due any moment.' She nodded and made her way back to her bedroom. At least it was something to do of an evening, something to keep her mind off things.

Chapter Eight

Lucy donned her Sunday best dress—the one her aunt had recently made for her. She also had a bonnet with a matching ribbon. She removed the ribbon from it, brushed her hair until it shone and tied it in her hair, allowing her locks to cascade on her shoulders. A pang of guilt washed over her when she thought of the time her aunt had spent selflessly sewing that dress for her when she had better things to do. She'd even stayed up late at night, squinting her eyes by candlelight to get it finished by morning. At the thought of that, she broke down into tears. None of this was Auntie's fault. How could she have been so stupid to think it was? She still had half an hour or so before she saw Smithy, maybe even longer as she hadn't even heard the coach he mentioned arrive as yet. That's what she'd do, she'd pop over to see her aunt right now and apologise to her for walking out like that.

On the way, she'd worked out what she'd say to her, *'Sorry, Auntie, I was so silly the other day, what you told me came as such a shock. I just couldn't deal with my emotions…'* Surely Auntie would understand? She sniffed, then dabbed at her eyes with a clean handkerchief she found in her dress pocket. Auntie thought of everything. How selfish was she turning on her like that when the woman had only been trying her best and had put a roof over her head all these years? If she'd been discovered by someone else she could well have ended up in the workhouse or even died that bitterly cold night.

***

As Lucy stood outside the front door of her old home, she felt ashamed of her earlier impetuous behaviour. She could only put it down to the shock of being told that her auntie was no real relation to her at all and that she'd been found abandoned as a baby on a bench in Whitechapel!

Gulping, she rapped on the door with its peeling paint, to find it eventually swinging open to the smiling face of Bert. That was most unusual for him. 'Sorry,' she apologised, taking a step back and ready to leave. 'I was hoping to see Auntie.' She knew that Bert rarely opened the door when Bessie was around as he saw it as being her duty as if she were some sort of skivvy for him. Not only that, but sometimes she got the distinct impression he was hiding from someone. She'd once overheard him being scolded by Bessie as it had become evident that Bert had run up a lot of debt all over Whitechapel. No wonder he didn't often answer the door and probably only appeared pleased to see her as she wasn't some burly bloke who had arrived on the doorstep to bash his brains out.

'She won't be long,' he said softly. 'Come inside and wait a while…' He gestured with his grubby hand. 'She's just popped out to the bake house down the road. She baked a very large batch of pies this morning and needed a bigger oven.'

Lucy nodded tentatively as she followed him inside, her eyes darting this way and that. 'Where are the boys?'

'Next door with Mave. They won't be long either.' He rubbed his chin as if mulling something over as he appraised her with his dark grey eyes.

A shiver coursed the length of her spine and she had no idea why except that maybe it was the intensity of his stare. 'I'd offer you a cup of tea but I'm not so good at making it, Bessie reckons it always tastes like gnat's p—' He purposely stopped himself from saying the word as if not to show himself up.

Lucy nodded, preferring not to be in his company, so she said, 'How about I make us a cup then?' It would be an excuse to put a barrier in the shape of a door and another room between them.

'That would be great!' Inwardly, she breathed a sigh of relief. 'Ain't you the grown-up lady now then, young miss?' The way he licked his lips made her flesh crawl as if he were a lizard about to devour a small insect. She was thankful of the chance to escape into the kitchen, closing the door behind her but leaving it slightly ajar not to alienate him. Hopefully, by the time she'd brewed up, Bessie might have returned. She wanted to close the door fully shut behind her but that would make the disgust she felt for him too obvious, so this was the next best option. She filled the kettle with water and put it on the hob to boil, then she located the tea caddy on the shelf above the range where it always was. As she waited for the kettle to boil, she sensed a presence behind her. Turning, Bert was stood there. How had he crept up so silently without her being aware of it? Maybe the sound of the boiling kettle and the shrieks and laughter from the alley outside had drowned out his footsteps. Or maybe he'd been that canny, he'd crept up like a cat on its prey, ready to pounce on her.

'Forget the tea,' he said, drawing closer as she swallowed hard.

'Sorry?'

'I said forget the tea…'

He was that close she felt his warm sour breath on the back of her neck as she felt a shiver run down her spine. Then she turned to face him so he might not take her off guard. 'Very well,' she said. 'But I would like a cup while I wait.'

'There's no need for it, you can have one later. Come and make yourself comfortable in the livin' room with me, darlin'. I've got a little present for you…'

'A present?' Since when had Bert ever given her a present?

When he could see she was adamant about making the tea, he said, 'I'll go and fetch it for you.'

What should she do? She had a chance to escape out of the backdoor, but it seemed rude to do so and maybe she was misreading the situation anyhow.

He returned within moments with something in his hand. Then he opened his palm wide to reveal a small dark blue velvet box. 'Open it, Lucy,' he said, using her name for the first time in ages. 'It's all yours if you want it?'

How on earth could he afford to buy her a present when Bessie made out he was always on his uppers and she had to keep bailing him out?

Out of curiosity, she took it from him and opened the box to see something blue and sparkling inside. It was a pretty blue stoned necklace, she'd never seen anything so lovely, apart from the silver locket Bessie had shown her.

Looking at him wide eyed with surprise, she gasped, 'But it's beautiful. Where did you get it from?'

'I've been saving up to buy it for you. I realise I haven't always treated you as I should have done in the past as you're not a blood relation. I know I can tell you this now as Bessie informed me that she'd told you the real circumstances of your birth. To be truthful, I feel ashamed of meself as I thought Bessie had dropped her drawers for someone when I was in prison…'

'She'd never have done that, Bert. She's a good, kind person. She worked hard when you were put away to put a roof over our heads and wouldn't have had time to go out courting someone else. I was only young at the time but I do remember some of it.'

'Aye, I know. Well do you like it?' His eyes widened in expectation.

She was now looking at Bert in a new light, maybe she'd misjudged the man and he did want to pour oil on troubled waters. 'That's very kind of you,' she beamed. No doubt, he and Bessie had gone to choose it together to make up for all the upset he'd caused her this past few years.

'Good, then allow me to put it on you,' he said.

She nodded as he fumbled in a clumsy fashion with the clasp and placed it upon her neck, letting the palms of his hands rest a little too long on her shoulders as she raised her hair with both hands, but before she could say anything, she heard voices outside as the boys burst into the kitchen. She didn't know why, but she felt it necessary to slip the necklace beneath the collar of her dress as if she didn't want them to see it and that made her feel very bad indeed, but at least they'd returned at an opportune time as she was feeling so uncomfortable with the situation. But it was a very pretty necklace indeed.

'W…would you like a cup of tea, boys?' she asked brightly.

They both nodded. 'Where 'ave yer been, Lucy?' Harry asked innocently.

'I've been back at the inn.'

He scowled. 'But I thought you were going to be staying 'ere for a few days?'

Before she had a chance to answer, Bert saved the day. 'Well, she was busy but she's here now and from my understanding, she still has a day's leave remaining, so we can all spend that precious time together.' He winked at Lucy as a hot blush seared her cheeks. She didn't quite know whether she liked this new version of Bert or not. She'd felt uncomfortable before when he ignored her or left her out of things but now, she felt even more uncomfortable as she had a feeling he'd be paying her more attention from now on.

***

Lucy had just finished her cup of tea when Bessie breezed in through the back door, her cheeks flushed from the cold and her hair slightly messed up from the wind outside. 'Lucy!' she exclaimed as her eyes lit up. 'I didn't think we'd be seeing you again the way you…'

'Walked out of here,' Lucy said, finishing her sentence for her. 'I'm ashamed of myself, honest I am. I've had time to think about things, and I am so sorry, Auntie. None of this was your fault. Over the years you've done the very best you can for me. Will you ever forgive me?'

Auntie's eyes filled with tears. 'Of course I will. I should have thought it through and not told you in such a manner. Come here and give me a hug!'

Then she was in her aunt's arms, safe and secure for a few moments until she heard Bert's voice interrupting a tender moment. 'What's for tea then, Bessie love?'

'Hold yer 'orses, Bert, the prodigal has arrived home and I'd like a little chat with her for a few minutes. Make yerself scarce before I ask you to do something for me and take the boys with yer.'

At the thought of having to do any work, Bert got out of his favourite armchair and rounded the boys up for a kick of the ball in the alley. While Bessie laughed until she almost cried. Wiping away her tears she said, 'I knew that would get rid of the lazy old bugger!'

Lucy smiled.

Her aunt's voice took on a tone of concern. 'What's the matter, gal? Something troublin' you?' How could she tell her aunt the thing that was troubling her had just left the room to play football outside with his sons?

'No, I'm all right. I'll leave after I've made you a cuppa and we've had a little chat.'

Bessie frowned. 'Yer not staying the night, then?'

'Er, I better not—I'm meeting my friend, Smithy. We're hoping to go to a magic lantern show later. I think I'd best stay at the inn tonight, but I'll be back soon you can be sure of that.'

From now on, Lucy decided she didn't want to be left alone with Bert. Maybe she was silly to have accepted that gift from him, but if it was harmless then she should tell Auntie as she'd know all about it, but something inside her told her Auntie knew nothing about it at all. And she didn't want to hurt the woman.

Chapter Nine

Breathless and exhausted from running all the way, Lucy made it back to the inn but when she arrived there, Smithy was nowhere to be seen. That was so strange as she'd been expecting him to be waiting for her.

She entered the kitchen by the back door to be faced with Cassie who had the sleeves of her dress rolled up to the elbow, her face all puffy and red. When she saw Lucy, she wiped her forehead. 'What's the matter with you gal, want to come back to work on one of yer days off, do yer?' She carried on speaking before Lucy had a chance to intervene as she splashed about in the old stone bosh washing the dishes. 'Been busy as hell 'ere it 'as an' all, could have done with yer help a bit earlier. A couple of coaches turned up unexpectedly.'

Lucy nodded in sympathy as she knew full well what it was like when they were descended upon. Meals had to be cooked and prepared at short notice, pots and pans washed and stacked away and the bar area would be heaving, though the landlord loved that. He was a great host as he'd question the customers where they'd come from and where they were off to. 'I'm looking for Smithy, we were supposed to go to a magic lantern show together but I'm a bit late.'

'Ain't seen him for some time, gal. He'd 'ave been helping the ostlers I expect. Go and check the stables, maybe he's having a kip.'

'Thanks.'

'Sure yer don't want to stay and help me? There's a bit of left-over pie fer yer trouble if yer do, like.'

Lucy shook her head vehemently. She was looking forward to the lantern show and she needed to apologise to Smithy, she didn't like letting him down like that.

'All right then, off you go, gal!' Cassie said with a resigned tone. 'I fink if I were in yer shoes I'd be the same meself. Make the most of it while yer can as you won't be 'aving any more days off fer quite some time.'

Lucy said her goodbyes and ran off in the direction of the stables. A young ostler was just leaving, he looked tired. His face grubby and his clothing was dishevelled. 'You seen Smithy?' she asked in expectation.

'Er...no,' he mumbled as his face flushed beet red. There was something about his manner that warned her the lad was being a bit shifty as his eyes darted this way and that. 'He's definitely not in them stables.'

Lucy thanked him but as soon as he'd departed, he headed in the direction of the kitchen, for a slice of Cassie's meat and potato pie no doubt. She turned on her heel to check the stables. There was no sign of anyone in the first stable, not even a horse but it still stank to high heaven of manure. To tell the truth, she'd half expected to find Smithy flat out on a bale of hay snoring his head off like Cassie had thought, but her stomach slumped down to her boots when she saw he wasn't there. Still, there were other stables to check. She looked in them all but it was the same story, they were empty, apart from one that had a horse stabled in it.

'Why does life have to be so difficult?' she asked the chestnut brown mare.

The horse snorted as if it understood as she smoothed its head.

There was one more stable to check out, a smaller one that was rarely used on the opposite side of the courtyard. As she approached, she heard a giggle and then a cough. Who on earth was in there? That light, high-pitched laughter sounded like it belonged to a female. But who?

'Oooh that bleedin' tickles! Watch yer hands they're icy cold!'

Feeling a sense of dread wash all over her, Lucy made her way tentatively towards the stable entrance.

'Go on, yer know yer want to, Nellie, me love...' She heard a familiar voice say in a husky tone that was thick with lust. Her heart sank when she realised it was Smithy and what he was up to. Should she confront the pair? Or leave now while she had a chance of not being spotted? Her stomach was churning at the upset of it all. Although she hadn't known Smithy very long and they'd hardly had a chance to develop their relationship, the betrayal cut through her like a knife. Nellie should have known better than to try to get off with someone else's fella. At that point something came over Lucy that was no longer dread as it fired her up like she hadn't been fired up in a long time. It made her heart almost pound out of the bodice of her dress with anger.

As she approached the darkened stable that was only lit by a small flickering lantern on a window ledge that cast large shadows of the pair, she snapped,

'Couldn't even wait half an hour for me, could you, Smithy?'

Smithy emerged from a tangle of arms and legs where he'd been entwined with Nellie and, from the state of her dishevelled dress as the bottom of it rode high above her knees in a scandalous manner and her mobcap was all skewwhiff on her head, it was obvious what the pair had been up to.

On seeing Lucy there with her hands on her hips and her chin jutting out in a proud fashion, Smithy stopped what he was doing and his hands went immediately to his sides as if by altering his body posture Lucy would think that he hadn't done anything at all. How silly was that? She had all the evidence she needed. He opened his mouth to say something then closed it again. 'L…Lucy, my girl!'

She shook her head as the lump in her throat increased in size. 'Well, after that little display you can be sure I am no longer your girl, Smithy! And as for you, Nellie Brown, I thought better of you than this, letting a lad get free with his hands! What will Mr and Mrs Harrington think?'

Nellie's hands flew to her face in horror. 'Yer wouldn't tell them, would you, Lucy?'

'And why not? If I can't trust you, how can they?'

Lucy had no intention of humiliating herself in front of the landlord and landlady by carrying a tale of what had just occurred, but it wouldn't harm Nellie none for her to think she would. She turned on her heel, leaving the pair who had been discovered in flagrante in front of her, in silence. Maybe it was better for her to find out what Smithy was like right now. No way did she want to end up like one of those fallen women, bare foot and pregnant as they walked the streets searching for food and shelter only to end up at the local workhouse or whorehouse. No sir, she did not!

***

It wasn't until Lucy returned to Bessie's house that she had a little weep. Bert, thankfully, had scarpered off to the pub, so they'd both been left chatting by the fireside as the boys had gone off to bed.

'Well, I think it's best that you found out now, dear,' Bessie said, sagely. 'No good in a few months when you've really fallen for the cad!'

Lucy nodded. She had to agree but that still didn't help her broken heart. She had really liked Smithy and hadn't thought him capable of this sort of behaviour. How was she going to carry on working at the inn now with him around? She saw him regularly during the day as he'd turn up at the back door of the kitchen trying to scrounge a bite here and there, or else he was in the bar room, trying to pilfer off customers who were loaded and had no more sense than to get inebriated and leave their valuables lying around for fast fingers to get to work. Smithy had told her they deserved it and they ought to share their wealth with the poor. He was only trying to do what Robin Hood and his Merry Men did, after all. Maybe to Smithy that gave him permission to do as he did as he was rewarded for his efforts with some coinage from Mr Casper, but Lucy knew it was wrong and she didn't like it one bit.

***

It was her final day at the house and now Lucy had settled back in she just didn't feel like returning to the inn, knowing what Smithy and Nellie had been up to behind her back. Bert had been unusually quiet and she began to figure that maybe she'd just misjudged the man. After all, it couldn't have been easy for him coming out of prison to find his wife was now bringing up another child that was most definitely not his! No wonder he'd been tormented by her. She still wore the pretty necklace beneath the bodice of her dress. Apart from the silver locket she'd had on her when Bessie had found her as a baby, they were the only beautiful items she owned.

'I wonder if you can help me out tonight,' Bessie said as she stoked the fire. Mave has asked me to go to the music hall with her. There's a lady who's top billing there who has come all the way from America and they say she has such a lovely voice! I'd love to go but someone needs to feed my lads and Bert of course…' Bessie looked at her in expectation. What could she say but 'yes'?

'Of course, I can, Auntie. I'll make them some stew if you like with that left-over scrag end of lamb you've got left in the larder.' She didn't really mind at all, as long as she wasn't left alone with Bert, which she shouldn't be, then all would be well as she'd be back working at the inn tomorrow and who knew when her next leave would be? Not until Christmas, she supposed.

'That's settled then.' Bessie rose to her feet and replaced the poker in its holder near the fire place. She sat herself down in her favourite armchair and Lucy did the same in the opposite chair. 'I'm still thinking about getting new premises,' she said. 'I've heard there's one going but it's near that No Man's Land area.'

'No Man's Land?' Lucy frowned. That was a new one to her.

'Yes, that area what goes through that archway a couple of streets from here on the way to Adam and Eve Court, there are often beggars and all sorts there.'

'Do you mean that place where ladies of the night ply their trade?' Lucy asked. She'd seen them in their gaudy bright dresses, flaunting off their ankles trying to lure men into the shadows to fleece them of their wages.

She nodded. 'Yes, that's the place.'

Lucy's eyes widened. 'I do know it and don't like it there to be honest, it gives me the blooming creeps! I never knew it was called No Man's Land.'

'Aye, it is by the locals. That's the only thing that's putting me off though—the area where the house itself is, is much nicer than around here. We'd have more room and a place for a small bakery too. The letting agent says I can rent it for time being but the owner is interested in selling it eventually.' She rubbed her chin as if in contemplation. 'I'm thinking that if me pie business really got off the ground, that in time, maybe I could buy the place.' Her eyes lit up like two shining stars in the sky as she spoke.

'That sounds a good prospect. You'll have to go and take a look at it at least.' Although Lucy wanted to remain positive for her aunt's sake she doubted very much if the woman could afford to rent never mind purchase a property like that.

Bessie carried on, her eyes gleaming with enthusiasm. 'I've viewed it from the outside and it does look in need of a lick of paint, but the house itself looks sound enough. There are some in that street that look very nice indeed. Of course, those ones are well decorated. I'm told that even a doctor lives in one of them!'

'A doctor! My, my, Auntie, you're really going up in the world!' Lucy chuckled, but secretly she liked the idea of them living in a respectable street even if that No Man's Land stood between the haves and the have nots of the area. She just hoped her aunt wouldn't be disappointed if she couldn't afford the place.

Bessie smiled. 'Aye, and maybe about time and all. I've been on the bottom rung of the ladder most of me bloomin' life!'

The only cloud Lucy could think about for her aunt was Bert because as fast as Auntie was earning money, he appeared to be spending it. She would do well to get rid of him, but she wasn't about to say so.

As if reading her mind, Bessie spoke in a hushed tone, even though he wasn't around. 'I'm also doing this for Bert as he can work at the bakery with the boys. It will give him back his sense of pride once again. One of the boys can help him put the pies I make in the oven and the other can help the delivery lad take stock to shops and pubs locally.'

Lucy had to admire her aunt, she had it all worked out. If only life were that simple though. She realised that Bert was no worker and would mooch off whenever he got the chance. There'd be no way he'd do any of the hard graft. How she wished he was no longer around.

Auntie's joyful expression suddenly changed as her eyes took on a pained look as she touched her neck with both hands. 'By the way, Lucy, have you seen my necklace anywhere? It's one what was given to me years ago by my mother. I can't find it where I normally would in my little trinket box on the dressing table.'

Lucy's cheeks seared with embarrassment. So, Bert hadn't bought her that necklace with Bess as she'd thought, he'd stolen it from his wife. What should she do? 'Fess up or say nothing and pretend she'd found it for Bessie? Would she have chance to do so without getting caught in the act? At that moment, she heard someone enter the house through the backdoor.

'It's only me, Bess!' a familiar voice shouted, interrupting Lucy's thoughts. Mave breezed into the room, her cheeks rosy and flushed and her voice animated in her excitement. Now might pose an opportunity to slip the necklace somewhere safe so her aunt could find it and be reunited with it once more. Whilst the two women were nattering away by the fireside discussing their proposed night out together, Lucy slipped upstairs, undid the clasp from the necklace around her neck, and then hid the pretty blue stoned necklace on the wooden floorboards just beneath Bessie and Bert's double bed. When her aunt went to the bedroom later, she would draw her attention to it. As much as she disliked Bert, she didn't want to be the cause of trouble between the pair.

Heaving a sigh of relief, Lucy went back downstairs and joined the women, who were so deep in conversation that they'd hardly missed her at all.

***

As Bessie busied herself to get ready to out for the evening, Lucy sat on her own bed watching her as she pranced up and down the bedroom trying on this and that. She finally opted for a green flowered dress and an old fox stole she'd picked up for a song at Spitalfields Market a month ago. Now was Lucy's chance.

'What's that glittering by there, Auntie?' she asked.

Bessie stopped in her tracks to turn to face Lucy. 'What, me love?'

Lucy pointed. 'There, on the floor beneath your bed, something just caught my eye.'

Bessie stooped to take a peek, lifting the bed covers as she did so. 'I can't see nothing?'

'There, look!'

Auntie took a closer look. 'Well, bless me soul if it ain't me missing necklace! I can wear it tonight, you clever girl!'

Lucy smiled and let out an inward sigh of relief. 'Let me get it for you, you don't want to be crawling under there in your best garb.'

'There's good you are to me.' Bessie puffed as she pulled herself upright by holding on to the bed.

And after a moment of scrambling beneath the bed, as Lucy had placed it well beneath not for Bert to see it, she handed it to its rightful owner. Bessie hugged her. 'What a blessing you've been to me, child!'

Seeing the look of sheer happiness and relief on her aunt's face sent a surge of guilt coursing through her, but Lucy reassured herself that at least she'd eventually done the right thing by drawing Auntie's attention to where she thought she'd lost it.

Bleeding Bert Harper! The good for nothing layabout! Thieving from his own wife like that—would the man stop at nothing?

After making him and the boys supper tonight, she wouldn't have to come near the letch for months as from now on she was only going to visit when he was well out of the way. She didn't need to sleep over ever again either, as now she had her very own room which was sparse and clean. The bed was comfy and she had a wardrobe to hang her few clothes in, a washstand with a pretty jug and matching basin and a small table and chair where she could read or write. There was a smashing view from the window down onto the street below where she could see the comings and goings of customers and even horses and carriages slowing down to enter beneath the archway to stay at the inn.

A voice in her head kept sending her a reminder though but for now she chose to ignore the repetitive warning. *Tell Auntie Bessie that Bert stole her necklace!*

Chapter Ten

It was a quarter past ten and Lucy was dozing in the armchair by the fire. She startled for a moment. Where on earth was Bert? The boys had gone to bed ages ago having enjoyed eating the stew she'd prepared for them. Should she go to bed anyhow? Bert could warm up the stew for himself, but she had promised Bessie she'd give him his supper. She was just about to make herself a hot drink when she heard a clatter in the yard outside which sent her hackles rising and her skin peppering in goose bumps. With no adult in the house she realised how vulnerable she was. The back door was unlocked for Bert but Bessie had her own house key for the front door. In all the time Bert had been back home, Bessie had never again allowed him his own door key—so he was in effectively, at her mercy. If he wasn't home by ten o'clock after one of his drinking sprees, then he got locked out. And on more than one occasion, he'd arrived home looking dishevelled with bits of straw in his hair or stains on his clothing the following morning. Lucy had no idea where he kipped down on those particular nights but she guessed it could have been in an old barn or on a park bench some place.

Her breathing had returned to normal as she decided it must have been a cat that had caused the clatter outside when she went to the kitchen to put on a saucepan of milk to boil. As she waited, she had that creeped out feeling once again as if she was being watched. The kitchen curtains were open, so she quickly drew them and went to lock the back door. She didn't care now if Bert got locked out or not, her safety and that of the boys was the most important thing.

But as she went to turn the key in the lock, she felt some resistance as if someone had hold of the door handle on the other side. She fought to lock the door but the person on the other side was too strong for her and then she stumbled backwards as the door was forced open. And there stood Bert, swaying slightly and smelling strongly of alcohol. That sickening smell she often noticed at the inn when blokes were lairy and their hands roamed towards the barmaids there. It didn't seem to matter whether they were toffs or not, they all seemed the same under the influence of alcohol.

'Bert!' She blinked several times. 'Thank goodness you're home. You scared me for a moment there, I thought there might have been a prowler in the yard!'

He grinned at her. 'Sssh, darlin', come here…' he stepped towards her as she took a step back. 'Those nice ruby lips of yours look fit for kissing. Did you expect your boyfriend here, then?'

'Most certainly not!' she said, feeling affronted. 'I ain't got a boyfriend. Well no more anyhow.'

His eyes widened. 'Did you let him get a bit free with you? A lovely looking young girl like you?'

'No, of course not.'

She suddenly remembered the pan of boiling milk and turned towards the hob to switch it off. After she'd done so, she turned back to find that Bert had invaded her space and was inches away. 'Come on now, gal. You can't tell me that a nice looking ripe young lass like yourself isn't taking advantage of some young lad some place. I bet they'd do anything for you to get their hands on…'

Her stomach flipped over at the lustful glint in his eyes. 'Please, Bert. Don't talk that way. You know I'm not like that…'

'Believe me, darlin', you're all the same. Bessie was about your age when I first met her and nice and rounded and buxom too. I deflowered her in my marital bed as I couldn't resist the little blossom.'

Lucy's heart began to pound, if he was seeing her the way he'd first viewed Bessie then she was in big trouble. Why, oh why, had she been so foolish? She knew deep down the way he'd been looking at her the past few weeks that he had designs on her. She'd developed some womanly curves and it wasn't just Bert who looked at her twice, it was Smithy and some of the ostlers too and some customers at the inn who were old enough to be her father or even grandfather. Sometimes she wished she was just a young, carefree girl again where she didn't warrant such attention from the opposite sex, but even then, in Whitechapel she'd heard of dreadful things happening to very young girls. Age wasn't a boundary for some. It made her shudder to even think of it.

'W…would you like some warm milk, Bert?' she asked in a vain attempt to change the subject but he wasn't listening to her. Instead he grabbed her arm and roughly pulled her towards him. His stare was penetrating as though he wanted to devour her whole there and then on the spot and she felt her body tremble.

'Please, Bert. Please don't do something you might regret, I'm only a young girl and what about Bessie?'

'That's how I likes 'em, love. Young girls haven't lost their bloom, not like Bessie. She looks like a bleedin' matron. More like me mother. It's a chore for me to get fresh with that one, not that she wants it of course. These days she'd rather do anything else than have time for her beloved Bertie.'

If only she could keep him talking to quieten things down. 'I'm sure that's not true, she loves you very much, Bert.'

He shook his head, 'No, she doesn't. She stopped coming to see me when I was in prison. And afterwards.'

'But you went to live with another woman, didn't you?'

He nodded slowly. 'Yes, but that was only because Bessie had gorn orf me. What's a man to do?'

'But she eventually took you back though, so she must feel something for you?'

He shook his head, then pulled her closer towards him and she gulped. Should she try to struggle to get away? She was frozen to the spot, afraid to move a muscle as he ran his hand across her cheek. 'Hmmm those ruby red lips,' he murmured.

The pan of hot milk was just behind her and, if she could only just reach it, she could throw it in his face. She tried to move her hand behind her but the pan was just out of reach.

He dropped his hand to her breast and squeezed. No man had ever done that to her before and no lad had either. She grimaced in horror. She hadn't even allowed Smithy to do that. The inevitable was about to occur, so she raised her knee and tried to give him a swift blow to the groin but he was too quick for her and grabbing her by the hair, marched her over to the kitchen table.

His eyes had now taken on a different look, they were hard as steel and he appeared to have sobered up. 'Lie on there,' he ordered, pushing her towards the table , 'or I'll give you a whack around the face that will ruin those pretty little features of yours forever.'

She began to whimper but she did as told as he moved his hands towards her neck. 'I could squeeze the life out of you right now,' he said in a sinister tone of voice. 'So, do as you're told, then you'll come to no harm. All right?'

She nodded, unable to speak as he had his hands so tightly on her neck. A bit tighter and she'd pass out altogether, or worse.

He released his hands and stood back. 'Now remove yer bloomers and hurry up about it.'

She did as told, struggling to get them down over her boots as he released the belt around his trousers and began to fiddle with his trouser buttons. She couldn't believe this was happening to her and not with someone who Bessie professed to love, the father of her children.

'Now stay put on that table, me lovely,' he said, 'and you won't get hurt. You might even enjoy it from a man of experience!'

She was just about to do as asked as she felt she had no other option, when she heard the front door unlock.

'Quick,' he said, 'hide those in your pinny pocket...' he flung her drawers at her, 'and not a word to Bess, understood? Or I'll punch your lights out!'

She nodded and did as told, sliding herself off the table, she pulled herself to her feet as he tidied himself up. Bessie breezed into the kitchen. 'Ah, I see you pair have been getting on well, then?' she said. Her eyes sparkled as if she'd had a great night out, and Lucy guessed maybe she'd had a glass or two of porter as well.

'Yes, we've been getting along famously, haven't we, Lucy?' He glared at Lucy as if testing her. Lucy nodded, but her legs felt boneless as she recalled what had almost happened to her. 'She was just making me a cup of warm milk before bed, weren't that nice of her, Bess?' He stepped forward and gave his wife a peck on the cheek, then he patted Lucy on the head like she was a little child.

As Lucy turned away, a tear ran down her cheek and she wiped it away with the back of her hand not for her aunt to see there was anything wrong. Then when they had both left the kitchen, she ran outside to the yard to throw up the contents of her stomach. For now, she had to act as if nothing had happened at all. She couldn't hurt Bessie, so she waited until she noticed the oil lamp being lit in the bedroom upstairs, a sign they had both gone to bed, then she wiped away her tears and returned to the house.

Chapter Eleven

The following morning, after very little sleep, Lucy said her goodbyes to Bessie as her pig of a husband snored his head off upstairs. It had been hard to sleep with the brute just feet away from her in the bedroom but he hadn't bothered her all night. He wouldn't have dared with Bessie beside him in bed. The boys were already out in the alley playing pitch and toss, she'd say farewell to them on her way out. For a brief moment, she wondered if she ought to tell her aunt about what occurred last night, but she couldn't bear to break her heart. But one thing she knew for certain, she must never return to this house whilst Bert still lived in it. There was one other thing though, Bert often called into the inn and she feared encountering him there, but on the other hand, what could he do with so many people around? The landlord watched out for her against the customers' wandering hands, anyhow. But in truth, she hadn't seen Bert at the coaching inn for a couple of weeks which seemed most odd and she wondered why he hadn't called in.

***

When she arrived back at The Horn and Bugle, Cassie had her feet up by the fireside in the kitchen, taking a well-earned break. Her eyes were half closed and a clay pipe she smoked from time to time which had been wedged between her teeth, was now beginning to look as if it might fall into the grate at any given moment. Lucy stooped to gently remove it. It had already gone out and she placed it on the mantelpiece. Cassie stirred and mumbled something and then she startled and sat bolt upright. 'The coaches are here, oh heck!' she shouted.

Lucy smiled. 'There are no coaches due here at the moment, Cassie, you've been asleep.'

Cassie yawned and rubbed her eyes. 'My pipe?' Her eyes darted around the room.

'It's all right, it was about to drop out of your mouth so I feared it would crack on the grate. I put it on the mantelpiece for you.'

'There's good you are to me an' all, Lucy. Now you're due back to work here this afternoon, that's right, isn't it? I've not dreamt that?'

Lucy nodded. 'Yes, my shift will begin at noon, but I can help you now if you like?'

'Aye, well I could do with some help peeling some potatoes and carrots.'

'Don't worry, I can do that, I don't mind starting early.'

Cassie studied her face. 'There's something troubling you, I can tell. Sit down a minute, I can spare the time as you'll be helping me later.'

Lucy hesitated for a moment, then took a seat opposite the woman. She placed her hands on her lap, then found herself twisting them this way and that as if not knowing what to do with them.

'Come on, you can't fool old Cassie. Something's gone wrong on this visit home, hasn't it?'

Lucy nodded as she felt a lump in her throat and tears prick her eyes. 'It was only last night that something awful happened, and oh Cassie, I am so glad to be back here…' For the first time since she asked, Lucy looked into the woman's eyes and saw a lot of compassion there.

'Who has upset you, gal?'

'It was Bert.'

'Bert? I know he can be a bit of a bounder at times especially when he comes here and starts his capers but I didn't think he was 'orrible or nothing.'

'Usually, in the past he's left me well alone. He never liked the fact that my aunt took me in as a young baby while he was in prison, but he's never caused me any harm. Just lately though, he's been looking at me in a different way.'

Cassie clucked her tongue and rose to take her clay pipe for the mantelpiece. She took a spill from the glass jar and leaned over to catch a flame from the fire to light her pipe, reseated herself and stared intently in Lucy's direction.

'It's only been happening since I've developed curves and such.'

'Since you've become a young woman, you mean?' She took a puff on her pipe sending out a plume of acrid smoke. Usually, Lucy didn't like the smell of tobacco smoke but for some reason she found it comforting this morning.

'Yes. He's been looking at me in a strange sort of way for the past few weeks, like sort of undressing me with his eyes and it's made me feel uncomfortable.'

Cassie nodded. 'I know the sort of thing you mean, gal. But he's not touched you in that way, 'as he?'

Lucy shrugged. 'Not exactly but...'

Cassie sat forward in her chair. 'But what?'

Lucy swallowed. She was just going to have to spit it out no matter how hard the words were to say. 'Last night my aunt went out to the music hall with our next-door neighbour. It's rare for her to have a night out. Anyhow, she asked me to make supper for the boys and for Bert. He had been gone for hours and I was tired and wanted to go to bed but when he returned home...'

'Bert?'

'Yes. He started trying it on with me saying how I had nice ruby lips. It was obvious what he was after, then he got really nasty with me and his hands went around my neck. Oh, Cassie, it was awful...' She began to sob as she relived the whole experience. Up until now she had managed to swallow her sadness down as she hadn't wanted to upset Bessie or the boys.

Cassie stood and said, 'Come here, lass,' and in an instant, Lucy was in her arms, crying on her shoulder. 'You let it all out.'

When she'd finished crying, Cassie encouraged her to sit back down. 'Do you feel you can talk any more about this?'

Lucy nodded and sniffed.

'After that, he told me he could punch my face in and ruin my features for life.'

'The bloody bastard!' Cassie's eyes bulged with fury. 'I'll get Mr Harrington to ban him from here for life!'

Cassie now looked like a blur as she peered at the woman through glassy eyes. 'Yes, please. But if you do so please warn him not to tell my aunt when she drops the pies off here. I couldn't bear that.'

'Lucy, love, I do think she ought to know in time though when you feel ready to tell her,' Cassie said softly.

'Maybe, but not right now.'

'Anyhow, what happened after that?'

'He…he instructed me to remove my underwear so it was obvious what he had planned. I couldn't even resist as I was that frightened of finding those hands on my neck again, squeezing the life out of me.' She let out a long breath of composure. 'Then, fortunately for me, I heard the front door open and Bessie had arrived in the nick of time.'

'What did she say though when she saw you in that state?'

'She didn't, by then Bert had told me to hide my drawers in my pocket and not to say a word to her so I had to act as if all was well. He told her I was making him a cup of hot milk, so Bessie in her innocence, thought all was well. In fact, she thought we'd been getting on like a house on fire, I could hardly tell her.'

'You've been through the mill and no mistake and you will be upset by this for a while for certain. But this is how I see it, yer've had a very lucky escape. A warning if you will. So what we have to do is make sure you are never put in that position with Bert again. Like I said, Mr Harrington can ban him from coming 'ere. Bert owes him money—he's been getting his drinks put on the slate and the landlord was thinking of stopping him coming here anyhow. He's not going to repay it, he thinks Mr Harrington is a soft touch, but he's not. That man will only take so much. Now, what you need to do when you feel up to it is tell your aunt. It's not fair that she doesn't know. Chances are if Bert has been trying it on with you, he's been trying it on with other young ladies, too.'

Lucy's mouth popped open. 'I hadn't even considered that! You really think so?' She angled her head as she waited for the reply.

'I know so and I know men like Bert Harper. They're chancers. I was a young gal meself many moons ago and I've seen how they work and believe me, their wives are always the last to know. Do your aunt a favour and tell her, love. She won't want him under her roof no more.'

Lucy nodded seeing the sense of what Cassie had just said. The trouble was, how and when was she going to let Bessie know?

***

Later that afternoon while Lucy was washing up at the sink, she heard a light tapping on the window. Feeling startled and edgy as she feared it might be Bert coming after her, she almost toppled off the old wooden crate she was standing on to reach the sink.

'Lucy!' a voice she recognised called out to her. She should have been angry but after what happened last night with Bert, it was almost a relief to hear Smithy's chirpy voice.

She clambered down from the crate, wiped her hands on a towel and opened the back door.

'Where 'ave you been, gal?' he asked and then his eyes cast downwards as she realised he felt ashamed of himself and was making an effort to speak to her.

'Been staying at my aunt's house but I'm back now.'

He looked at her and blinked and then a big smile covered his face. 'I'm so glad of that, I ain't half missed you.'

'I thought you'd have had Nellie to keep you company?'

'Don't be daft, she ain't a patch on you. Girls like Nellie are only good for one thing, she's not like you, Lucy. Yer a lady!' He said proudly.

At the sound of him saying that, she felt herself blush. 'Oh, go on with you.'

'So, are you still my girl?' His eyes widened with expectation.

He had a right cheek on him. She hesitated a moment before replying. 'I shall have to think about it. You hurt me that night I found you with Nellie. And we hadn't even broken up, I was just late coming to meet you that was all.'

'I know, darlin'. I am so ashamed of meself. I thought you'd dumped me.'

'But why on earth would you think something like that?'

'Because one of the ostlers was winding me up and he told me he'd seen you walking with a fella over towards Spitalfields area when you were supposed to be waiting for me! 'Cos you didn't show up I thought he was telling the truth!'

'That was a load of rot!' She placed both hands on her hips and tossed back her hair. 'I had gone in that direction but I wasn't with no fella, I went to see my aunt to apologise to her.'

'I am sorry. Will you forgive me? I never done nothing with Nellie anyhow, it was only a bit of slap and tickle. Honest.'

'It might have been for you, Smithy, but that girl has designs on you and you can bet she'd have allowed you to take certain liberties with her.'

He nodded. 'Aye, I realise that but I was glad in a way that you walked in on us when you did. I don't mean that I'm glad you were hurt but we were getting carried away a bit and I don't have any special feelings for her like I do for you, love.'

She felt her face flush and all of a sudden, she had warm feelings for Smithy too, but she couldn't forgive him just yet, she had to teach him a lesson. 'That maybe so, but I am going to have to think long and hard whether or not I give you another chance, Smithy.'

He nodded. 'Yes, I do understand.' He looked past her for a moment. 'Meanwhile, any left-overs from dinner time?' He asked hopefully.

'There might be,' she teased.

'Oh, go on gal, me stomach feels like me throat's been cut!'

'I'll slice you a piece of Cassie's corned beef pie and give you a couple tatas, that's all I can spare as there's a load need feeding at the inn tonight.'

He nodded. 'Any gravy?'

She laughed and flicked his face with the towel she was holding. It was good they were on speaking terms once again.

Chapter Twelve

If Bessie was wondering if there was something wrong, she wasn't saying so. She was her usual bright and breezy self when she dropped off a couple of baskets of pies at the pub a couple of days later.

'Now's yer chance, gal,' Cassie urged.

Lucy cleared her throat and went to greet her aunt. 'Everything all right at home, Auntie?'

Her aunt smiled warmly when she caught sight of her. 'Yes. Bert is going to back me with this new house, we're both going to view it later.' Now more than ever she realised she needed to tell her aunt what had been going on before that man had a chance to move in with her at the new house and fleece her of all the hard earned cash she'd acquired from her pie making business.

'What's wrong, Lucy?' Bessie studied her face. 'Is it because you don't want me to move house?'

Lucy shook her head, vehemently. 'No, it's not that, Auntie, honestly it's not. Can you come into the kitchen a moment please so I can speak to you in private?'

A look of apprehension swept over Bessie's features as she followed Lucy to the kitchen where Cassie had just removed a large sizzling joint of pork from the oven. On seeing them both there, she said tactfully, 'Mrs Harrington wants me in her living quarters a moment, I'll be gone a few minutes…' then as she passed by, she winked at Lucy without being seen by Bessie.

Lucy beckoned for her aunt to sit down by the fireside and she took the chair opposite her.

'I can't help feeling that something dreadful is going to happen next, Lucy,' she said tentatively. 'This is going to be bad news, isn't it?'

'Yes, in a way, but what I am about to tell you, and this is for your benefit as much as mine, will have a bearing on your future…'

'I don't much like the idea of that, Lucy, love. Me heart is beating at a mile a minute here.' She placed her hand on her chest.

'I'm sorry but this needs to be said.' Lucy played with a handkerchief between her fingers. 'It's Bert.'

'What about him?'

'I um…er…The other night when you were out at the music hall with Mave, he got fresh with me.'

'Fresh?' Bessie blinked several times as if she could hardly believe her ears.

'You mean he was flirting with you? Oh love, he's often like that with all the ladies, he means nothing by it. It's just his way that's all.' She smiled as if relieved.

Lucy leaned forward in the chair and took her aunt's cold hands in both of her own warm ones. No doubt she was perished from delivering her pies around the pubs. At least when she had the new place, Jacob and Harry would be helping out. Lucy paused a moment as if finding the right words to say. She looked into her aunt's eyes. 'No, it was more than that, I'm afraid.'

'More? I don't understand.'

As Lucy related the story to her Aunt, the woman's eyes widened and her hands flew to her mouth in horror. Then her eyes rolled back in her head as she appeared to pass out from the shock of it all.

'Auntie, wake up! Oh, what have I done?'

At that point, Cassie returned to the kitchen. 'Tap her face, Lucy, I'll fetch a glass of water.'

Lucy did as told, all the while tapping Bessie's face gently. Eventually, Bessie stirred. 'I've just had an awful dream…' she mumbled.

'It wasn't a dream,' Lucy said. 'I am sorry I told you though as it's caused you to faint off.'

'It might have been the cold this morning. It's perishing outside. Have you eaten this morning, Mrs Harper?' Cassie asked.

Bessie brought her hand to her forehead. 'No, I didn't have time. I overslept and had to get me pies out to the pubs. And you're right, it is perishing.'

'Here drink this water,' Cassie instructed. 'I'll brew up a cuppa and you can have a couple of rounds of toast to eat.'

'I don't think I could manage a thing,' Bessie said looking at Lucy with tears in her eyes.

'Look,' Cassie said forcefully, 'I mind me own business. You pair have things to discuss so I'll make meself scarce while you to carry on.' She handed Lucy a toasting fork with two slices of bread. 'I've put the kettle on to boil and if you can't manage two rounds of toast, I'm sure Lucy will help you out with the other.'

Lucy smiled at the woman. At first when she'd come to work at the inn, she'd viewed her as a harridan of a woman. How wrong she'd been—she had a heart of gold.

Once Cassie had departed, Bessie studied Lucy's face. 'She knows?'

'Yes, I had to tell her as she could sense something was up and I'm glad I did. She's also asked the landlord to bar Bert, but not told him the whole story. He owes money to the man anyhow, so he won't miss his custom.'

Bessie rolled her eyes as if it was no surprise to her at all. 'That's good then. What do you think I ought to do?'

For a fleeting moment, Lucy thought that Bessie was going to give in and not do anything at all about the situation but then she said, 'About buying that property, I mean. As for Bert, he's already gone as far as I'm concerned. I'll never 'ave the same looks on him again. I know I should never have taken him back. I'm sorry for that.'

'But you weren't to know,' Lucy said, standing and swooping down to peck her aunt on her cheek.

'Maybe not, but I knew the type he was. After all, he seduced me when I wasn't much older than you, but to be truthful back then he was a 'andsome man and I didn't take much seducing.' She laughed for a moment, then her face took on a serious expression. 'I should have guessed he'd go for a young 'un again sometime. I never told you this before as you were only a baby at the time and it wouldn't have seemed right badmouthing Bert when he was put away in prison, but he was carrying on with a young girl then who worked at the Ten Bell's Pub. So, I do know what he's like…' Her voice trailed off into nothingness and Lucy felt desperately sorry that she'd been the one to break the bad news to her aunt. Yet, at the end of the day it was for her own good.

'What'll you do now?'

'We were supposed to go to view the property tomorrow afternoon, but of course we won't go together now. I don't much feel like it anyhow.'

'I'll tell you what... I'll come and view it with you instead. I'm sure Cassie can cover for me while I take an half hour or so off from my duties to come with you.'

Bessie's sad eyes lit up. 'Oh, would you, love? I'd really like that, but first I have to get home and send someone packing.'

'Where'd you think he'll go?'

'I don't much care to be honest, but one thing's for certain, I am going to make him say goodbye to the boys first, he never did that when he went to prison of course as there was no time, but it's the least he can do.'

Lucy nodded and she had to admit she agreed.

***

Half past two the following afternoon, Lucy met her aunt outside her small house where she was already stood waiting for her in her Sunday best, she obviously wanted to make a good impression.

The house no longer felt foreboding, but she had to ask. 'Has he gone?'

Bessie nodded. 'I gave him his marching orders as soon as I left you before he'd even gone to the pub. That way I knew my words would get through to him.'

'Did he admit what he'd tried to do to me?' Lucy asked in a soft voice.

'No, well not at first, but then he did and said he just hadn't been able to resist you. I think he was going to make out you led him on but I know better than that, love. I'm a pretty good judge of character and if I'm being truthful, I only took him back because I felt sorry for him in the first place—more fool me. And when I did, he abused my trust so that he whittled away at every last bit of love I had left for him. I feel quite empty inside now to be honest with you.'

Lucy squeezed her aunt's hand. 'You'll see, Auntie, things will change for the better sooner than you think. How did the boys take it?'

Bessie shook her head. 'Bert threatened to take them away with him, to hurt me I suppose. But neither wanted to go with their father. They're both too big now for him to push them around, particularly Jacob, who could floor him with a fist to the face.'

Lucy nodded. 'Yes, he's a young man now.'

'Do you know though in the end they were glad to see the back of him! I wasn't expecting that but Jacob said he was sick to death of being woken up by a drunk in the middle of the night and Harry looked relieved. He said he was a bit scared of him. He's not the father they remember, that's for sure.'

'Come on then,' Lucy said with a smile on her face. 'It's time to get going.'

'It is indeed. This will be a new chapter for us all!'

***

As they made their way, walking at a brisk pace along the frosted pavement, Lucy took a look at the roofs of the higgledy piggledy houses. They reminded her of the iced cakes she'd seen Bessie make last

Christmas. The cold from the pavement travelled through Lucy's boots and seeped upward to her legs, chilling her to the bone. No wonder Bessie had fainted yesterday if she'd been walking in these sorts of conditions, hawking her pies from pub to pub. Now she wished she'd donned an extra shawl and worn her mittens to protect her from the biting cold.

The cold didn't seem to be affecting Bessie though as she marched with extreme purpose towards their destination. The area was becoming drearier looking as houses appeared to be almost on top of one another. Some had broken, dirty window panes that were stuffed with old newspapers in a vain attempt to keep out the cold. They were now entering the area known as No Man's Land.

A rotting, sickly sweet smell hit Lucy's nostrils, causing her to gag. The last thing she wanted to do was let Bessie down by being ill, so she held her breath until they got away from the nasty niff. According to Bessie, even the police feared setting foot here as it was full of criminals. People lodged in some of the dwellings and came and went as they pleased. The people here lived off their wits and employed look outs as various goods were pilfered from those that could afford it and fenced to be sold for sizeable sums.

The afternoon's dying sun cast a sombre shadow over the area. Lucy shivered, this time not from cold but from fear as they walked through the narrow passage way towards the archway which separated them from the more civilised area and people beyond.

Lucy heaved a sigh of relief once they set foot in the other area. No doubt most living around here would consider it a nobs' area to live. The street of four storey houses was quite neat and tidy with black wrought iron railings and flowery shrubs near the front doors. One or two houses looked like they needed more attention décor wise than the others and Lucy guessed the one they'd come to view would be one of those. Stopping outside number ten, they looked up at its uneven looking steps and the blue paint peeling off the door, though its wooden panels appeared pretty strong looking, so it was nothing a fresh coat of paint couldn't put right.

'What now?' Lucy looked at her aunt.

'We wait for the owner to show us around.'

'But it's bleedin' freezing out here,' Lucy said as she hopped from foot to foot with the cold.

'I know and I'm sorry about that but we are a few minutes early,' Bessie said in a clipped tone of voice. Oh dear, she wasn't annoyed with her, was she? But presently her annoyed expression turned into one of expectation as a carriage pulled up outside and a smart looking gentleman alighted from it. He wore a long black frock coat and top hat, and his chiselled features made his face astonishingly handsome.

He stood before them.

'Mr Knight?' Bessie asked.

'At your service, ma'am. And you must be Mrs Harper?'

She nodded. 'Yes, and this is my niece, Lucy,' She introduced.

'Pleased to make your acquaintance,' he said, tipping his top hat towards them both. This was a gentleman and no mistake about it.

'So, what now?' Bessie asked.

'I have the keys so I'll show you both inside. Take your time looking around, but I have to tell you there are other interested parties.'

Lucy felt her heart slump to her boots. 'How many other interested parties?' she asked.

Mr Knight's face reddened as if affronted by a direct question from such a young person.

'It's all right, Mr Knight, Lucy here is privy to all my business ventures and she might end up living here.'

Lucy beamed when her aunt said that. Imagine living in such a large fancy house.

Mr Knight nodded. 'Well, obviously like I informed you by letter, this is for rental for the time being but the owner will consider selling at some point in the future.'

'You mean you're not the actual owner then, Mr Knight?'

'Good heavens, no. I am working on behalf of the owner whose name shall remain a secret for time being.' He tapped the side of his nose with his index finger in a furtive manner.

Lucy, who couldn't be doing with all the cloak and dagger stuff, tugged on the sleeve of Bessie's dress. 'Maybe we'd better leave sharpish,' she hissed. 'I think you're being messed around if you ask me. It's daft that you can't know who's selling the place and it's being dangled like a carrot in front of your nose. Others are after it too, then it might be sold to you but only if the owner approves.'

Bessie's eyes clouded over and then she pursed her lips and crossed her hands in front of her like she did whenever she got cross. 'Mr Knight, I think you are just toying with me. No doubt, you've already received some good offers, so I think you'll waste our valuable time no longer, so we'll bid you, good day!'

Both of them turned on their heels to set off in the direction they'd arrived from.

'Whoah, ladies!' Mr Knight shouted after them. 'You have totally got this wrong...'

Bessie and Lucy turned to face him. 'Have we now? I don't think so!' Bessie said forcefully.

Mr Knight drew up in front of them. 'Look, I'm sorry if my manner upset you. There is only one other interested party and I think it's doubtful they can raise the funds. Between me and you, people are put off this property as it is a little run down and near a notorious area. As for the owner wanting to keep her identity private, there is a very good reason for that which will be revealed in good time.'

'So, it's a lady then, is it?' Bessie stared at the man.

'It is indeed,' Mr Knight said, smiling. 'Please, won't you both step inside and then if you don't like it, I promise I shan't badger you any further.'

Bessie nodded. 'What do you think, Lucy?' she asked in a tone loud enough for Mr Knight to hear.

'I think we should take a look at least—we've come this far.'

'I agree,' Bessie said, winking at her.

They followed the agent up the steps, then he pulled a bunch of keys from the inside pocket of his coat and unlocked the door.

Chapter Thirteen

Lucy and her aunt followed the agent inside the house. Although the décor had seen better days, Lucy was amazed by the splendour of it all. She could well imagine that in its day this house might have been quite opulent. Maybe the Master and Mistress had a few servants too as she'd spotted a set of servant bells near the door. There was a drawing room and a living room, a large kitchen, four bedrooms and two small attic rooms that maybe the servants had slept in at one time, and a good sized basement too. Outside was a small garden with a vegetable patch and beyond the back gate, the other side of the lane, was a red brick building belonging to the house.

Auntie's eyes lit up when she saw that. 'That could be fitted out as a bake house!' she exclaimed.

Lucy had no doubt about it at all but one thing troubled her greatly, how on earth could her aunt afford to rent a place like this? While Mr Knight tried various keys in the door of the brick building, she whispered to Bessie. 'Are you sure you can afford this place? It looks quite grand to me even if it needs some attention.'

Bessie nodded. 'Yes, the letter assured me I can.'

Lucy nodded and thought to question her aunt later about that letter. It was the first she'd heard of it.

Mr Knight unlocked the door, if Auntie had any doubts about it, there were none at all now. She stepped inside and gazed around its interior. 'Yes, yes!' she exclaimed with a beaming smile on her face and tears of joy in her eyes. 'This is just what I need to get the business going properly!' She clasped her hands to her chest. 'I can have a couple of ovens fitted here and counters over there,' she said as she pointed a finger to the facing wall, 'And there are a couple of windows and a chimney too. It's ideal for my bakery business!'

Lucy had to admit that it was, but some niggling doubt deep inside her told her this was all too good to be true.

Auntie thanked Mr Knight for his time and he promised he'd be in touch when the necessary paperwork was drawn up. As Lucy watched him climb into the cab, she wondered what his particular world was like and where and how he lived. She walked back home with Bessie, and along the way, expressed her concerns. 'So, tell me about the letter you said you'd received?'

Auntie let out a long breath. 'It arrived a couple of weeks ago addressed to me personally, saying there was a house to rent with a suitable outbuilding that would be ideal as a business premises at a very affordable price.' She puffed out a breath into the cold afternoon air.

Lucy stopped walking for a moment and taking her aunt by the arm, spun her around to face her. 'But don't you think that was strange? Had you contacted any agents about a new property previously?'

Auntie shook her head. 'No, that's the odd thing but it seems to be the answer to my prayers.'

Lucy shook her head. 'Auntie, I think you should try to find out more before you sign anything.'

Bessie's frame slumped as if all the air had been sucked out of her body and now Lucy felt guilty for bursting her bubble. 'But how can I check things out?'

'Well, you question the neighbours for a start to see if any of those know who owns the place!'

'That's a good idea. I suppose you're right, it does all seem to be too good to be true, mind you.'

'I just think the rent Mr Knight suggested you pay seems far too low for that sort of property. Maybe he's a con man who just has the keys to the place and he's trying to get money from all sorts who think they're going to rent it.'

Bessie brought her hand to her mouth. 'Oh no, I do hope not. He seemed such a gent an' all.'

'Appearances can be deceptive. All I'm saying is try to find out more before you sign anything or part with any money.'

'When did you get to be so wise?' she asked and then chuckled. 'Ah, maybe it was all a pipe dream anyhow.'

The pair fell into step once more, she so hoped that someday Auntie would see her dream come true but she wanted the woman to err on the side of caution first.

***

Lucy heard no more about the property for several days but then, Bessie turned up at the inn, her eyes twinkling and cheeks flushed. 'I need to speak to you for a few minutes, love,' she said when she found Lucy clearing away some glasses from the bar area.

'Come on through to the kitchen…' Lucy wondered what on earth her aunt had to tell her.

They both sat near the fire. It was a perishing cold morning again, even colder than the last time her aunt had visited.

'I went to find out more about that house,' Bessie said, warming her hands by the roaring fire.

'And?' Lucy blinked.

'Well, I spoke to both sets of neighbours either side and they said the same, that it's owned by an elderly posh lady who lives up west. They've only met her a couple of times but she told them she used to live in the house many years ago. The house has been empty for years and years and that's why it's so run down. They've never known anyone to live in it since they've been there.'

Lucy narrowed her gaze. 'That's so strange.'

'Yes, and that's not all. They once heard noises inside there and assumed it was some sort of ghost as they could hear a woman crying.'

'Was it the old woman though?'

Bessie shook her head. 'The one neighbour, a Mr Potts, told me that the following day he saw a young woman in a black cloak leave the house. He assumed she was in mourning for something and he never saw her again.'

'So, what are you going to do? Are you going to rent it or not?'

Bessie nodded. 'Yes, I've made up my mind that if that other person who is after it doesn't want it, I'll sign as soon as possible.'

Lucy had a feeling that there was no other person and she wondered why the elderly woman who owned the house was so keen for her aunt to live there.

***

On the day Auntie moved house, Lucy arrived early to help as she had been given the morning off work. Mave and her husband, Jim, and Jacob and Harry, had helped load up the few possessions they had onto the back of a borrowed horse and cart. Bessie had left her old house as clean as a new pin with Lucy's help and they made their way to number 10 Court Terrace, walking behind the cart across the cobbled streets with Jim holding the reins in his hands at the helm.

When they arrived at the new house they were in for a surprise as previously it had been unfurnished. But now every room in the house had furniture! There were beds in all the bedrooms and a smart, plum velvet chaise lounge and highly polished table in the drawing room, with a set of empty mahogany book cases. All it needed now was a grand piano and a crystal chandelier, Lucy thought.

'I can't believe this!' Bessie said with tears springing to her eyes. 'There was no mention of any furniture when I signed the rental agreement. These classy pieces are going to make my worn old bits and pieces look very shabby indeed!'

While her aunt was in a state of disbelief about the situation, Lucy narrowed her eyes and tried to take it all in. Why would some elderly woman want to help her aunt so much? It just didn't make sense. It was as if she were some sort of benefactor to her and the fact she didn't want to reveal her identity made it all so creepy in her eyes. For now, her aunt was over the moon with it all and she didn't want to upset her. But she feared it might all come crashing down if she wasn't careful. She loved Bessie so much that she didn't want to see her hurt in any way.

***

As the days and weeks went by, Lucy's fears abated. Bessie and the boys settled well into the house and Bessie's savings were used to purchase an oven for the bakehouse and a couple of wooden counters. She'd decided to just purchase the oven second hand for time being as she feared getting into financial difficulties, but all was well. The business was booming with the help of the boys and she even took on Mave as a bakery assistant. Word soon spread around the area about Bessie's delicious mouth-watering pies. Soon she was supplying new pubs and shops with her baked goods, and trying out different recipes every so often.

One afternoon when Lucy was visiting, Mr Knight showed up to collect the rent as he always did each week. Now was Lucy's chance after he'd had a cup of coffee and been given payment by Bessie, and she felt a strong urge to question him.

She approached the kitchen table where he was sat reading a newspaper with his empty coffee cup and a half-eaten sponge cake in front of him. 'Mr Knight, might I ask you something?'

He smiled and then he patted down his moustache and folded his newspaper away. 'Go ahead, young lady, I shan't bite you!'

She giggled and then said, 'Would it now be possible for us to meet the lady who owns this house as my aunt would like to thank her.'

Bessie, who was sat beside Mr Knight, stared at Lucy and her eyes widened in surprise.

He simply shrugged. 'I have to be honest with you, I don't know if that would be possible. She rarely leaves the house these days.'

'But please would you ask her for us? I'm sure if she can't leave her house, that you could take us to visit her?'

He shook his head. 'To be honest, she is somewhat of a recluse these days. I can't see her wanting to see any visitors, but I promise that I'll ask for you.'

Lucy brightened up. 'I think I'd like that, thank you very much.'

When Mr Knight had departed and Lucy watched him getting into his carriage from the drawing room window, Auntie said, 'I don't think you ought to hold up your hopes about meeting the lady too much, Lucy. It sounds to me as if she is a bit closed off from the real world. I'm just thankful for the chance she's given me in living here and having a new business premises.'

'But aren't you curious at all?'

'I am, yes, but you know about curiosity, don't you?'

'Should I?'

'It killed the bleedin' cat!' She said sharply, then she turned on her heel and left the room.

***

Lucy was getting along surprisingly well with Smithy and he did eventually take her to see a magic lantern show. Nellie, on the other hand, became quite haughty towards her and she feared the girl would cause her some trouble if she wasn't careful. It was quite obvious that she was jealous of her. Not only did Lucy have the bedroom she wanted for herself because she'd been working at the inn the longest and saw it as her absolute right, but Lucy also had the boy she liked as well. It didn't help matters either as the

Harringtons were showing favour to Lucy a lot and Nellie was left with all the dirty jobs, but what could she do about it? It wasn't her fault that she wasn't asked to empty chamber pots or light all the fires at the inn. She decided to just take things in her stride and hope it would all blow over soon. She tried to be kind to the girl like calling her into the kitchen for a cuppa whenever she and Cassie were brewing up, but Nellie wouldn't have it. She always claimed she was in the middle of something or other, rebuffing every little effort Lucy made. There was nothing she could do about it, and for now, she decided that maybe it was no longer even worth trying.

***

A couple of nights later, Lucy was stood at the sink washing the dishes when Smithy turned up, he had a young lad with him who only looked a bit younger than them. He wore a flat cap just covering his large eyes, a pair of tattered breeches and a jacket that swamped his small frame. His eyes widened when he caught sight of her.

'This, here, is Lucy!' said Smithy proudly. 'She's me girlfriend.' At hearing him say that, Lucy felt all warm inside. It was the first time he'd ever said so in front of anyone else.

Lucy smiled and batted her eyelids. 'Hello!' she said, as she scrubbed away at a pot covered in soapy suds.

'Hello!' said the boy. 'My name is Archie.'

'Archie's helping me with the horses and he's brought his dog, Duke, with him! He's an orphan. Never known his father and his mother died not so long ago.' Smithy declared. She could tell he was trying to take the lad under his wing and she admired him for doing so but she hoped Smithy wouldn't get him into any trouble.

Lucy smiled. 'Cassie told me that you had someone helping you, Smithy. Now I know it was Archie.' Lucy's heart went out to the lad as she knew what it felt like to be a newcomer working at the inn and to have no mother or father—that couldn't be easy for the lad. She felt she ought to offer the pair something as Archie looked so small and frail. 'Cassie's left some food in the oven for you. It's been in there for some time but it should be fine for you to eat if you don't leave it any longer.'

Smithy opened the oven door. 'Smells 'orright to me, don't know what it is though?'

'A nice bit of rabbit for you both with some veggies and gravy.'

She stood down from the old wooden crate which she'd been using to reach the sink. She dried her hands on a towel, then brought out two tin plates with a dinner on each for both of them. 'Sorry, it's a bit dried up,' she explained, 'we had a lot to feed tonight and they all ate a lot earlier. You pair were busy with the horses and the coaches for so long I thought you were never going to sit down to eat.'

Lucy hoped that poor little Archie wouldn't be introduced into the thieving that went on at the inn, but somehow, she knew he would.

***

Lucy awoke the following morning before first light as the mail coach from York was due. As she helped Cassie cook the bacon, eggs, black pudding and fried bread, she heard a commotion in the corridor outside.

'What's going on?' she asked Cassie.

'I'm damned if I know!' Cassie looked a bit cross as they had a lot of work on whenever mail coaches arrived.

A gentleman barged in the kitchen taking them unawares.

''Ere what's going on?' Cassie complained. Lucy knew she hated anyone trespassing in her kitchen. He'd overstepped the mark in Cassie's book.

He was dressed in a long dark coat with a velvet collar and around his neck he wore a silver-grey cravat. He sported the thickest bushy white whiskers Lucy had ever seen in her life. 'Well, I'm alerting the police!' he yelled at Cassie and Lucy. 'I've already told the landlord that someone in the bar stole my wallet last night. I know it was a young person as I walloped them around the head. You wait and see, whoever it was will be in trouble for this and I guess an adult must have been involved as well!' He glared at Cassie as he raised his cane in one hand. For a moment, Lucy feared he was going to beat them with it.

Cassie's nostrils twitched. Her face grew red and her eyes appeared to bulge out of her skull. She did not like people entering her kitchen unless she either invited them or they should have been there.

'You, sir!' she shouted and pointed a finger at him. 'Can ruddy well get out of my kitchen and stop accusing people because we have done no wrong!'

The man drew nearer and raised his cane even higher above Cassie's head as if about to strike her, when Mr Harrington suddenly appeared. 'Please sir, someone has gone to get the police, we shall sort this all out right now. Please leave these ladies alone, they are merely cooking breakfast.'

The man glanced at the frying pans of bacon and eggs and turning one more time to Cassie said, 'You have not heard the last of this! Heads will roll! There was a lot of money in that wallet!'

When he'd left, following Mr Harrington out of the kitchen, Lucy sank to the floor and wept.

'Now get up, young Lucy. There's no need to be taking on so.'

'But I haven't done anything, Cassie. I would never do that. I know some thievin' goes on here, but I don't do that sort of thing. I don't want to lose my job.' She stood, but now her legs felt like jelly. How was she going to be able to concentrate on the breakfasts now? She hadn't felt as bad as this since Bert had assaulted her.

Cassie wagged a finger in her face. 'Look, luvvy, I don't know what went on in the bar last night and to be honest I don't want to know, sometimes it's best not knowing these things. But what I do know is yer honest as the day is long.'

Lucy knew that Cassie was involved with Mr Casper and that he was a bit of a rogue, so she wouldn't be surprised if he was behind this. But did Cassie take that wallet? She wasn't sure. More likely it was Smithy, though. She'd warned him about doing that sort of thing but he'd told her that him caring for the horses when there were experienced ostlers around was all a front. If he didn't do as he was told, he'd be out on his ear. And if he was out on his ear, poor little Archie would be too. Oh dear, what would happen now?

***

Lucy was running around in a blind panic trying to get things sorted as they'd fallen behind with the breakfasts. Cassie was trying to calm the situation down as Smithy and Archie entered the kitchen by the back door.

'What's up with yer pair?' Smithy asked.

Lucy explained what had happened.

'But it was…' Archie said.

Lucy noticed Smithy roughly grab hold of the boy's arm and kick him on the back of his leg.

'Was what?' Lucy's eyes widened and she wrinkled her nose.

'It was shocking, weren't it, Archie?' Smithy said. 'Old Casper just told us.'

Archie nodded. 'Y…yes.'

'But why do people think it's one of you two?' Smithy asked.

'Because we were both in and out of the bar room at some point during the evening. According to the customer, who it appears is some fancy London lawyer, a young boy bumped into him in the bar. The landlord says no, there was no boy in the bar last night whatsoever, he'd have noticed. So now the customer thinks it's one of us!'

'Can't he remember then?' Archie asked.

Lucy shook her thick curls. 'No. All he remembers is some young person bumping into him and he gave them a clip around the earhole. He was blotto, I remember him slurring his words. Now people will think it's definitely me and not Cassie as I'm so young.'

Archie let out a long breath as if he'd been holding something back and Lucy wondered what that was. Had he watched Smithy nick that wallet, she wondered?

The lads ate the buttered crumpets Cassie had put to one side for them, in silence. Then they returned to the stables with some left-over bacon scraps stuffed into their jacket pockets for Duke, the dog.

When they were gone, Cassie closed the back door and looking at Lucy said, 'It was definitely one of those what took that rich lawyer's wallet, you mark me words! I've got a nose for these things!'

***

Lucy noticed the detective and uniformed constable's arrival at the inn and her stomach somersaulted over. The detective had bushy red sideburns and, every so often, puffed on a pipe. The uniformed constable was dispatched to fetch people at the inn for interviews while the detective sat in a leather highbacked armchair in the coffee room. Although Lucy hadn't done anything wrong, she felt a surge of guilt as to what was now occurring. Deep down she knew there were light fingers in operation, but she had chosen to ignore it up until now. When it was Archie's turn to be questioned, the detective stood with his hands behind his back.

She watched as the constable marched Archie into the room, holding him by the collar of his jacket like he was a sack of spuds and when the door was closed behind them, she listened intently outside. She could just about make out the men's muffled voices inside but had to strain to hear what Archie was saying as he spoke in such a quiet voice.

She heard Archie give an explanation which was something about cleaning the coaches and then having some grub and going to sleep in the stables afterwards, then he was asked if he'd seen the gentleman whose wallet had been stolen.

The door creaked opened a little, causing her to move away and she heard Police Constable Salmon being summoned. She hid in the kitchen for a couple of minutes and once Lucy heard him going inside, she returned to listen at the door but she had to quickly disappear again as the constable was sent to fetch the man who had been robbed. Apparently, his name was Mr Fortescue.

As she watched through a crack in the kitchen door, she noted a looming figure entering the coffee room. He was well dressed in a fancy waistcoat, and the long black coat she'd seen him wear the night before. Once the door to the coffee room had been firmly shut behind him, she returned to listen.

'Is this the boy you smacked around the head, Mr Fortescue?' the detective asked.

'I can't say for certain, but he's about the right height of what I remember. I was tired and I admit I'd partaken of a little too much gin.'

So, he'd been drunk that much was evident! How could he possibly know who had taken his wallet then?

Then she heard the detective shout: 'Bring in the girl and we can compare their heights; it has to be one or the other. All the other young folk who were present at this establishment have good alibis. That

Smithy lad was seen by several people, including the coach driver, cleaning down the coach, though interestingly enough, none saw this young man stood before me!'

Lucy quickly ran back the short distance to the kitchen and began clattering around with pots as pans as though she was busy at work and hadn't been eavesdropping at the door.

The constable called out to her. 'Excuse me, miss, I know you have work to be getting on with but you're wanted in the coffee room for questioning.

All was quiet as she entered and she felt Fortescue's eyes boring a hole into her. The detective, who was seated in a chair, didn't give anything away with his face, it was totally deadpan and that unnerved her somewhat.

She began to tremble and felt a lump in her throat. Oh dear, she didn't want to break down crying. She glanced at Archie who appeared as nervous as she was, he looked at her with a great deal of sympathy in his eyes.

The detective addressed her. 'Where were you, miss, from 10 o'clock onwards last night?'

She swallowed hard. 'I'd been helping the cook in the kitchen, served the men grub, then I went to the bar room.'

'And what were you doing there?'

'I was helping to take drinks to some of the men and collecting their empties. I was a bit irritated to be 'onest with you, sir.'

'And why was that?'

She hesitated before answering as she thought back to how demanding the work had been that

evening, she'd been rushed right off her feet.
'Because I was busy enough in the kitchen as it was. I had a stack of pots and pans that needed washing full of hardened on food, so they'd wanted some good ol' scrubbing an' all. I thought to meself, how can I be in two places at once? Well, it's just not possible is it?'

The detective nodded. 'Have you ever seen this gentleman before?' He pointed to Fortescue.

'Y…yes. He was in the bar last night and I also saw him check in earlier on that day.'

The detective turned his attention to the man. 'Did you see this girl in the bar room last night, Mr Fortescue?'

'I don't rightly remember. I don't take much notice of skivvy sorts…but she could be the right height of the person I walloped after they bumped into me.'

Lucy's cheeks flamed. The man was insulting her. She noticed how Archie was gritting his teeth beside her and turning his hands into fists, there was no doubt about it, he was angry.

There was a silence as if the detective was mulling things over. 'To be honest with you, I think there is a lack of evidence in this case.' He turned to Constable Salmon. 'Did the men check the boy's sleeping area and the girl's?'

The constable nodded. 'Yes, sir. Nothing was found.'

'Turn out your pockets, both of you!' the detective demanded and he narrowed his gaze as he glared at them.

Lucy gulped and she hoped and prayed that Archie would have nothing on his person.

Slowly, he pulled out the pockets of his kegs and his jacket and the constable checked them. 'Nothing here, sir,' he declared. She noticed a look of relief sweep over Archie's face which no one else seemed to have noticed as now they turned their attentions on to her.

The constable then checked Lucy's dress and apron pockets which made her feel like a criminal. 'Nothing here either, sir,' he said.

Whew, that was a close one for Archie. If he had taken the wallet, where had he stashed it? Or did Smithy have it somewhere?

The detective got out of his chair and, staring Mr Fortescue in the eyes said, 'From what I can see, you were very careless last night and drank too much spirit, sir. You should have had your wits about you in a place like this.' Then he spat out the words, 'People like you are prime targets for pilfering!'

'W...what?' The man seemed taken aback now the detective was turning the tables on him.

'If you had remained sober last night, this would have been an unlikely occurrence. I suggest in future you stay off the gin and keep your valuables under lock and key. And I am far from impressed that you can't even tell the sex of the young person who bumped into you. Now, I could bring a case against you, for wasting police time!'

Fortescue's eyes widened with rage and his lips narrowed, then he shouted, 'And I, sir, have the powers to bring a case against *you*, as I am a top city lawyer.'

The detective just smiled at him as if he was dealing with a deranged person from the local asylum. Then he turned to Lucy and Archie and said, 'You are both free to go.'

Archie let out an audible breath of relief and Lucy felt like she wanted to cry but fought to hold back the tears. Though this time they weren't tears she'd fought to keep back out of fear and frustration, this was a feeling of consolation now that she was being absolved of committing a crime she'd been falsely accused of. She was well aware that there'd be no apology though but for now, getting her name cleared was all that mattered to her. But was Archie as innocent as the detective seemed to think? That thought bothered her a little. She became aware of him trailing behind her as she left the room and she felt she had to say something to him so she knew the truth.

Once outside in the corridor, Lucy hugged him. He looked startled for a moment. 'I'm so pleased the police didn't catch you, Archie.'

He blinked several times. 'You knew?'

She nodded, feeling she needed to warn him about what could happen to him if he was caught stealing, 'They bring in new lads here all the time to do that job and Smithy always takes advantage of them when Mr Casper asks him to help out on their first time. If you stay here much longer then you really will get caught by the police and you could end up transported to Australia.'

He gulped. 'I was just thinking that myself. But where can I go, Lucy?'

Cassie emerged from the kitchen and looked at the pair of them. 'You young folk know nothing!' She seemed annoyed. 'Transportation to Australia ended a few years back!' She walked off in a huff, leaving them speechless for a moment.

Archie's eyes widened as he trembled.

Lucy laughed as she knew Cassie's bite was far worse than her bark. 'Don't pay any attention to her,' she reassured Archie. 'I think her brother was sent there for nicking a leg of lamb from the butcher or something, she's never got over it!'

'I don't know if it's still going on but I don't want to end up there! I need to find a safe place to stay.'

An idea began to form in Lucy's mind, so she whispered, 'I've got an auntie who might be able to sort you out, she runs a bakery a few streets over. As long as you're a willing worker, which I can see you are, she might take you on. Meet me first light in the morning, come to the kitchen door and I'll take you there.'

If there was any way she could help Archie by getting him away from the inn then she would.

Now the boy was not in Smithy's company, she felt she could ask him things as he seemed a bit quiet when the older lad was around. 'How come you ended up here, anyhow?'

He sighed deeply. 'It's a long story, but I was taken in by my rich Uncle Walter after my mother died. You wouldn't believe it looking at the way I'm dressed right now, would you? I look more like a tramp than a bloomin' toff!'

She shook her head. 'So, how come you're down on your luck then, did you run away or something?'

'No. I was beginning to like living there. I was kidnapped by this chimney sweep who worked at the big house and he brought me here with his girlfriend

Flora. Flora has a little boy called, Bobby. Anyhow we both had to go up chimneys to earn a living.'

Lucy gasped. 'Oh, Archie, you poor thing.'

Archie's eyes filled with tears. 'Yes, all I want to do is get back home and I want to help Flora and Bobby, too,' he sniffed.

'Why, what happened to them?'

'We all of us escaped when Bill Brackley, he was the sweep, was drunk one night, we even took Duke with us as you know. Flora has found work at a big house as a maid and they've allowed her and Bobby to stay there but they wouldn't take me.'

As soon as he'd said it, he broke down in tears, huge wracking sobs took over his little frame. So much so that she took him in her arms to comfort him. 'You poor thing. Well, if I can get my auntie to take you in you won't have to worry any more. She helped me when I needed it. You see, she's not my real aunt.'

Archie stopped crying and looked at her through glassy eyes. 'She must be a really good person then.'

'Oh, she is. She found me when I was a baby abandoned on a park bench at Itchy Park.'

'I know the place!' Archie exclaimed, 'we had to sleep there the night we escaped. It scared me half to death. It's just as well your aunt found you then, who knows what would have happened otherwise.'

Lucy nodded. She had a lot to be thankful for because even if no one had harmed her that night, she would surely have died from the biting cold if she hadn't been taken by Bessie and given a home.

***

Archie and Lucy had to sidestep several piles of horse manure and rubbish underfoot as they walked towards Bessie's house. The whole area stank so badly that they gagged a couple of times on the way. Archie, who had been trailing behind, soon caught up with Lucy after he tried kicking a pile of what he'd thought was rubbish only the rubbish got up and walked and he realised it was a vagrant lying on the floor. He finally caught up with her. Breathlessly he asked, 'What's the rush? I know you have to get back to work, but you seem on pins?'

'It's not a good area at all this part,' she explained, her dark brown curls bouncing on her shoulders. 'Be very wary if you have to come here. They'll slit your throat as good as look at you for a few pennies!'

Archie's eyes widened with fear. 'We saw some rum sorts that night we all slept in Itchy Park. Just as well Duke with us to guard us on the way.'

Lucy looked at the dog, he was the dearest thing and even though he was a very big dog who she thought was probably a Great Dane, she realised he was a softie at heart. At least he was with both of them, but just as well if he could frighten people, especially in this area.

After walking through a narrow, dark passageway which scared the living daylights out of the lad, they finally emerged through the arch facing the street where Bessie lived. Lucy held firmly on to her basket. 'I'm going to pretend I was borrowing some suet from my aunt, in case I get asked any questions on my return,' she explained to him.

Archie blinked. 'Why? Won't they allow you some time off?'

'It's not that so much. It's Nellie.'

'Nellie?' Archie frowned.

'Yes, she has it in for me. She's works mainly in Mr and Mrs Harrington's quarters as their maid but occasionally helps out in the bar.'

'I think I know the one you mean, I saw her mopping the floor in the bar this morning. But why has she got it in for you?'

Lucy blew out a hard breath. 'I think she's jealous as I was allotted the bedroom she wanted and she has to sleep in the attic one. I'd rather swap with her not to cause all this hassle but I daren't approach the Harringtons about it as it was their decision. Also, she's got her eyes on Smithy.'

Archie laughed. 'Ha, I definitely know who you mean now, she was making eyes at him last night and he told her to get knotted!'

Lucy giggled. It was reassuring that Smithy was keeping to his word about staying away from the girl and was only true to her.

They stood outside the house and Archie stared up at it for a moment. 'Not as posh as your uncle's house?' Lucy asked.

'No, but it's a lot posher than most houses I've seen.'

'That's probably true,' Lucy smiled. 'I think Auntie plans to get it painted soon.'

He followed her up the steps and she knocked the big brass knocker.

Presently the door was opened by Bessie who, when she saw them there, wrapped her arms around her with tears in her eyes. Lucy knew why, because she'd already visited her last night and mentioned

Archie's predicament to her. She was so warm-hearted and wanted to help in any way she could. Bessie began to smile and chat with them, and then looking over Lucy's shoulder at Archie, waved at him as he tied Duke's rope lead to the railings.

They all had a nice little chat inside and when Lucy was about to return to work, Bessie insisted Archie bring the dog inside. She whispered to Lucy and winked. 'I can give him and the dog a roof over their heads and he can help out delivering pies around the place.'

Lucy felt such a sense of relief.

As Lucy was leaving, Mr Knight's carriage drew up outside the house. She watched as he alighted. 'Ah, Miss Harper,' he said, 'just the person I wanted to see…'

Chapter Fourteen

Lucy stood in front of Mr Knight and blinked. What on earth did he want to see her about?

'Is there anything wrong, sir?' she asked.

A sense of mischief seemed to play about his eyes. 'No, not at all, my dear. It's just that I relayed your request to the owner of this house and much to my surprise, she has agreed to meet with you. She'd like me to bring you to her at nine o'clock sharp in the morning.'

Was this all a dream? Never in a million years did she think the woman would agree to her request. 'But I don't know if I can get the time off from my duties at the inn,' she said, frowning.

Mr Knight's expression became more solemn. 'To be honest, I wouldn't break this appointment, Miss Harper. As I previously told you, the lady in question has become somewhat of a recluse lately. She never leaves the house and refuses all visitors, apart from myself and her even more elderly brother.'

'Oh, I see, I didn't realise quite how bad things were…' Lucy fought to think as to what she could do. She could ask Nellie to fill in and cover her duties she supposed, but to do so she'd have to bribe the girl with something. Maybe one of Bessie's delicious pies?

Mr Knight's persuasive voice penetrated her thoughts. 'I'll bring the carriage around here at half past eight in the morning to collect you?' He tilted his head to one side in a questioning fashion.

She was relieved he hadn't suggested picking her up at the inn as that would pose some difficult questions. 'What about my Aunt Bessie? Might she be allowed to come?'

He shook his head. 'No, I'm sorry. The lady has made it clear that it's only you she wishes to see at this point and believe me, that will be quite enough for her for time being. She's of quite a delicate constitution and I wouldn't wish to upset her.'

Lucy nodded. What the devil was this lady going to be like? She feared it might be like treading on eggshells to be around her. Finally, she said firmly, 'Very well, then. I shall be ready and waiting at half past eight.'

'And there's just one more thing…' He looked both left and right in a conspiratorial fashion.

'Yes?'

He lowered his voice a notch as he spoke behind his leather gloved hand. 'You are not to tell your aunt about this. For time being this is between yourself and the lady.'

As much as Lucy disliked deceiving her aunt, her curiosity was now getting the better of her. 'I understand,' she said. 'When you pick me up though, you'd better park your carriage a way down the street in case my aunt sees and asks questions.'

Mr Knight smiled and his eyes glittered with amusement, causing Lucy to bristle. 'I don't see what there is to grin about?'

'I'm sorry. I can't explain to you right now, but you remind me so much of someone I know.'

Lucy shook her head, baffled by his quip and the whole mysterious set up in general, and then she strode off at a fast pace in the direction of the inn. She had spent more time at her aunt's house settling

Archie in than she intended and she didn't want the likes of Nellie to make trouble for her by embellishing tales of her disappearance behind her back.

***

When she arrived back in the courtyard at the inn, all seemed to be quiet; too quiet for her liking. She walked over to the kitchen door which was ajar. Cassie was asleep by the fireside, her mouth wide open. She'd even managed to wash all the pots and put them away by the look of it, which made Lucy feel guilty. She had told the woman she was popping out to see her aunt but hadn't intended to stay away so long. She removed her shawl and donned her pinafore which was hanging on the back of the door.

Cassie stirred and then snorted loudly in her sleep which woke her up. She rose to sit forward in her armchair and blinked. 'So, you're back then, girlie!'

'I'm sorry, it took longer than expected.' She hadn't told Cassie the reason she'd gone to her aunt's as the less people knew the better in her book. 'Is there anything I can do to help you right now? I am sorry for not being back in time to wash all the pots and pans.'

'It's 'orright, I guessed you might have been gone for a while so I ordered Nellie to do them, she didn't look best pleased, either!' she chuckled.

Oh no! That would immediately set the girl on edge towards her and she needed a favour for tomorrow.

She paused for a moment before saying, 'I have to go somewhere important tomorrow morning and I was thinking of asking Nellie to fill in here for me.'

Cassie harrumphed. 'What's going on, you swanning off like this all the time?' She frowned.

'It is important, please, Cassie. And it's my only chance.'

'Yer only chance to what, might I ask?'

'I've got the chance to meet a lady, I can't say anymore for time being as I've been sworn to secrecy.'

Cassie appeared to mull it over in her mind for a while, then she smiled and said, 'As long as you don't make a habit of it and can get cover. I can't do all the breakfasts on my own.'

'Oh, thank you, Cassie.' She ran over to the armchair, knelt down and wrapped her arms around the woman.

'Hang on there, missy, people will think I've gone soft in me old age,' Cassie chuckled.

Lucy stood back and faced her. 'The only problem is I don't know how to persuade Nellie to work here and cover for me. She doesn't like me at all and I know she won't want to do it. I did think of bribing her with one of my auntie's pies.'

Cassie nodded. 'You just leave Nellie to me, I've thought of a way I can get her onside and I won't tell her you're going to meet no lady, either. I'll just say you've had some personal business to attend to, that's all she needs to know for time being.'

'I'd appreciate that. Thank you. Maybe I'll be able to tell you someday what this is all about but I don't rightly know what it's about myself as yet.'

Cassie lifted her silver brows. 'Well, whatever it is you seem to be so curious about it all so it would be a shame to stop you in your tracks, my girl.'

For a moment, Lucy feared Cassie would add, 'And you know what curiosity did? Killed the bleedin' cat!'

***

The following morning, Lucy was up and dressed bright and early and helped Cassie in the kitchen until a quarter past eight, which would allow her a quarter of an hour to run to Auntie's street to get the carriage. They were half way through serving the breakfasts as another couple of coaches had turned up unexpectedly and doubled the work load. 'I do feel awful leaving you like this!' Lucy said to the woman.

'Never mind that, you go and get Nellie here right this minute and then you can leave. You don't want to be late.'

Cassie was right of course. Lucy searched the Harrington's living quarters where Nellie could usually be found lighting the fires and sweeping the floors, but she was nowhere to be seen. She wasn't in the bar room either, and by the time Lucy had climbed all the way to the attic, she had a sinking feeling in her stomach.

Nellie's doing this on purpose to get back at me! She knows I need to get away.

She checked the kitchen one more time to see if the girl had shown up in the meantime, but Cassie shook her head as she dished up several plates of fried egg and bacon for the customers. 'It's no good, I'll just have to stay behind! You've got too much work on to manage on your own!' Lucy wailed.

'No, you will not, my girl!' Cassie said firmly. 'You get going. I'm going to serve these meals and then I'll see if there's anyone else who can help me here. That Nellie one is going to get her ears boxed when I catch hold of her! You'll see if she doesn't!' Cassie raised a fist in the air which made Lucy smile. She kissed the woman's rough cheek. 'Thanks so much. I'll be back as soon as I'm able!'

'Don't worry, I'll cover for you!' Cassie shouted after her, but Lucy'd already left the kitchen and was making her way across the cobbled courtyard.

What on earth did Nellie think she was doing going missing like that?

Lucy walked through the arch of the coaching inn and glanced at the church clock opposite. It was five minutes later than she thought. She could make it if she ran very fast, and so she did. She hoisted her skirts and made her way running across the road, dodging the heavy traffic of carts going to the market place and the odd carriage here and there. She was in such a rush that for once No Man's Land held no fear for her, and she arrived just in time, panting heavily as Mr Knight's carriage drew up at the end of Court Terrace.

Puffing profusely, she took a moment to catch a breath as Mr Knight alighted from the vehicle, looking astonishingly handsome in his black coat with its astrakhan collar and his shiny top hat. He appeared most amused to see how breathless and worked up she was. Then in a solemn tone of voice he said, 'I do apologise, Miss Harper. The lady realises she is impinging on your time, you can rest for a while in the carriage. Let me help you aboard...'

Lucy nodded and smiled tentatively at the thought of the journey ahead of her and where it might lead.

***

The carriage took a turn at the end of the road and then they were on their way. She longed to ask Mr Knight where they were going, but by the look of devilment in his eyes, she decided against it. He'd only laugh at her and tease her along the way, she just knew he would. He closed his eyes for a moment as if resting them. He really was a good-looking man: his dark, almost black hair, was neatly combed into place and she guessed he'd used a little pomade to gel it down. The skin on his face looked soft and clean shaven, apart from his thin, pencil style moustache which suited him very well indeed. Mr Knight was a total contrast to Bert, who'd often sported a five o'clock shadow and looked so scruffy unless he was going out to meet his floozie, then he'd taken more care of his appearance. She shivered at the thought of that man and forced herself to think of Mr Knight instead. She imagined he had his very own barber who kept him immaculate like that. His clothing was well tailored and she noticed beneath his fancy coat, his pinstriped trousers, crisp white shirt and navy silk cravat which was held in place with what appeared to be a diamond pin. He looked most business like this morning. Who was this man to the owner of the house? Surely, he was more than an agent to her?

She quickly averted her gaze in case he opened his eyes and caught her staring at him. There were people milling along the streets outside the carriage, all on their way some place. Work most probably as this was a working-class area. Those not fortunate enough to be engaged in regular employment, though, took on occasional work off sweaters from various factories to keep a roof over the heads of themselves and their families. And there were others that lived off their wits by either taking in washing and ironing or engaging in illegal or criminal activities. Such was life in the Whitechapel area of London.

She wondered what she'd say to the lady when she met her. She'd deliberately chosen to wear her Sunday best dress with a pair of lace white gloves that she cherished. Bessie had given her the gloves a couple of years ago as a birthday present, and although a little too small by now, at least they gave her a smart appearance. All of this was topped off with a new grey cape Bessie had sewn for her when she went to work at the inn. She'd have been mortified if she'd had wear an old knitted shawl to a grand house. She'd brushed her hair one hundred times that morning and affixed a cornflower blue satin ribbon in it. She wasn't quite a lady but she was doing the very best she possibly could.

It was about a half hour later after they'd entered a more countryfied, treelined area, that the carriage ended up turning into a leafy lane. It was nearing the end of autumn but there were such beautiful colours on the leaves as they fluttered off the trees towards the ground, spreading out as a gold and russet carpet. Lucy gulped as the carriage carried on through a pair of wrought iron gates, leading up to a long drive. 'Is this where the lady lives?' she asked.

Mr Knight nodded. 'Yes, and you'll get to meet her shortly.'

'But why does she want to meet me? I just don't understand. It's my aunt she's been helping out with that house not me. Please Mr Knight, why has she been charging my aunt such a low rent and furnishing her house with expensive furniture?'

Mr Knight coughed as if he couldn't believe that she'd worked things out for herself. 'It's not for me to say. If you have any questions then you'll have to ask Mrs Dowager for yourself.'

So that was her name, Mrs Dowager!

'I'm sorry,' he chuckled 'that's my nick name for her.' He put his gloved palm to his face and said in a surreptitious manner, 'Please don't tell her I call her that, will you?'

She shook her head. 'So, what is her name then?'

'It's Lady Fanshaw-Smythe actually, but everyone calls her Lady Fanshaw, she dropped the last part of her surname a few years ago.'

Lucy gasped, she'd never been introduced to a person who had a double-barrelled name before, it all sounded so posh.

When they arrived at the top of the drive, there was an ornamental fountain with flowing water, which fascinated her. This was surrounded by pretty flowerbeds of flowers she had never seen before but they were such pretty colours: yellow, fuchsia pink and lilac.

The house itself was grey-stoned and turreted, a little like a castle and the windows were leaded in a criss-cross fashion. In the centre, above the main doorway was a clock which showed the time as just gone past nine the hour. It was the largest house she'd ever seen in her life apart from Buckingham Palace of course. Someone could get lost in that house if they were staying there. To the right of the property, there was even an archway which reminded her of the one at the inn with its courtyard. No doubt that's where the carriage would end up finally parking up. She supposed there were ostlers and stable hands working here too, all ready to fly to the driver's command as he pulled up.

The carriage drew to a halt and Mr Knight clambered off it first, and then he waited whilst the driver helped Lucy down. As she stood beside it, her legs felt like they needed stretching but she didn't complain; there would be time enough when she had to get back to the inn later and she'd have to walk all the way from Court Terrace.

'Now, I must warn you that Lady Fanshaw is a little snappy, dear. But don't you worry, her bark is far worse than her bite. In fact, I recommend that you hold your ground if she argues with you, she's like that. She'll have far more respect for you if you show your strengths rather than your weaknesses.' He twirled his moustache both sides between his thumb and forefinger.

What was this lady like? She sounded like an old dragon to Lucy. Oh dear, what had she got herself into? Why had she insisted on meeting her when her connection appeared to be with Bessie and not herself?

They were greeted at the door by a lady in a black dress with a set of keys dangling around her waist. The woman looked quite stern at first to Lucy but she welcomed them both.

'Is Lady Fanshaw ready?' Mr Knight asked.

The woman nodded. 'She's waiting in the drawing room and I have to warn you, she's particularly fractious this morning!'

Fractious? Where had Lucy heard that word before? Oh, she remembered now. Bessie had been speaking about a lady she knew who'd had a baby and the baby had been fractious when she was teething. It was beginning to sound as if this lady was going to be hard work.

'I'll leave you to it,' Mr Knight said, looking at Lucy.

'B…but aren't you going to stay?' She couldn't believe he was leaving her here to face the lady all alone.

'I'm sorry, but I have some urgent business to attend to. I'll return in a couple of hours to pick you up.' He smiled and then, turning his back, left her standing there on the doorstep, feeling as though she were about to enter the dragon's den.

***

Lucy followed the woman inside the house and was immediately overawed by the splendour of it all. The crystal chandeliers, the black and white marble tiled flooring and the exquisite mahogany winding staircase, were all things that in her world, she was not a part of.

There was no conversation from the housekeeper as she worked hard to keep up with the brisk pace she walked, the only sounds being the click clacking of the woman's heels on the tiled floor and Lucy's own heartbeat thudding through the bodice of her dress.

Presently, after walking down a narrow corridor lined either side with various artwork of vibrant country scenes and portraits of people Lucy guessed might be long since passed away going by their style of dress, they arrived outside a heavy looking oakwood door.

'The mistress is expecting you,' the housekeeper said, and then for the first time she smiled at Lucy, causing her to smile nervously back at the woman. 'I'm Mrs Tavistock, should you need to summon me!'

Lucy nodded.

The housekeeper gave a sharp knock on the door, then stepped back, and Lucy heard the word, 'Enter!' from behind it in a weak, shaky voice. She gulped as the housekeeper turned the knob of the door and pushed it open to reveal a room with large leaded windows, heavy leather padded furniture and dark wood book cases that were packed to the rafters with all manner of books. It was a few seconds before she spotted the woman sitting in a high-backed, winged armchair, near a roaring fire. Beside her was a small occasional table with a crystal decanter and glass on top of it, the glass itself was half empty. After stepping inside the room, she was unaware of the housekeeper closing the door behind her to attend to further business elsewhere.

'Come inside, child, I'm not going to bite you,' the woman said, looking up from her armchair. She had the whitest hair Lucy had ever seen and was dressed top to toe in black. The only other colours on her were the white laced edged collar and cuffs to her dress and a faint rose blush to her cheeks, which Lucy guessed was either down to being sat beside such a big fire or from whatever it was she'd been drinking in that glass, or maybe it was from both.

'Good morning, Lady Fanshaw.' Lucy felt like curtseying but wasn't quite sure what she should do in such circumstances, so she stood awkwardly for a moment, with her hands behind her back. And then, she tried to fill the conversation with words as the woman seemed to appraise her with piercing blue eyes that reminded her of a sapphire diamond she'd once seen at the museum: all shiny and many faceted as it reflected the light. 'I'm Lucy Harper,' Lucy continued, 'and I live…'

'I'm quite well aware of who you are and where you live,' the woman said, in a clipped fashion. 'In fact, I know far more about you and your aunt than you might care to realise.'

'You do?' Lucy blinked in astonishment.

'Yes, indeed. Come closer so I might get a better look at you, my eyesight isn't as good as it used to be.' She gestured with a wave of her hand for Lucy to draw near and then squinted to make her out.

Tentatively, Lucy walked towards the woman and as she approached, she felt almost beaten back by the heat of the fire. How on earth could she stick being as close to it as that? For some reason the fire they had in the kitchen back at the coaching house never felt as warm as that but maybe that was because of the draught from the back door and the fact windows had to be left open sometimes to leave the steam of the cooking out. People were always passing through, opening the main door which led to the corridor inside.

'Yes, I can see all the features there,' the woman said, holding up her gnarled and thin-skinned hand, outlining Lucy's face from a distance as if painting a picture with it.

But what did she mean by that? She could see all the features? That didn't make sense at all to her. Or was she referring to her bad eyesight when said that? Whatever she meant, maybe she'd find out in due course. Meanwhile, she'd do her best to be polite to the woman.

'Do you like my house, Lucy?' the woman asked.

It seemed like a random question because she hadn't viewed much of it as yet. 'Oh, yes,' Lucy replied enthusiastically. 'Though so far I've only seen outside, the corridor and this room, but it does look very grand indeed.'

The woman smiled, closed her eyes and nodded. For a moment Lucy thought that maybe she'd dozed off to sleep after drinking the alcohol but then both her eyes flicked open and she said, 'I'm glad of that. Now have you eaten?'

'No, ma'am. I was up bright and early to come here and had some tasks to carry out at the coaching inn as I wanted to help Cassie before I left as she's making the breakfasts this morning and I…'

'Slow down, child. I get the picture. I'm going to ring for the maid to bring you something. How about some hot buttered crumpets and a glass of buttermilk, will they do?'

Lucy nodded and then, remembering her manners, said, 'Yes, please, ma'am.'

'Sit down then, child. And then I'll tell you why I wanted to meet you.'

Lucy did as asked, and waited as Lady Fanshaw lifted a small brass bell on the table by the side of her and jangled it. Within moments, a young maid appeared and curtseyed. 'You rang, ma'am.'

'I did indeed.' Her eyes held a glint of mischief about them. 'Now could you please bring a plate of hot buttered crumpets, a pot of tea for myself, Indian and not Chinese, and a glass of buttermilk for Lucy?' she asked.

The maid nodded. 'Certainly, ma'am.'

When she had departed, Lady Fanshaw chuckled. 'A good-looking girl but as dull as dishwasher and as slow as a tortoise!'

Lucy smiled. She yearned to ask why the woman wanted to meet her, but now her conversation had gone off at a tangent and she was speaking about how cold it was for the time of the year and how all the red berries on the holly indicated there would be a hard winter ahead. She watched as the lady donned a pair of spectacles.

Being bold for once, and maybe that was due to the curiosity inside her, Lucy said, 'You were saying, Lady Fanshaw…'

'About the berries…' she peered over the top of her gilt covered specs.

'No, before that.'

'Ah, yes, what was I saying, now?'

'Something about the reason you wanted to see me?'

'Yes.' Recognition finally ensued. 'It's because I need a lady's companion.'

A companion? What does the lady mean by that?

'Someone to come and sit with me during the day and help me out as my eye sight isn't what it once was. Someone to write letters for me, read books and newspapers aloud to me, escort me for walks in the grounds, maybe even accompany me to the odd social event, I haven't been out in such a long while. That sort of thing.'

Lucy was silent for a moment and then she said, 'But I have a job at the coaching inn, Lady Fanshaw.'

Lady Fanshaw smiled. 'I know you do, Lucy, but I would pay you a nominal sum and you'd have a room of your own and freedom in your spare time to read anything from my extensive library. You could learn skills like embroidery, how to play the piano—I would employ tutors for you. You'd learn how to become a lady. Will you think about it, at least? I need some company and conversation in my dreary, drab life.'

Lucy's heart went out to the woman, she was obviously not in the best of health and utterly lonely with her own company all day long. She nodded. 'I promise I shall think about it, Lady Fanshaw, but one thing I need to know…' Lady Fanshaw angled her head on one side. 'Why are you offering me this opportunity, I just don't understand?'

'Take it from me,' the lady said, with a serious expression on her face, 'all will become clear in good time.'

Before Lucy had a chance to say anything else, the maid arrived carrying a tray on top of which was a silver salver and refreshments.

'Thank you, Mary. You can put it down on that table over there.' She pointed to a small table which had a chair either side in front of the bay window. It was a relief for Lucy to move away from the fire place as her legs felt red hot and she imagined Lady

Fanshaw's must be like two mottled red sausages beneath her dress.

***

'I'm telling you, Cassie,' Lucy said, when she was back at the coaching inn, 'you should have seen that flippin' house, it's the biggest house I've ever seen and there were wall to wall paintings in fancy frames and statues all over the place, and then Lady—'

Cassie smiled, but Nellie, who was stood next to her with a mixing bowl and wooden spoon in her hand said, 'I'm fed up of hearing you go on and on, I don't believe a word of it. You're making it all up!' Cassie had obviously finally managed to rope the girl in to doing some of Lucy's work.

'I tell you, I'm not!' Lucy yelled at her.

'Look, girls,' Cassie said, in an attempt to calm the situation, 'I believe this is true, but we have got work to be getting on with. We've just had an extra coach draw up without warning and I need us to bulk out what we've already got. So, then Lucy, you go cut some slices of bread, and Nellie, put that bleedin' cake you're making in the oven, you've stirred it enough by now! And then you can leave the kitchen and get back to your other duties now Lucy has returned.'

Nellie nodded and then turned to Lucy. 'Well, if you are telling the truth, why on earth would a lady of fine breeding want to invite a young rag o'muffin sort like yerself for breakfast?'

Lucy couldn't answer that as she didn't know herself. She wasn't going to tell Nellie either that she had been asked to become the woman's companion but she did intend telling Cassie later when she'd gone.

'Can't answer, can you?' Nellie said in a smug manner. 'That's because it's all made up and you were elsewhere this morning while you were needed here!'

Cassie shot Lucy a look which warned her not to say anything, and in doing so, it caused Nellie to get her cake ready for the oven and leave the room. If Lucy had responded they would have been at it like hammer and tongs all afternoon long.

When the girl had left, Lucy turned to Cassie and said, 'It is true, Cassie. But I don't know why the woman would pick me, nor rent her house out in Court Terrace for a pittance to Bessie. It doesn't make sense.'

'Well, I believe you, and I agree, but there has to be some good reason for it and it's my guess you'll find out in good time.'

Chapter Fifteen

A few nights later, Lucy noticed a man in the bar room that she didn't much like the look of. He was well-built with scruffy dark hair and an unkempt appearance which made her think of Bert. But it wasn't just that, her instincts told her he was bad news. He had a young boy beside him, who looked out of place. The lad's eyes were doleful looking as though he feared everyone around him, particularly the man whose company he was in and he cringed as the man bellowed as he spoke to all and sundry, half of whom looked as petrified as the boy and they appeared to nod in agreement to whatever he said, just to keep the peace.

The man then chatted to the landlord across the bar for a while and whispered something in his ear. Then he carried a drink in a glass over to the boy and appeared to warn him about something. He left the lad alone and disappeared with a woman who worked at the coaching inn, called, Ginger. Lucy knew what she and some other sorts got up to there, taking men back to their rooms. They were getting paid handsomely for their services by the look of it, and there were rumours that sometimes they stole from customers. But that man looked like he could handle himself; no one would dare mess with him.

Lucy watched as the young lad took a sip of his drink and scowled. Whatever it was, he didn't like it.

He gulped as she approached his table. 'What are you doing on your own, little 'un?' she asked, with one hand on her hip, the other with a round metal tray held firmly to her body so that it was tucked under her arm.

'I'm waiting for Mr Brackley to come back...' he said meekly. Brackley? Wasn't that the name of the man that Archie had escaped from? She immediately felt a sense of dread and compassion for the lad. 'Oh, so he's the gentleman just gone with Ginger to her room?'

The boy shrugged. 'I don't know what her name was but she was collecting glasses in here not long since,' he replied.

She nodded. 'Aye, that's her. They'll be gone a while yet, if I know that one!' She chuckled. Then her face took on a more serious expression. 'What are you drinking there?' She narrowed her eyes.

'Gin. Bill bought it for me and told me to sup it by the time he returns.'

She shook her head. 'And I'm betting you'd much rather a lemonade or ginger beer, right?'

He nodded enthusiastically. She swept the glass away with her free hand, then seeing his worried expression, said, 'Don't worry, little 'un, I'm only going to swap it for lemonade for you. I'll pour the gin back into the bottle that way Mr Harrington won't mind as he can sell it twice over!'

He smiled broadly, obviously at the thought of no longer having to appease Mr Brackley by drinking that gin.

Lucy returned with a cold glass of lemonade for him. 'I'm Lucy,' she introduced herself. 'What's your name? I can't keep calling you "little 'un", can I?'

After taking a long swig of the sweet cool drink, he set down his glass, wiped his mouth on the back of his sleeve and said, 'Bobby. My name is Bobby.'

'That's all?' she frowned. 'What's yer last name?'

He shrugged his shoulders. 'I don't rightly know, miss.'

'Well, your last name, your surname should be the same as your father's.'

'Don't have no father.'

Oh dear, was he an orphan like she was? 'Oh. I see, well never mind. At least I know your first name is Bobby now and you know my name an' all, so we're practically friends! I have to get back to work now,' she whispered, as she noticed the landlord glance over in her direction.

Bobby nodded, obviously sad to see her go and she wondered if she'd ever see him again.

***

When she had the chance a few days later, Lucy called to see her aunt as she wanted to check up on Archie to find out how he was settling in and to tell him how she'd seen Mr Brackley with a young lad.

Bessie was amazed by her news about visiting Lady Fanshaw and the fact that she was their benefactor. 'Well, knock me down with a bleedin' feather!' she said. 'I can't believe you arranged all that behind me back, though!' At first, she thought the woman was annoyed with her, but then a twinkle lit her eyes. 'I do think you ought to consider becoming a companion for her, it will give you a great start in life, better than being at the coaching inn where you're on your feet most of the day and at night as well! But I really don't understand why that lady is helping us out and appears to know who we are?' She scratched her head.

'Neither do I. I don't like to ask either as she can be a bit sharp at times!'

Auntie smiled. 'Well, if anyone can handle her ladyship, it's you, Lucy Harper! Like I said, it might be worth you working at the big house and leaving the coaching inn behind for good.'

'I suppose you're right, Auntie, but I do enjoy working at the inn.'

'I know that, but is it because you don't want to leave that lad who is sweet on you called Smithy?'

Archie frowned by the side of her. She knew what he thought about the lad. He realised he was a wrong 'un and would be gunning for him as he'd left with Duke like that.

When Auntie had left the room to bring them some refreshment, Lucy whispered to him, 'How are you settling in here, Archie?'

He glanced around the room as if he feared being overheard. 'I like living here well enough and working for Mrs Harper but...'

'But what?' she eyed him intently.

'But that Jacob one is a bit of a bully!'

'I know what you mean. You just have to stand up to him that's all, his bark is much worse than his bite.'

He nodded. 'I've made a new friend though!' His eyes lit up.

'Oh?'

'Yes, Mr Baxter the butler at a house where I drop off deliveries. He's ever so kind to me, let's me have a break in the kitchen with him when I arrive!' He smiled broadly.

'That's good. I'm glad it's all working out for you. And Duke, does he like it here?'

'Yes. Mrs Harper gives him lots of leftovers and he's allowed to sleep in the house with me overnight. She reckons it's too cold for man nor beast to be outside right now.'

'That's good. Just take care with Jacob though and hold your ground,' she advised. Archie nodded. 'By the way, didn't you tell me that the man you escaped from who sent you to sweep chimneys was a Mr Brackley, Archie?'

Archie frowned as if he didn't want to be reminded of the man but Lucy knew she had to warn him. 'Yes, why do you ask me that?' His eyes became large as if filled with fear.

'Because he was at the coaching house in the bar room the other night.'

He breathed a sigh of relief. 'Thank goodness I left the inn when I did!' he said, looking pleased with himself. 'Thanks for helping me to escape, Lucy.'

'That's not all though, Archie. He had a young lad with him and he was making him drink gin. When he'd left the room, I swapped the boy's glass of gin for lemonade, which he was grateful for.'

Archie nodded. 'He used to make me and Bobby drink that stuff. Yuck it was 'orrible! We used to leave it dribble down our chins onto our clothing to make it look like we were drinking it, or when he weren't looking, we tipped it on the floor.'

She narrowed her gaze. 'Bobby, you say?'

'Yes? Why?'

'That was the boy's name, I'm almost positive of it!'

'What did he look like?'

Surely there couldn't be two Bobbys taken on by Bill? That would be a big coincidence. 'Small and frail, about eight years old. He looked so sad, too.'

'But I don't understand why he's back with Bill. He went to stay with his mother as she got a job at a big house. Thinking about it, mind, he could well have kidnapped Bobby if he found out where he was staying, like he kidnapped me.'

'Just you be careful, Archie, when you're out and about delivering those pies in case he catches hold of you. I'm going to warn Auntie when she comes back in.'

Within moments Bessie arrived, smiling, carrying a tray containing a couple of steaming hot meat and potato pies and two glasses of her homemade lemonade. 'What's wrong with you pair? Especially you, Archie. You look like yer've seen a flamin' ghost or something!' She said, setting down the tray.

Lucy was determined more than ever that her auntie needed now to protect Archie from the brute.

***

Lucy was on her way out when she decided to see Mr Harrington to tell him where she was off to. She was dressed in her bonnet and shawl and over the crook of her arm she carried a wicker basket.

She turned and saw the man sat in the corner, who was cradling his pint in a pewter tankard. It was him again—Bill Brackley. A shudder ran through her.

'I'll get you those pies then from my auntie's place!' She called across the bar room to the landlord as she didn't want to lead the man to Archie when she was going to visit her aunt. Did he know her connection with the lad? There was something about the way he'd looked her up and down that creeped her out. It reminded her of the way Bert had sized her up with lustful eyes. But then again, surely, he had no idea that she and Archie were friends? He wouldn't have seen them together. She made sure he was still sitting in the corner when she left the room and made her way to her aunt's house.

She needed to pass No Man's Land again, but wanting to see Archie and her aunt spurred her on. Every so often she thought she heard footsteps behind her, but each time she turned to glance over her shoulder, the footsteps would stop and then she'd begin again. Thinking she was imagining things, she carried on walking. By the time she passed through the alleyway, she knew she was safe. She turned one final time to see a lady and a gent walking behind her. Maybe it was them she'd heard in the distance and now they'd finally caught up with her.

She climbed the uneven steps to the house and rapped on the door, experiencing an emotion of relief when Auntie opened it and allowed her in.

'What's the matter, Lucy?' She asked. 'You're white as a sheet?'

Her mouth felt dry from anxiety and her hands trembled as she spoke about what had just occurred. 'I thought I was being followed by that Bill Brackley I told you about. He was at the coaching inn earlier and was sizing me up. I kept turning around when I heard footsteps but there was no one there. Maybe it was all in my imagination.'

'Aye, maybe you let your thoughts get carried away,' Bessie said, but her look of concern told Lucy otherwise. 'Anyhow, come in. I'm not letting you return to that inn on your own later when it's dark. Who knows who is about, never mind Bill Brackley!' She closed the door behind them.

***

Archie finally showed up after he had finished work for the day, with Duke at his side, wagging his tail in excitement to see Lucy. She knelt down to hug the dog, burying her head in his fur. 'Good boy!' she said. And the dog showed his affection by licking her cheek but for some reason his eyes looked sad today.

'Everything going well today?' she asked Archie.

'Yes,' his eyes lit up with excitement. 'Mr Baxter says he's going to ask his employer to make enquiries to find out where my uncle lives so I can go back there!'

Lucy stood to embrace him. Holding him at arms' length she said, 'I am so pleased for you.'

'I feel bad though,' he said shaking his head.

'But why's that?'

'Because you've all been so good to me, particularly Mrs Harper.'

'I wouldn't worry about that, Archie. Auntie only wants to see you happy in life and when you return home, we can all still be friends.' She noticed the tears in his eyes. 'Come here, soppy!' And she embraced him once again whilst Duke looked on in great amusement and he gave a solitary bark as if to say he approved.

Bessie decided to celebrate Archie's good news by preparing a special tea for them both of miniature cucumber sandwiches, fondant fancies and long glasses of ginger beer.

'Don't worry though, Lucy,' Archie said, 'I'll write to you so we can keep in touch and maybe you can visit the big house someday.'

'That would be lovely!' she sighed. 'But don't send any letters to the inn, not for Mr Casper or Smithy to see them. Send them to my auntie's house instead, that way I'll be sure to get them.'

He nodded. 'I will, no fear.'

'Now then, Archie,' Bessie said finally, 'it's getting dark so we'd better leave Lucy get back to the inn.'

'I'll walk you,' Archie offered.

Lucy frowned. 'What if Mr Casper sees you?'

'Well I can at least walk you part of the way,' he enthused.

She looked at her aunt who nodded in agreement. 'Come straight back then, Archie!' she called after the pair. 'Take Duke with you.'

'Come along, Duke!' he called. Duke lifted his head from beneath the table and whined as if he couldn't be bothered to make the effort.

'I don't know what's the matter with that dog today,' Mrs Harper tutted, 'he's not been himself at all. Maybe you better leave him behind in case he's sickening for something…'

Lucy looked at Archie and nodded. It was most unusual to see the dog acting like that and she hoped Duke wasn't ill.

***

As the pair set off for the inn, they were unaware that someone was lurking in the shadows. The pair walked through the archway that led them to *No Man's Land*. No matter how many times Lucy took this route, she couldn't help gagging from the smell of something rotten permeating her nostrils. It was like a mixture of rotting vegetables and festering flesh.

When Lucy was a stone's throw away from the inn, she turned to Archie. 'I shall miss you when you return home, Archie.'

He was quiet for a moment and then to Lucy's surprise, he leaned over and planted a kiss on her cheek, taking her aback. 'I'll miss you too, Lucy,' he said. 'You take care of yourself and remember to write to me!'

She nodded, shyly. This past few weeks, Archie seemed to have grown up a lot, not just physically, but he seemed older as well. She couldn't help worrying about him though as she waved him goodbye and walked off on her own. This time there were no echoing footsteps behind her, and for that she was grateful. Soon she would be safely back at the inn, but she didn't want anyone to catch sight of the boy, it was just too risky.

When Lucy passed the front of the inn, she peered through the steamed up bay window to see lots of gesturing figures inside—there seemed to be much merriment taking place, and she guessed another coach party had landed for the night. Nellie was collecting glasses from the bar with a big scowl on her face, so she stepped away from the window before the girl caught her looking in. She hurried through the archway across the cobbled stones of the courtyard where the ostlers were sorting out the horses and sprucing up a couple of coaches, and let herself in through the back door of the kitchen where

Cassie was having a snooze by the fireside. She was just about to put on a pan of milk to boil to make some cocoa, when Smithy entered the back door, and speaking in a whisper not to wake Cassie because she got in a temper when she hadn't had enough kip, he asked, 'You seen that Archie one, have you?'

A rush of blood suffused her cheeks at the thought of not long since being in Archie's company and him kissing her. She turned to face him and swallowed hard. 'No, why do ask?'

'I thought you might know seeing as how you helped him to escape.' He narrowed his eyes.

'I might have helped him get away from the likes of you and Mr Casper's thieving ways but it doesn't mean I know where he is now. I ain't seen him since.'

'Well if you do 'appen to see him, like, tell him that Bill Brackley is looking for him.'

Lucy's heart began to thump so hard she could hear it pounding in her ears. 'I will, yes, but I'm unlikely to see him, he told me he was trying to get back to his uncle's house. When was Mr Brackley asking?'

'A couple of hours ago in the bar room. I didn't speak to him meself, but I overheard him talking to Mr Casper. He's dead angry the boy left him in the first place, he had taken him on as a chimney sweep he said and the lad had run off. That must be when I bumped into him on the street and brought him here. Archie seems to have a way of being offered work and board and lodgings and then running off as that's what he's done to me too. I've a good mind when I find him to drag him by the lughole over to Bill's place. 'Spect he'd pay me for the privilege too, the bleedin' rapscallion needs punishing!'

'No, Smithy!' Lucy said vehemently. 'He's only a boy. Leave him alone!'

'Leave him alone? What's going on 'ere, gal? You got feelings for him or somefink?' he stared hard at her as if he was trying to read her mind.

'No, of course not, he's a couple of years younger than me. He's just a little boy. I feel sorry for him as he's an orphan and it can't be easy for the lad.'

'Well, I understand all about that as I'm one meself, but he should never bite off the hand what feeds him!'

It occurred to Lucy it might be best if she wasn't so outwardly sympathetic toward Archie as it appeared to incur Smithy's wrath. If he found out anything he could cause trouble by going to Brackley.

She placed her hand on his shoulder and said, 'You're right, Smithy. He abused your hospitality, after all you've done for him and all.'

Smithy nodded and then moved away to get back to his work. Once he approached the door, he hesitated for a moment, turned to face her, and then said, 'Promise you'll tell me where Archie is if you find out?'

'I promise, cross my heart,' she said. But what Smithy didn't see was that she had her fingers crossed behind her back.

***

The following morning at five o'clock after a restless sleep due to worry over Archie, Lucy got washed and dressed and went downstairs at the inn to begin lighting a fire in the kitchen, so at least they'd be warm while they worked as it was perishing cold. Cassie hadn't stirred from her bed as yet. She usually rose about half past the hour, and by then, the fire was underway and the kettle put on to boil. But before Lucy had a chance to take over Cassie's tasks, there was a sharp rap on the back door.

Lucy unlocked it to find Bessie stood there looking all of a flap. Something was wrong, she could sense it. 'Oh, Lucy, did Archie stay here last night?'

'No. I said good night to him and assumed he'd gone back to your house. You'd better come in out of the cold, though I haven't lit the fire as yet.' She guided her aunt inside the kitchen.

There were now tears in Bessie's eyes. 'I should have insisted that he take that dog with him but we thought Duke must be ill because he's looking so sad this morning as if he's missing his master. Though I don't think he's unwell, he just senses something, you know?'

'Look, sit down a moment while I light the fire and we'll have a think about this,' Lucy said kindly.

Auntie nodded and she took Cassie's armchair by the fireplace, Lucy didn't have the heart to tell her that Cassie didn't like anyone else sitting in it, but chances were by the time the woman arose, Bessie would be gone long since.

The fire was already set with coal and kindling, so Lucy took a box of matches from the mantelpiece and struck a light to it. Soon there were flames catching up the chimney. She filled a kettle and put it on to boil on the hob, then she seated herself opposite her aunt.

'Smithy called to the kitchen last night to tell me Bill Brackley was looking for Archie.'

Auntie quirked a brow. 'What time was that?'

'Apparently it was a couple of hours before I got back. You don't think he was watching Archie walk me home last night, do you?'

Bessie frowned. 'I wouldn't put it past him. I've met that man before as he knows Bert and they're both cut from the same cloth if you ask me. If they see an opportunity they grab it with both hands!'

Lucy tried to persuade her aunt to stay to have something to eat, but she insisted on getting back in case Archie turned up.

It was going to be a long day as neither of them would rest until they knew that Archie was safe and sound.

Oh, Archie, where are you my friend? A solitary tear coursed Lucy's cheek.

Chapter Sixteen

Lucy had been finding sleep difficult for the past couple of days as she was so concerned about Archie's welfare that she tossed and turned all night long. She found being busy during the day kept her going, but the nights were long and seemed never ending.

Poor Aunt Bessie was going out of her mind with worry about the lad too. Archie's disappearance seemed to be taking a toll on the woman's health as she fought to keep the business going now he was no longer around to make his deliveries. When Lucy had suggested she take on a new boy to help, she wouldn't hear of it. No one would be good enough to take Archie's place, so as a result, the woman ran herself ragged making his deliveries as well as her own and baking her pies.

There was nothing they could do—it was all a waiting game to see if the lad showed up. And when Aunt Bessie had suggested they go to the police station, Lucy warned her that Archie wouldn't want that as he might get into trouble if he was found stealing on the streets if Bill was up to his old tricks again and getting him involved in his nefarious activities—that was if he had him in the first place. There was no way of knowing as Bill Brackley appeared to have gone to ground and was no longer calling at the inn for a pint or to see Ginger to meet his lustful desires.

Lucy sighed to herself. There was plenty of work here to be getting on with for time being.

The stack of dirty dishes she was carrying almost toppled from her arms when she heard a sudden noise behind her. She turned to see Archie and Bobby stood in the kitchen, but then she smiled and set the dishes down on the counter. They had taken her unawares and must have sneaked in as the back door was ajar. She opened and closed her mouth, unable to believe her eyes, but she was so pleased to see them but had to ask. 'What are you doing here, Archie? My aunt has been looking for you? And Bobby?'

'It were 'orrible, Lucy. Bill threatened me in the alleyway with a knife after I left you, he'd been watching us!' Archie said breathlessly.

'Oh that's awful, Archie…' she gave him a hug. 'What an ordeal for you, but where have you been and how did you get away from him?'

'He took me back to his place and that's how I ran into Bobby, thankfully. I managed to get us both out of there when Bill was blind drunk and sleeping it off on the bed!'

Bobby's eyes were shining bright. 'I don't know what I'd 'ave done if Archie hadn't rescued me,' he said, as he looked at the boy with admiration shining in his eyes. 'He got the key from Bill's pocket and we ran away. That man half-starved us.'

There were tears in Lucy's eyes as the boys took it in turns to tell her what happened, barely bothering to pause in the excitement of it all. Then Archie explained something else that made Lucy's eyes enlarge in horror. 'I heard Bill talking to Mr Casper when he called around one night. They were both having a drink together and thought we were fast asleep. Oh, Lucy, I don't know how to tell you this, but he's been watching you here at the inn…'

'I know, I've seen the way he looks at me and it gives me the creeps!'

'He plans to kidnap you too and I don't know what for exactly, it can't be to go up chimneys or nothing like that, but I know he has bad intentions for you.'

Lucy nodded. She could guess what Bill wanted her for, the same thing that Bert was after. She shuddered at the thought of it.

'Come with us to your aunt's house,' Archie urged, 'you're not safe here anymore, Lucy!'

She nodded. 'I'll just fetch my shawl...' She located it hanging on the peg on the wall, and the three of them crept out of the kitchen and into the courtyard just as Casper and Smithy made an appearance. They were speaking to someone inside a coach that had just pulled up. Smithy's mouth fell open when he spotted the trio and he nudged Casper to attract the man's attention.

'When I say make a run for it, we all scarper!' Archie said. 'But try to keep together, understood?'

Lucy and Bobby nodded. Then the three children ran for their lives past the coach, out through the archway and onto the street outside. In the distance, there were muffled shouts arising from Casper and Smithy.

Lucy snuck a glance behind her but she couldn't see them. Old Casper's arthritic legs couldn't keep up she supposed, and she knew the mail coach was due in any moment, so Smithy must have had second thoughts about leaving the inn.

'My auntie will be so pleased to see you, Archie,' Lucy said breathlessly as they ran, 'she's been that concerned about you.' The trio moved as fast as they could to get to Bessie's with less concern for passing No Man's Land than being apprehended by Bill Brackley.

When they arrived at the kitchen door, Bessie was there to greet them. She almost broke down in tears when she saw Archie stood before her. 'Come in all of you!' she said, 'I've been so worried about you, Archie. Your Uncle Walter has been here and taken Duke home with him and he said I was to send word to him if you show up. What happened?'

Uncle Walter had finally been tracked down by Mr Baxter's employer at the big house as promised. It was such a shame that after Archie had been separated from his uncle for so long that when he'd shown up at Bessie's house, the lad was thought still missing and feared to be in Brackley's clutches. There was no way of Bessie knowing Archie would turn up unexpected like this on the same day and within an hour or so of his uncle's departure.

By the time Archie had gone through the whole story of what happened to him and Bobby too, with a sprinkling of how Lucy was under the threat of danger while she remained working at the coaching inn, Bessie looked right worn out with the worry of it all.

'Well, you're quite safe here for time being,' she explained. 'You all look as though you could do with a good feed and a nice glass of me homemade ginger beer.'

Bobby was so overcome with the woman's kindness that he burst into tears and she cuddled him like he was her own son. Soon they'd all eaten a meat pie each with thick gravy and some mashed potatoes too and they sipped her ginger beer. Later they sat in front of a roaring fire, Bessie rocking in her chair, her mind mulling things over. 'I'm trying to think how best to get word to your uncle, Archie,' she said. 'I could send Jacob over in the pony and trap?'

Archie didn't like the sound of that one little bit; he didn't trust the lad. 'Don't trouble yourself, Mrs Harper,' he said. 'Best thing would be for me to see Mr Baxter, the butler over at Nightingale Terrace. He'd want to help again, I'm sure.' Archie trusted that man with his life.

'Very well then,' Bessie said, with a look of uncertainty on her face. 'I do think we should contact the police though.'

At the mention of the police, Lucy watched the colour drain from Archie's face. She realised that was the last thing the boy wanted, all he wanted right now was to get back home to his Uncle's house.

***

The children sat around the fireside while Bessie spoke words of reassurance to them as she rocked back and forth in her wooden rocking chair and chatted amicably.

Lucy noticed Bobby glancing at the back door with a look of horror on his face.

There, stood against the door jamb was a large looming figure, no one had seen enter the house.

Bill Brackley. Lucy swallowed.

'Come along now then, boys, you're coming with me!' he said firmly, with a snarl on his face.

Bessie carefully got out of her chair and reaching over to the fireplace, stood with a poker in her hand.

'Be careful, Auntie!' Lucy shouted.

The man laughed and pushed Bessie down in the chair again. 'Ain't nothing you can do to stop me taking those boys,' he sneered. 'And given time, I'll take the girl and all!'

A shiver of fear coursed Lucy's spine at the thought of what that man intended taking her for.

Suddenly the door leading to the hallway opened, causing Bill to turn around, and to Lucy's relief, Harry stood there, with a determined look on his face as his eyes flashed. 'Just what do you think you're doing to my mother?' he demanded. Harry was almost as tall as Jacob these days and she'd never seen him in this light before. Come to think of it, it seemed some time since Jacob had bullied him as now, they were almost the same height.

Bill didn't flinch, but Lucy knew who was coming behind him as it had all been pre-arranged by the look of it. Mr Baxter was to tell the master and bring his coach over. Standing behind Harry was a well-dressed gentleman with two burly police constables. Harry must have been responsible for this as his mother had explained what had gone on this past few days.

Quiet, affable Harry.

Bill trembled; he didn't look so clever now. He scrambled to get away from the room and back out into the yard to make a getaway, knocking over a potted fern plant in its holder in the process, but the policemen had a strong hold of him. 'We've been after this one for a long time,' said the younger of the two, who had Bill's arm locked behind his back. 'He's been breaking the law sending lads up chimneys and soliciting women and now we can add kidnapping of children to the list! Which is an offence under the Offences Against the Person act of 1861! Section 56 to be precise!'

The inspector smiled and patted the young policeman on his back. 'We've trained you well, P.C. Parker, put him into the Black Maria but cuff him first.'

They all watched as Bill was led away in handcuffs. 'Bread and water for you from now on,' said the constable as he pushed him roughly out through the door.

The gentleman introduced himself to Archie as Mr Worthington, Mr Baxter's employer at the house Archie had delivered pies to.

'Thank you for bringing the police, sir,' said Archie.

Mr Worthington patted him on the head. 'I'm just glad you're out of danger, young Archibald. The inspector will have to take some details from you all and then my driver will take you back to your uncle. I'm sure Mr Baxter would be happy to accompany you seeing as how you've become good friends lately.'

Archie smiled and he watched as the inspector got out his notepad to take down some details. It was decided that Bobby would be taken to his mother at the same time and Lucy guessed she would be out of her mind with worry about the lad.

Lucy had tears in her eyes as she said goodbye to both boys.

'Don't forget to write, will you, Archie?' she said wiping away a tear.

'No fear,' he said, planting a kiss on her cheek. 'I won't forget to write nor will I forget you, Lucy!' Then Archie thanked Bessie for her generosity as she hugged him to her breast and, taking his belongings from her grasp, he left the house with both men and Bobby. He was going home at last.

Lucy didn't know how she'd cope without her only true friend in the world. They'd formed a bond with one another that she never wanted to break.

Chapter Seventeen

When Archie and Bobby had departed, Lucy slumped down in the fireside chair.

'What's the matter now?' Bessie asked, 'Shouldn't you be happy for them both?'

'Oh, I am, but I shall miss Archie so much. I hardly got to know Bobby though, but he's a nice young lad and I'm so glad he can be reunited with his mother. It's just...'

'Just what, Lucy love?' Auntie's eyes were full of concern.

'It's just I've been thinking about the offer Lady Fanshaw made me and I think this has decided it for me, I'd like to become her companion. As much as I've loved living with you and working at the inn too, I feel there are not many opportunities for a young woman in this neck of the woods. It's either settle down and become a wife and mother or take on working long hours for very little pay.'

'I know. It's a hard life for a young woman around here. Very well then, Lucy. When Mr Knight calls for the rent money, I shall tell him about your decision.'

'Oh, would you, Auntie?' Lucy had no further doubts about taking the position as she could hardly return to the inn now.

And so, it was arranged that Lucy begin work at the big house as a companion to Lady Fanshaw. Bessie, who by now was doing so well with her bakery business that she could afford to shell out some extra coppers for rolls of pretty material, escorted Lucy to a local dressmaker to have some gowns made for her new role in life. Bessie could have sewn them herself, she was skilled enough, but she said she felt she wanted the best for Lucy.

Lucy stood admiring her reflection in the long oval mirror at the dressmaker's home.

'So, what do you think then, Lucy?' Bessie asked as she took a step back to get a better view from behind. There were exquisite seed pearls handsewn into the back of the prettiest gown.

Lucy smiled into the mirror, admiring the image of the young lady reflected back at her. She had never owned anything as beautiful in all her days. She ran her hand over the smooth lemon taffeta material. Nellie would be so jealous when she discretely called to say goodbye to Bessie at the inn and it served her right too for being so beastly to her. 'I love it, Auntie, thank you so much!' She turned to face the dressmaker. 'And thank you for all your hard work, Mrs Perkins.'

The dressmaker, who was a small weedy looking woman with eyes like a little bird, darting this way and that behind her glasses, nodded looking quite pleased with herself.

'And we'll have to purchase a decent trunk for you to take your belongings with you,' Auntie said, more to herself than anyone else. 'And you'll need some new shoes and boots. A pair of sturdy boots for the winter and walking and a comfortable pair for around the house during the day, a pair of carpet slippers wouldn't go amiss either and maybe a smart pair of shoes if Lady Fanshaw wishes you to accompany her anywhere. Can't have you going somewhere posh and letting the side down, gal!'

Lucy chuckled. 'I've never had many pairs of shoes before.'

'Aye, I know,' Bessie shook her head. 'If I'd have got rid of Bert a bit sooner, you'd have had a lot more. A few nice dresses and such, but that blaggard was spending me money as fast as I was earning it. Still, he's dead and buried now as far as I'm concerned.'

'Do you know where he is?'

'Nope. And I don't want to find out either. Now then, if you can wrap these up for us, Mrs Perkins, I'll make full payment to you and we'll be on our way.' Bessie sniffed.

'I can arrange for someone to deliver them to the house, if you like?' the woman offered.

'Even better! But if you can arrange it for tomorrow evening as I'll have finished all my work by then. And there'll be a nice tasty pie ready for the delivery boy for his trouble an' all.'

The woman smiled. It was probably unusual for someone to pay her upfront like that as a lot in the area liked things on tick. They eked out what they had from week to week, trying to pay the most urgent bills before the rest. Board and lodgings always needed to come first but some dodged the rent man and spent it on food instead. Others, like Bert, just whittled it away.

'Come on then, Lucy,' Bessie said, 'get changed back into your clothes. I want to catch that shoe shop before it closes for the day!'

Lucy smiled but she'd noticed the dark circles beneath her auntie's eyes and hoped she wasn't over doing things. Glancing out of the lace curtained window, she could see it had already gone dark. Only another three weeks and it would be Christmas. She was so excited; she would leave for her new position the following week and Bessie had promised her if she wanted to return for Christmas, she could but she'd understand if she wanted to stay in such a grand house instead. Imagine the sort of Christmas fayre that would be there! Lucy decided she'd better buy some Christmas gifts for Bessie and her boys before she left as who knew when she might see them again.

Swirling snow was falling as they left the dressmaker's home to make their way down the frosted street, chilling them to the bone. Gas lamps had been lit, pooling a warm yellow glow on the streets below. People hurried hither and thither, some to get home before the fall got too heavy.

'It's only a couple of streets away,' Bessie said brightly. 'Then we can go home.'

As they rounded the corner, Lucy thought for a moment that she spied Bert entering a pub named The Goose and Peacock, but on second glance it wasn't him, just a gentleman who wore a similar flat cap and muffler. Imagine if it had been him though? What would they have done?

'Come along, Lucy, don't dawdle,' Auntie warned as Lucy turned her attention back to the road ahead. This was to be a new beginning for her. The best chance she had in life. And she wouldn't forget to write to Archie either. She'd send him her new address and a Christmas card too.

Auntie seemed to be out of puff a lot lately and it concerned her. The woman rushed around a lot having so much work on and although she had help from her sons and Mavis, she liked to do a lot herself when maybe she should have been having the time to put her feet up. She was going to tell her what she thought before she left, she didn't want the woman to run herself into the ground.

Lucy's fingers were cold to the touch. And for a fleeting moment, thoughts of the locket her mother had left with her as a young child on such a cold winter's night came to mind.

Oh, Adella, whatever happened to you?

Before she left for the big house, she was going to ask Auntie if she might take it with her. She didn't think she'd mind.

But before she had a chance to think any further, a costermonger's horse and cart careered around the corner, mounting the pavement in the semi darkness. The horse seemed to be frightened by something as if it had just bolted. She quickly jumped out of the way.

'That was a close call, Auntie…' she said, but when she turned around Bessie was lying on the floor, groaning. She knelt down beside the woman to attend to her. 'What happened? Did the horse and cart bump into you?'

'No, it didn't touch me, I just lost me balance from the shock of it. Must be the cold freezing me brain. Can you help me up, gal?'

Lucy took Auntie's outstretched hand and gently pulled her to her feet, steadying her by taking her by the arm to support her. 'I think we should visit that shoe shop some other time; we need to get you home in the warm so you can put your feet up.'

'I wouldn't disagree with that,' said Bessie sounding relieved as she leaned on Lucy's arm as if it were a crutch to prop her up with.

'A visit from the doctor wouldn't go amiss either,' Lucy added.

'I don't want to see no doctor, I'm fine honestly. I'll be back to normal tomorrow.'

But the following day, Bessie was far from normal and Lucy sent Harry to fetch the doctor who lived in the same terrace.

Doctor Mortimer followed Lucy as she climbed the narrow stairway to the woman's bedroom.

'Do you need anything, Doctor?' she asked.

He shook his head. 'No, not for time being. Now can you tell me what happened to you, Mrs Harper?'

Bessie explained the circumstances of her fall and Lucy told him how she thought the woman was overdoing it. He removed his hat and coat and placed them on a chair along with his medical bag to get a closer look at the woman.

He lifted her wrist to feel her pulse. Then without showing any real emotion on his face said, 'Can you poke your tongue out for me, Mrs Harper?' Bessie did as told. 'Hmm, that's not a healthy looking one!' He shook his head and Lucy wondered what he was thinking.

Lucy realised the woman didn't like being an invalid in bed and would prefer to be downstairs in her kitchen rolling out the pastry for her pies, rushing from pub to pub delivering her wares, or else trying to drum up lots of business.

'Yes, it looks as if you're a bit run down. You can close your mouth now, Mrs Harper.' Bessie obeyed and closed her eyes momentarily as if it was all too much for her. 'Overwork has weakened your immunity, I'm afraid. You have no reserves to fight off illness.' He scrabbled about in his leather medical bag and brought out a stethoscope to listen to her lungs.

'It's as I suspected,' he said eventually, removing the stethoscope from around his neck and replacing it in his bag, 'you are stressed out from overdoing things I think, and that's why you collapsed in the cold like that. I'm going to prescribe a tonic for you to take. You need to eat plenty of fruit and vegetables and take a month off from your work.'

Bessie blinked several times. 'But I can't possibly do that, Doctor!'

'And why not?'

'Because it's my busiest time of the year, that's why!'

'You can defy my orders if you wish but the consequences from doing so will mean further ill health which could end up irreversible. You need to rest and look after yourself and possibly take on more people to help you if you wish for your pie business to continue.'

Lucy took her aunt's hand. She had an idea. 'I can help you instead of going away to stay with Lady Fanshaw. Mave and I can manage making the pies between us, you have the boys to work in the bakery as usual, and perhaps take on another delivery boy or two now Archie has left us. I think that's why you've got yourself in this state as you've also been delivering out in all weathers as well as completing your normal duties.'

Bessie huffed out a breath. 'Aye, maybe you're both right but I won't have you give up on your new job before you even get started, my girl. I'll take someone else on to help in the kitchen.'

'You could ask Cassie!' Lucy said excitedly.

'But doesn't she already have a busy job? She'd never fit both in,' Bessie looked alarmed. 'She'll end up like me if she's run ragged.'

'No, you misunderstand me. She'd finding the work there too much for her. I think she'd appreciate it. Would you like me to ask her for you?'

'Yes please, Lucy.'

'That's settled,' said the doctor. Then he reached into his bag and brought out a brown glass bottle with a cork stopper in the top. Then looking at Lucy, he said, 'Give her this tonic three times a day after meals and make sure they're nourishing ones.'

'Thank you, Doctor.' Lucy watched as the doctor packed up his bag and donned his hat and coat, then she showed him out of the house.

As he was leaving, he said, 'And you, are you all right, young lady? I heard you had a terrible scare with that chimney sweep fellow?'

'Yes, I'm fine thanks. I don't work at the inn anymore—I have a new job lined up working at a big house as Lady Fanshaw's companion.'

The doctor lifted his eyebrows in surprise. 'Ah, I remember her, as of course she owns this house. I believe she might have been renting it to a young lady at one time. The lady was here for a while and then mysteriously she disappeared one day and we never saw her again.'

'Oh, that's strange, Doctor.'

'Yes, we've never got to the bottom of it all. Then the house was left standing empty for many years, like a mausoleum of sorts.' She didn't know what one of those was but if she got the chance and she could spell it, she'd look it up in one of those dictionaries at Lady Fanshaw's house. 'I hear she's a bit of a recluse these days?'

'It seems that way, Doctor. I think that's why she wants me to work as her companion. I still don't understand why she's renting this house to Auntie for a peppercorn rent, mind.'

The doctor raised his silver brows. 'That is most odd indeed. It makes you think, doesn't it?'

Lucy nodded.

He lifted his top hat and replaced it on his head once again as a mark of respect. 'Bye for now, dear. Do let me know if your aunt gets any worse, but I don't think she will if she takes my advice.'

Lucy breathed a sigh of relief when she closed the door behind him. She would be so distraught if anything ever happened to her aunt.

Chapter Eighteen

Dunraven House was nestled in amongst the trees and seemed to Lucy far away from civilisation, nevertheless Lady Fanshaw seemed to like it. But what puzzled her the most was, if it were true that the lady had been a recluse for so many years, why would she suddenly yearn to come out of her shell like this?

Lucy had been staying at the house for several days and it played on her mind. As she walked the corridors whilst the lady was asleep in her bed chamber, she marvelled at the oakwood panels and the mysterious paintings on the wall. Some upstairs were of landscapes that featured rugged mountains, quaint farmhouses and flocks of sheep, whilst others were more exotic in nature. Those ones featured beaches at sunset and tropical islands. Her attention was drawn to a painting of an attractive young woman in a turquoise, shimmering satin ball gown. She looked as if she should be happy as if a great occasion had taken place at the house. Although the woman was beautiful, her deep brown eyes told another story, they reminded her of Duke's eyes that time Archie had gone missing. There was a longing and an emptiness within.

I must ask someone who that is? She thought to herself and then went off in search of her tutor, Miss Meadows, who would be arriving for the first time to give her piano lessons that afternoon. She'd been told to meet her in the drawing room at precisely two o'clock. Lady Fanshaw always had an hour or two's extra kip in the afternoons. Initially, Lucy wondered why that was so, but then she realised after noticing how much brandy she knocked back during the morning and then a glass of wine with her lunch, that it was a no wonder that she slept like that. She hardly ate either, preferring to nibble away like a little bird at everything. Lucy wondered why she drank like that and why she had so little appetite? It was almost at times as if something inside her had died. She felt so desperately sad for the woman.

Miss Meadows was waiting for her when she arrived, she had her back to her and was staring out of the window. She was a young woman of around eighteen years old who cut an elegant figure before her. Suddenly, she turned to face Lucy and recognition ensued. 'Ah, you must be Lucy Harper?'

'Yes, miss!' Lucy answered and she felt totally in awe of the beautiful lady in front of her in her cornflower blue fitted dress with leg o' mutton sleeves, over which she wore a fur mantel. This was how Lucy wanted to look when she was older.

'And I am Miss Clara Meadows,' she smiled a warm smile that reached her blue eyes and beyond as if she could see into Lucy's soul and understood her very thoughts.

Clara removed her mantel and draped it over the chair. Then she untied the matching cornflower blue ribbon of her bonnet and placed it carefully on the table. Lucy knew she was a lady because if that had been her, she'd have just tossed it on the table instead. There was a lot she could learn from this young woman.

'And have you had any experience of the pianoforte, Lucy?'

Lucy shook her head. 'No, not really, miss.'

Clara arched an eyebrow. 'How do you mean, not really?'

'There's an old upright one at the coaching inn where I used to work, in the bar room. I used to tinkle about on it when I was cleaning there. Usually when there was no one else around to hear it.'

Clara laughed, a whole hearted yet ladylike laugh that lit up her eyes. 'I see. Let me hear the sort of thing you used to play.'

Lucy blushed, but then she took her seat behind the elegant walnut grand piano. Lady Fanshaw had told her it had come all the way from Vienna in Austria. She couldn't imagine why when there were piano shops all over London.

She flexed her fingers and then began playing *Greensleeves*. As her fingers danced over the keys, she forgot her inhibitions and played other little ditties she recalled from memory.

Afterwards, Clara clapped her hands with delight. 'Bravo, young lady! But I thought you said you didn't really play the piano?'

Lucy turned her head to face her. 'No, I don't, not like what proper pianists do. I don't follow no music sheet or nothing, I just hear a song and try playing it until it sounds right.'

'But don't you realise that's quite a talent you have there?' Lucy couldn't understand for the life of her what all the fuss was about, so she shook her head. Clara smiled. 'You are a natural. But I will teach you all the scales so in the future you can read sheet music too.'

'Will you really, miss?'

'Most certainly,' Clara smiled. 'Now let's begin with something simple. I'll just bring a chair and sit beside you.'

Immediately, Lucy jumped off her piano stool, no way did she want Clara to have to carry a chair across the room. She, herself, was used to hefting furniture around in the bar room.

'That's very kind of you, Lucy.'

And so, they spent the rest of the afternoon going through various scales on the piano. And Clara pencilled in some notes beside the sheet music to help her along the way. 'I shall ask Lady Fanshaw if for now, I might pencil the notes onto the piano keys to make it easier for you, Lucy. It will be easy to clean off and that way you'll pick it up much quicker. Next lesson, I'll teach you how to play my favourite Christmas carol: *The Holly and the Ivy!*'

Lucy beamed, deciding she was going to enjoy taking piano lessons very much indeed. If only Archie could see her now.

***

Later that afternoon, Lucy took tea in the drawing room with Lady Fanshaw. Cook had set out a small china cake stand with such delicious delicacies as custard and jam tarts, currant buns and miniature cucumber sandwiches with the crusts cut off. All of this was topped off with a large matching china tea pot, enabling them to pour copious cups of tea for themselves.

Lady Fanshaw just nibbled away at a custard tart, causing Lucy to glance at the lady sideways as she wondered if she'd ever finish it.

The woman's eyes met hers. 'What are you staring at, girl!' she snapped.

'I'm sorry, ma'am, I just wondered why you eat so little? Every time I see you, you eat like a little bird.'

Lady Fanshaw swallowed a morsel and wiped her mouth with a cotton embroidered napkin, then flung it down on her plate and pushed the plate away from her as if it provided too much temptation. There was still half a tart there going to waste and many of the starving in Whitechapel would have fought to the death just for a taste of a mere morsel of that.

The lady narrowed her eyes. 'Not that it's any of your business, but there is a good reason why I eat so little and it's because years ago there was a tragedy in the family. To be truthful, I've never really got over it and I'll say no more about it.' She swallowed hard and looked away as if trying to blink back the tears that were threatening to spill.

Going by the clipped tone of her voice though, Lucy thought she was beginning to get angry, so she didn't probe any further. To change the subject she said, 'Lady Fanshaw, I am going to write a letter to my friend, Archie, this afternoon. Have you any letters you'd like to dictate to me?' She had been writing letters of correspondence all week for the woman, so thought she'd offer her services up. After all, that's what she'd been employed to do in the first place.

'Not at the present. When you have finished here, you are dismissed!' she said in a curt manner.

They hadn't been enjoying their tea for more than a few minutes but Lucy felt hopeless and awkward in the woman's company as now she seemed so affronted. Whatever tragedy it was that occurred had cut deep and she vowed never to mention the woman's eating habits ever again. After excusing herself and replacing her napkin on the table, with tears in her eyes, she rose and left her half-eaten plate of food behind.

'You may take your plate with you,' Lady Fanshaw said as she also rose and took her seat by the fireside.

Lucy nodded and returned to the table for the plate of food to see the woman was staring into the flames of the fire as if she were in her own world. She failed to look up as Lucy left the room.

***

The winter light was fading fast as Lucy stared out of the window of her bedroom. The slate grey sky brought a promise of snow later, something she normally found a sense of joy in, but not today. She had upset Lady Fanshaw earlier and she didn't understand why. The woman had been quite cold towards her and dismissed her at her behest.

In the corner of her beautiful bedroom, beside her bed, was an elegant looking mahogany escritoire. It was there, she decided to pen that letter she intended sending to Archie.

Dear Archie,

I hope you are happy now you're back home at Huntington Hall? I've begun that position what I told you about with Lady Fanshaw. I'm beginning to wonder if I've done the right thing in leaving the coaching inn. At first, I liked it here but I find the lady's moods hard to cope with. I seem to upset her

*and I really don't know what I am saying or doing
that is so wrong.*

In her frustration, she picked up the piece of paper,
scrawled it up into a ball and threw it into the fire.

*I can't send that to Archie, it might only concern
him.*

She picked up her fountain pen, dipped it in the ink
well on the desk and began again:

Dear Archie,

*I hope you are happy now you're back home at
Huntington Hall? I've begun that position what I told
you about at Lady Fanshaw's beautiful home. You
should see it, Archie. It's like the biggest house I've
ever seen in me life. But I suppose it's similar to
where you're living though I haven't ruled out going
back to the coaching inn to work if this doesn't work
out, I'll be quite safe now Bill Brackley is behind
bars. I'm having piano lessons from Miss Clara
Meadows. She says I have a good ear for music as I
can already play some tunes that I've picked up
meself at the inn. I've also got a tutor for school
studies. I never went to school much when I was
young and Lady Fanshaw thinks if I am well educated
that it shall help me in life. You should see the library
at the house, Archie. I never seen so many books in
me whole life. Are you excited about Christmas? I
am. I don't know yet whether I'll be staying here for
the season or going back to stay with Auntie. She
hasn't been well and has been told by the doctor to
rest.*

*Well I must close for now as I have a lesson to
attend and Lady Fanshaw is a stickler for punctuality
and so is my tutor.*

I'll be in touch again before Christmas and might have a little surprise for you. I've written my new address on the back of this page.

Your friend always,

Lucy

Feeling satisfied on her second attempt, Lucy blotted the page with blotting paper and carefully folded it, before slipping it inside a white envelope. She'd been informed by Mrs Tavistock that any letters should be taken to Mr Grimes, the butler, by eight o' clock of an evening and he would summon a young lad to take the mail to the post office early next morning, or if it was near, the lad would deliver it himself by hand. None of Lucy's letters would be delivered by hand though as both Archie and Bessie were living a few miles away.

She wondered what Archie was doing right now. She imagined that maybe he'd be well dressed and dining with his uncle. How different life must be for him now. How he'd suffered at the hands of that Bill Brackley. Thankfully, the brute was now behind bars. Auntie had told her that but how long he was put away for she wasn't quite sure. In her last letter she had joked that maybe he and Bert were banged up together and enjoying bread and water at Her Majesty's Pleasure. If Bessie was being humorous like that then she guessed the woman must be feeling a whole lot better.

How she missed her though. Life at Dunraven House made her feel lonely at times. It was such a large building with echoing corridors and sometimes the silence was deafening. The only respite for her were the times she spent with her tutors or the kitchen staff, who invited her in for an impromptu cuppa and a chat. There, she got to hear all the gossip about what was going on. How Mr Knight was really fond of Lady Fanshaw and although she didn't show it, she was really fond of him too.

She couldn't let Auntie down and return home no matter how much she desired it. Her aunt had bigger and better things in mind for her.

She decided to change her dress for dinner. She didn't want to upset Lady Fanshaw, who insisted herself on donning a fresh gown for her evening meal. It seemed to be what the woman referred to as, *Ett-eee-kett*, but Lucy had no idea what the word meant. She intended to ask her English tutor, Mr Maskell, next time she saw him.

Opening her fancy French Queen Anne design wardrobe, she looked at the rack of pretty gowns. The ones Bessie had purchased for her from the dressmaker, paled into insignificance beside those Lady Fanshaw had insisted she wear. The truth was, she didn't feel too comfortable in any of them as yet, as she wasn't used to looking and acting like a lady. She let out a long sigh of frustration. Was it going to be an evening of her sitting one end of the dining table with the lady on the other, with little or no conversation?

She selected a pretty pink dress which had a low waist and square neckline. It was quite unlike anything she'd ever worn before, and according to one of the maids at the house, the height of fashion. The dress had a white overlay of lace which, apparently, came all the way from Belgium, no less. She should have been excited at the prospect of wearing such a dress as someone like Nellie would be green with envy, but it was no good, Lady Fanshaw's mood had rubbed off on her.

A knock at the bedroom door, startled her. She went to open it to be confronted by the housekeeper. 'How many times do I have to tell you, Miss Harper, you do not open the door yourself when someone knocks!' Her sharp beady eyes scanned the room behind Lucy.

'Sorry, ma'am.' She bobbed a curtesy to the woman out of respect.

'And you definitely *do not curtesy* to a member of staff at this house, it should be the other way around if you are to become a lady like Lady Fanshaw would like you to be.' She sighed heavily, then mumbled, 'Though to me it is akin to making a silk purse out of a pig's ear...'

What did the woman mean by that? Lucy looked around the room but could see neither a silk purse nor anything that resembled a pig's ear. Something else she'd have to ask Mr Maskell later.

Then the woman's face softened. 'I'll send Meg up to help you dress.'

'But I can dress myself,' Lucy protested.

'I dare say you can, but as a lady, you're not supposed to dress yourself. In any case, there are some tricky small pearl buttons on the back of that dress.'

Lucy nodded, seeing the sense in what the woman was trying to convey to her.

How she longed to be sat around Bessie's fireside right now with a plate of homemade mutton stew and a hunk of bread and butter, fighting and laughing with

Harry and Jacob while their mother looked on with tears of laughter in her eyes. Then she remembered that her aunt still wasn't well enough to be taking on domestic duties and she had Mave for that. The housekeeper left the room to attend to her duties elsewhere, and within minutes, the maid appeared by her side, smiling at Lucy. The girl only looked a year or two older than herself.

'Mrs Tavistock said I was needed here, miss?'

For a moment, Lucy didn't know what to say to the girl but remembering what the housekeeper had told her, she realised she needed to be in command. 'Would you help me slip into that gown, please?'

'Certainly, miss.' She bobbed a curtsey and her eyes moved to the bed where the dress was laid out. 'That's a truly beautiful dress, miss.'

Lucy had a thought for a moment. 'I bet you'd like to try it on?'

The girl's face reddened beneath her mobcap as if Lucy could read her thoughts and she opened and closed her mouth again as if she didn't quite know what to say in reply.

'Well, not now as I'm in a rush but I shall let you try on a couple of these gowns someday.' The girl nodded with delight. 'But whatever you do, don't tell anyone, will you? As I could get into trouble for it.'

'Oh, no, miss. I wouldn't tell a soul as I could get into trouble meself.'

Lucy smiled. 'Would you like to be my friend, Meg?'

The girl nodded. 'I would, miss, yes.'

'I need a friend as it's so lonely for me in this big house, do you understand? I've left all my friends and family to be here.'

Meg looked thoughtful for a moment and then said, 'I do know what you mean, miss. I feel like that myself 'ere sometimes.'

'Well consider me your friend then, Meg. But we better keep it our little secret, eh?'

Meg nodded and then went to undo the buttons of the dress as Lucy removed her day dress and placed it on the bed where the other had been. As Meg slowly lowered it over Lucy's head and she helped her on with it, she stood back in awe. 'Cor, miss. That looks real nice on yer. You look more grown up in that dress.'

Lucy studied her reflection in the long mirror, which was on a stand in the corner of the room, and she smiled with pleasure. 'You're right, Meg. It makes me look quite a bit older.' The dress nipped her in at the waist, showing off her curves. Thank goodness that Bill Brackley and Bert Harper hadn't seen her in this. Men like them were shameful.

After Meg brushed Lucy's hair and set a pearl hair slide in it, finally, she was ready to go downstairs to the living room. As they both walked the length of the corridor outside, Lucy glanced upwards at the portrait of the young woman with the sad eyes. She stopped and turned towards the maid who had been walking behind her, 'Meg, do you know who the young woman is in that painting there? She's very beautiful but looks so sad…' She pointed towards the picture.

Meg looked in the direction of the painting. 'I think she might be Lady Fanshaw's daughter, miss.'

Lucy stopped in her tracks. 'Really? I never knew Lady Fanshaw had any children. Where is her daughter now?'

Meg frowned. 'I don't rightly know, miss. All I know is that she used to live here a long time ago before I ever came here. Cook might know. She's been working 'ere at this house for donkey's years.'

In different circumstances, maybe Lucy could have asked Lady Fanshaw herself about her daughter but her reaction earlier had put paid to that. Now she felt she ought not probe too much about anything at all for fear of upsetting the woman.

'Yes, I'll ask Cook when I get the chance. Have you noticed how much alcohol Lady Fanshaw drinks, particularly in the morning, Meg?'

Meg nodded and then averted her eyes as if she was afraid to speak ill of the woman. 'Yes, I have, but I think she does it because she doesn't sleep much at night.' She lowered her voice, 'One of the other maids, who no longer works here, told me she used to hear her sobbing at night.'

'Oh, that's so sad. I wish I could help her.'

Meg looked directly at Lucy. 'But you are helping her, miss. She rarely spoke to anyone before you arrived, 'cept for Mr Knight that is. He seems to be her confidante. I really think you are helping.'

Lucy decided that maybe she needed to be more patient with the woman. Rome wasn't built in a day and bringing Lady Fanshaw out of her shell, inch by inch, would take time and persuasion.

Chapter Nineteen

Lucy had left the house to go to the market place with Meg. It was the time when she was supposed to be resting in her room for a couple of hours, so no one knew she had escaped the claustrophobic confines of Dunraven House, except for the girl herself.

'It's nice to have company, miss,' Meg said, swinging her wicker basket by the side of her. Cook had handed it to her to fetch some special cheese and biscuits that Lady Fanshaw liked to eat, along with instructions for a jar of sweet pickle and a bottle of port wine. This gave Lucy the opportunity to indulge in some Christmas shopping for Bessie and the boys. She decided to buy a little something for Cassie too as the woman had been so good to her, but the main present she wanted to purchase was for Archie himself.

As they set off down the lane, Lucy marvelled at the liberal peppering of red berries on the green holly bushes, all frosted with what appeared to her as a dusting of icing sugar. She recalled then what the lady had said to her about it being an indication of a hard winter ahead. Her fingers and toes were numb with the cold, even though she was wearing her fur-lined hooded cloak over a warm dress, and she wore a muff around her neck to insert her hands in to keep warm. Meg wore two knitted shawls instead of her usual one with a bonnet and she had thick woollen stockings on beneath her dress. If Lucy'd asked for permission to leave the house, she supposed she could have made use of one of Lady Fanshaw's carriages, but then questions would surely be asked and she certainly would not be allowed to take a servant with her, she was sure of that.

They walked at a brisk pace, the cold air hitting them making their breath appear as if they were puffing out clouds of steam. Meg's cheeks were rosy pink and fresh looking.

'Are you sent out shopping every day?' Lucy asked.

'Most days. It's a chance to get out and have some fresh air. I love going to the market place.'

Lucy smiled at the girl and how she took pleasure in the smallest of things, something perhaps wealthy sorts might not do. It brought her thoughts to Archie. Would having great wealth change him? She certainly hoped that wouldn't be the case.

As they approached the market place amongst the throng of the bustling crowd, Lucy was in awe of the covered stalls. There was one that sold vibrant looking fresh fruit and vegetables, another that displayed all sorts of fine materials: silks, satins and colourful cottons that Bessie would just love to get her hands on, another that sold homemade wooden toys and clockwork carousels, whilst others offered all kinds of cheeses, breads and homemade ginger beers and wines. Some stalls were decorated in a Christmas fashion with sprigs of holly and mistletoe. And then there were other smaller painted stalls, which were really glorified handcarts that sold steaming hot punch, jacket potatoes, roasted chestnuts, and various beverages. The vendors shouting out to the hordes to claim their attention to sell their wares. 'Roll up, madam! How'd you like some juicy fat pork sausages for your husband's tea?

Make the fellow happy! Come on now!' and 'Try
Doctor Henderson's Cure All for your cold, missus!
You can drink it or even rub it on your old man's
chest! That should cheer the bugger up!' The stall
holders' form of patter made the crowds laugh and, in
some cases, it was as interesting as the goods
themselves.

'It feels so Christmassy here,' Lucy said smiling,
as they passed a stall that sold decorated Yule Logs
and candles. 'I can understand why you like coming
here so much, Meg.'

'I've been coming to this open-air market 'ere
since I was a kid, me ma used to bring me.'

'Does she still shop here, then?'

'No...' Meg lowered her head. 'She and me pa and
my younger brother and sister, all died from
consumption,' she said sadly.

Lucy wasn't sure what to say next. After a
moment's pause, she touched the girl's shoulder. 'I
am so sorry to hear that. I have no mother or father
either. How did you survive yourself then?'

'I was lucky, I didn't get it as I was staying at me
auntie's house at the time when they all took ill. She
couldn't afford to keep me so I ended up at the
workhouse and boarded out at the big house. Then I
was taken on permanently. I was given the position of
the maid what I told you had left there.'

'Do you know why she left the place, was she
unhappy or something?'

'No, not at all, she loved her job, but Lady
Fanshaw said she had loose lips. I never got to the
bottom of it all but I think it was something the maid
had said about the lady's daughter.'

'Oh!' Lucy decided to say no more on the topic as she had obviously touched a raw nerve there and the girl was uncomfortable discussing it further.

They became aware of a melodious song drifting towards them. It sounded like someone playing a flute. And when they searched to see where it was coming from, they spotted a man stood outside the old medieval church, with his head angled to one side as he played the silver instrument. His long shoes, with bells on the toes, were curled up in a curious fashion like a court jester as he played what Lucy now recognised as the song, *I Saw Three Ships*.

'How delightful!' she exclaimed as she approached him.

There was an upended top hat on the floor beside him, where people tossed in spare coins. Unfortunately, Lucy didn't have any to spare until she worked out if she had enough to purchase her Christmas gifts. She'd been planning to buy presents for Bessie and the boys before she left home to live at the big house, but when her aunt had taken ill like that, all sensible thinking had flown out of the window… 'We'll be back later to put something in,' she said to the man, who smiled and nodded as he carried on playing.

While Meg went in search of the items for Lady Fanshaw's order, Lucy busied herself viewing the wares of the arts and craft work stalls. She spotted a pretty embroidered silk drawstring bag she could purchase for Bessie at a reasonable price and handed a silver sixpence over to the female stall holder. Thanking her, she made her way to the adjacent stall where she purchased a book about sea voyages around the world for Harry. He was mad on that sort of thing and had a big map on the wall in his bedroom, he was going to love it. Jacob, was a little more difficult to buy for, but then she spotted a leather case which contained a shaving brush, razor and comb and knew that's just what she needed to get for him. His voice had recently broken and he was sprouting hairs on his chin. His little goatee style beard was charming at first, but he had told her he thought he would eventually shave it off, so it would be a perfect present for him. For Cassie, she purchased a second hand book entitled, *Mrs Beeton's Cookery Book*. The book was a best seller and the woman, herself, had passed away eight years ago, but it continued to sell well and was thought highly of. Cassie would love it as she enjoyed cooking so much and loved to experiment. After Lucy'd placed all her purchases in her basket, she searched around to see if she could spot Meg, but she was no longer queuing at the cheese stall.

A slight panic took over her at not being able to locate the girl, the market had got even busier and it would be getting dark soon. In the distance, she heard the flute player still playing his songs and at the moment he was playing, *Deck the Halls*, which was a favourite of hers.

She breathed a sigh of relief when she noticed a familiar figure in line at the hot chestnut stall and they made eye contact with one another. ''Ere Lucy, do you fancy any of these chestnuts?' Meg called across to her.

'I'd better not as it will ruin my dinner with Lady Fanshaw later, but you go ahead. Let me take your basket for you.'

Megan smiled, 'Thanks. I managed to get everything, even the port wine, so that ought to put her ladyship in a better mood.' They both giggled as Lucy took the basket from the girl and she set it down on the ground with her own whilst she waited. As she stood there for some time as the queue was quite long for the chestnuts, she glanced around. Darkness was developing and some of the market stalls were beginning to light up their pitches with lanterns and candles as they would be here for a few hours more. They didn't just close down when it got dark. All she needed to do now was to think of something she could buy for Archie.

She noticed a gentleman in a top hat and black frock coat, taking a beautiful looking woman by the arm. They looked a lovely couple together and spoke to one another in an adoring sort of fashion, though she couldn't make out what they were saying. As they grew closer, wrapped up in one another's company and oblivious to those surrounding them, she recognised the pair and blinked in surprise. It was Mr Knight himself and the lady he had on his arm looked so much like the young woman she'd seen on the large portrait painting hanging on the wall back at Dunraven House. When they'd gone a fair distance past, she hissed to Meg, 'Meg! Did you see what I just saw?'

Meg emerged from the queue with a poke of hot chestnuts in her hands. She blinked, 'Er, no? What was I supposed to see?'

'That couple who just passed by, it was Mr Knight and the young lady in that portrait I spoke to you about, only now she looks a bit older, more like a woman.'

'Never! Where are they?' Meg looked both left and right amongst the throng.

Lucy pointed in the distance, but the couple was lost in the crowd. 'Somewhere over there!' She pointed in the general direction she'd last seen them heading towards.

Meg frowned. 'Are you sure you didn't imagine it?'

'No, of course not, I know what I saw. But I assumed Lady Fanshaw's daughter had died?'

'That's what I thought an' all? Maybe it was someone who just looked a bit like her.'

Now Lucy wasn't so sure who she had seen in Mr Knight's company. Maybe Meg was right, it was hardly likely to be a woman who had died years ago.

Meg offered her a chestnut and she took one, she'd forgotten all about keeping herself hungry for dinner. The chestnut was still hot to the touch as she split it in half, so she had to savour it slowly. The inside all sweet, earthy and succulent. She hadn't tasted anything as good in a long while.

'I expect you're right, Meg,' Lucy said, licking her fingers. 'I must have imagined that lady was the one in the painting.'

'Well, that's understandable, 'cos it's getting dark. Trick of the light I suppose!'

Once the girls had finished their feast, Lucy noticed a stall selling mugs of hot tea and drinking chocolate.

'Let's have a hot chocolate!' she announced, deciding she'd buy Archie his present next time. There were just too many good things here she wanted to see and experience. 'This is on me; I still have some money left over and enough to give the flute player a couple of pennies too.'

Meg nodded eagerly. 'Yes, please!'

As they sipped the hot chocolate which warmed them to the core, Lucy felt a feeling of well-being as she realised this was the first time since she'd been at Dunraven House that she'd felt any form of contentment.

When they'd returned their tin mugs to the stall holder and Lucy had spotted yet another stall she'd like to peruse, Meg suddenly yelled, 'Cripes! Look at the time on the church clock, Cook will 'ave me guts for garters, I was supposed to be back an half hour ago!'

The girls had been enjoying themselves so much that they'd both forgotten the time. And if Lucy herself didn't rush to get back, questions would be asked where she'd been to and she didn't want that as she needed to leave the house again next time Meg went out shopping to the market place or village.

***

Lucy had a quick wash, changed her clothing and made it to the dining room in the nick of time. Lady Fanshaw was already there waiting at the head of the table when she arrived. She nodded her head towards Lucy. 'You may seat yourself, Lucy,' she said. There was no way of telling if the lady was still annoyed with her or not, so she took a seat opposite the woman.

At that point a maid arrived carrying a silver salver in her arms, closely followed by Mr Grimes.

'Ah, dinner is served!' Lady Fanshaw beamed. Lucy couldn't quite fathom how much the lady's mood had changed from one day to the next, but she realised why when she heard a very loud hic, causing the maid to look at her in astonishment. Then she noticed the butler exchange glances with her as if to warn her not to take any notice.

The butler removed the lid of the salver to reveal a tureen of soup which he placed on a small serving table directly behind Lady Fanshaw. 'Asparagus soup, ma'am,' he said as the maid brought over a basket of bread rolls to the table.

Lucy's mouth watered. She was ravenous after all that fresh air earlier on and she hoped Meg hadn't got into trouble for returning so late.

Lady Fanshaw sipped at her soup and then began to giggle. 'ASS PA RA GUS!' She mouthed the words as if she were a naughty child, then she hiccupped loudly again causing her to bring her hand to her mouth. '*Excusez moi!*' she said.

Mr Grimes's face was deadpan so it gave nothing away, but surely, he noticed something was wrong?

'*She was Mary from the Dairy and she came from down the farm…*' the lady sang off key.

The maid's face flushed, she was obviously embarrassed by such behaviour but no one was doing or saying anything. If only Mr Knight were here right now, he'd know what to do.

The lady then rose from her chair and bellowed, 'I always wanted to be a singer but Mama would never allow it, she said it was for common women! Not for someone like me!'

Lucy noticed she had begun to hoist her skirts, revealing her ankles as if she were about to perform some sort of East End knees up. Oh no, someone had to save her from herself. It was like the story of *The Emperor's New Clothes.* Everyone knew what was going on but all were acting as if things were just dandy. The butler and maid were ignoring the fact that the lady was drunk. Lucy had seen enough of how Bert behaved to realise what was happening here. How would Aunt Bessie deal with this?

Thinking on her feet, she decided to try to get the lady to her bedroom for a lie down to save her from any further embarrassment.

'Mary,' she beckoned the maid over. 'Would you please help me to assist Lady Fanshaw to her bedroom?

Mary nodded, but the butler just stood there with his nose in the air. He was obviously used to such scenes and Lucy silently cursed him for his "turn a blind eye" manner.

Both girls took Lady Fanshaw by either arm. 'Wass going on hereeee?' she demanded to know as she slurred her speech. No doubt she'd been into that bottle of port that Meg had brought back for her earlier. And if she had, then she must have drunk quite a lot of it. Or maybe she was topping up on what she'd already been drinking all day.

Lady Fanshaw giggled as the pair led her away from the dining room as the trio swayed from side to side.

'Rule Britannia!' she shouted, raising an index finger to the ceiling and closing one eye. 'Where the devil are we going to, girls?'

'We're just taking you to your bed chamber for you to have a little lie down,' Lucy explained.

'B...but I haven't had my schinner yet!' She hiccupped loudly again, now both eyelids were closing.

'I'll ask Cook to bring you something up on a tray later when you've rested, your Ladyship,' Mary cajoled.

Following a little protestation, the lady finally gave in and allowed the two girls to lead her to her bedroom. Mary turned down the bedcovers as Lucy tried to prevent the woman from toppling over.

'Is she always like this?' Lucy hissed.

'Not always.' Mary joined Lucy in helping guide the woman towards her bed.

They managed to sit her down. 'We'd better not undress her, just remove her shoes and put her into her bed!' Lucy said, waiting for the maid to do the honours. 'Well, what are you waiting for?' Lucy was becoming impatient because as far as she was concerned, she didn't want the lady to make a bigger fool of herself in front of her staff than she already was, and needed her out of their view and sleeping it all off safely in her bedroom.

Mary took a step back, 'I don't like to, miss. You'd better do it!'

Lucy sighed. It was obvious that although Mary was a few years older than herself, she was scared stiff of Lady Fanshaw. At the inn, Lucy was well used to dealing with people, those from all manner of classes in all kinds of states. She remembered what Cassie often said, 'When the drink is in, the wit is out!' Which was perfectly true in Lady Fanshaw's case. But dealing with her was altogether something else.

She struggled for a moment to unlace the lady's shoes, but then, Lady Fanshaw smiled as she opened both eyes and closed them again, falling back on the bed, already asleep as she gently snored. Then Lucy lifted her legs up onto the bed and both girls moved her into the middle of her bed and brought the bed clothes up to her neck.

Mary turned off the oil lamp beside the bed and they left the room. Once outside, Lucy whispered, 'Cripes, how often does she get into that sort of state?'

'About once a week, I'd say.'

'And does anyone ever put her to bed when she's in that state?'

Mary shrugged and pausing for a moment, replied, 'No, not really.' Her face reddening with embarrassment.

Lucy frowned. 'What happens then?'

'Mr Grimes and Mrs Tavistock always insist we're to leave her to her own devices. More often than not, she'll find her own way to an armchair and snooze it off overnight.'

Lucy shook her head, thinking it was quite disgusting that the lady was left in that way by her senior staff at the house, and that something truly awful must have happened in the lady's life for her to repeatedly allow herself to get in such a state.

Chapter Twenty

The following morning, Lucy stared out of the window. There had been a little light snow overnight, but it didn't appear to be sticking right now. She watched down below as she saw a little robin search for food on the sculpted lawn. Robins always made her think of Christmas, and today was no exception. How could she possibly return to Court Terrace for Christmas and leave Lady Fanshaw in this state? She would have to pen a letter to her aunt explaining her predicament and hope she'd understand, then she'd post all the gifts she'd bought for everyone. It wasn't ideal, and she didn't relish staying at the house with the lady, but somehow, she didn't quite trust Grimes or Mrs Tavistock. She was going to have to do a little digging later and find out more about Lady Fanshaw's daughter and why Grimes and Tavistock were so callous towards her ladyship.

She was surprised when she entered the dining room to see Lady Fanshaw already seated at the table with a plate of scrambled eggs and toast in front of her as if last night had never happened. And, more astonishingly than that, she was tucking into her breakfast with relish. Grimes was serving her coffee from a silver pot. He glanced up when Lucy arrived and she could have sworn he was sneering at her as he said, 'Breakfast this morning is scrambled or poached eggs with toast, Miss. I told Cook not to bother with a full cooked breakfast after last night's er…' he coughed into his white gloved hand, '"fiasco".'

Lucy felt her temper rise and she gritted her teeth. There was no need for this, the man was obviously referring to Lady Fanshaw's inebriated state but looking at the woman, she seemed to be either ignoring his jibe or blissfully unaware of what Mr Grimes was referring to, or else she hadn't heard him.

'For heaven's sake, Lucy, take a seat,' she proffered. 'Do have the scrambled eggs, dear. The way Cook makes them they are all fluffy and light.'

'Thank you, I think I will,' she said, as she seated herself.

'Milk or fruit juice, miss,' Grimes asked.

'Neither. I'd prefer coffee, please!' Lucy said with some conviction. In truth, she'd never tasted it before as Bessie had told her it was a drink that was only for adults. But in this case, she intended to show the man just how grown up she really was.

Grimes filled her cup for her. 'Milk and sugar, miss?'

'Yes, thank you, Mr Grimes.'

Then he relayed Lucy's order to Mary and stood in the background while Lady Fanshaw chatted away, surprisingly good humouredly towards her. Had she totally forgotten about how she'd got herself drunk the previous evening and had to be put to bed? But as soon as Grimes left the room, she whispered to Lucy. 'Many thanks for what you did for me last night, Lucy. I won't forget it.'

'It was nothing, Lady Fanshaw. I just thought it would be helpful if you slept it all off.'

'Well, thank you anyhow for saving my dignity.'

Lucy smiled. So, she did remember what had happened but she wasn't about to say so in front of Mr Grimes, which made Lucy think that the lady didn't trust him herself. Not wanting to upset the woman, Lucy just made small talk throughout breakfast, then left the room in search of Cook. There were questions that just needed answering and as the person who had been employed at the house the longest, she would have all the answers.

***

When Lucy caught up with Cook, she found the woman in the kitchen scolding a young kitchen maid called Sylvia. 'Now, I've told you often enough…' she wagged a finger in the girl's face, 'you're far too heavy handed with that potato knife. I want to see thin peelings not half the potato and the peeling being tossed into the bin.' She rolled her eyes and tutted.

Oh dear, was this the wrong time to approach the woman?

But she needn't have worried as when Mrs Farley turned and saw Lucy stood behind her, her face broke out into a big smile. 'Hello, young Lucy, and what can I do for you this afternoon? Have you come to tell me that Lady Fanshaw has cancelled dinner yet again after all the fuss we've gone to?' Her china blue eyes twinkled with mischief.

'No, Mrs Farley. I wanted to have a private word with you, but I can see now as how you are busy.'

Cook touched Lucy gently on the shoulder. 'No, not at all. I always have time for you, dear. I'm due a break. We'll head off to the rest room. Sylvia, you carry on peeling them spuds and remember what I told you, girl!'

Sylvia's neck shrank down into the neck of her dress as she lowered her head. 'Yes, Mrs Farley.'

'And Jenny, you stir that boiled beef and carrots well in a couple of minutes, don't want it sticking to the pan like the last time!' The girl nodded. 'And I'd appreciate it if you could brew up a cuppa for us an' all. Me throat is so parched it feels like the bloomin' Sahara. And for heaven's sake, don't make it like thick treacle again! You left it to stew too long in the pot!' She turned to Lucy. 'Got to keep 'em in check,' Cook chuckled as she led her away. 'Me bark is worse than me bite!'

Lucy smiled, she liked the warm-hearted woman a lot and sometimes thought she'd prefer working in the kitchen than being a lady's companion as it was more of a familiar territory to her after working at the coaching inn. Though Cook was nothing like Cassie. Cassie could be terribly coarse at times with her use of bad language and her pipe smoking, and on the odd occasion she'd caught her spitting in the courtyard like a navvy. Cook was far more ladylike and Lucy would never dream of calling her by her Christian name, it was either "Cook" or "Mrs Farley", that was all. But in either case, she liked both women in different ways. Cook was sensible and had good advice to give everyone and Cassie had a wisdom about her from having such a hard life she supposed. So, in that way they were similar at least, even if one was a lady and the other a bit of a tramp.

Once in the rest room, which was a small room offside of the kitchen containing two armchairs, a stool and a small table, they seated themselves. It was nice and warm as there was a fire in the grate and the room seemed far cosier than some of the big draughty rooms in other parts of the house.

'Now, what did you want to ask me?' Cook raised her brows in anticipation.

'It's about Lady Fanshaw. Is it true she had a daughter, Mrs Farley?'

'Yes. She died about twelve years ago, I believe.'

'You believe?'

'Well, it's most odd if you ask me, her daughter was a vivacious young thing, everyone loved her. The life and soul of this house she was. But then she went missing one day and was never seen again. Then it was reported to the staff here that she was dead, apparently her body had been found in the Thames river. But if you ask me…' She pursed her lips and looked right and left as if for fear someone would overhear their conversion, then she lowered her voice, 'it's pretty bloomin' odd that there was never any sort of funeral if they found her body. We were never allowed to make any enquiries as Mr Grimes would shut down any conversation about it. Then the old girl starts going a bit bonkers with grief. Starts staying in her room and dressing in black all the time. I mean she still wears black during the day time now, but at least changes into a different dress for dinner.'

Lucy reflected for a few moments. 'That would make sense then why she is the way she is with regards to her drinking habits.'

'Aye, well, you're not wrong there, she didn't used to touch a drop of the hard stuff before that. It's a pity to see her the way she is.'

'About Mr Grimes, do you like him, Mrs Farley?'

She crossed her hands on her lap. 'Can't say I neither like him nor dislike him but what I do dislike is his snobbish manner sometimes. I've always had this feeling as how he knows stuff that the rest of us ain't privy to. He sucks up a lot to Mr Knight. Seems to fawn around the man, if you get me drift. A bit of a sycophant, if you ask me.' She sucked in a breath of disgust through her pursed lips.

Lucy had no idea what a sycophant was. Was it a bit like an elephant, she wondered? Yet another word for her to look up in the dictionary if she could work out how to spell it. Maybe not. So instead she asked Mrs Farley about the word.

'Sorry, don't mind me, I have a habit of using big words now and then. What I mean is, Lucy love, he's what me old ma would have referred to as a "boot-licker"!' She studied Lucy's face for a moment and then let out a sigh, 'I can see you don't quite get it. I mean he flatters Mr Knight in a way most others would not and I think he does so to get what he wants from the man. It's obscene the way he hangs around him and agrees with everything he says.'

Lucy nodded, now she was starting to get it. 'So, what do you think he wants from him?'

'Information, maybe. Things that he might discover to his own ends, I reckon. And don't be telling anyone else this mind...' Lucy shook her head as she waited with baited breath in anticipation of what Mrs Farley had to say next, 'I reckon he's on the take in some form or another. Lady Fanshaw is so unhinged half the time, she wouldn't know what was missing and what was not. But Mrs Tavistock reckons that some of the silverware has gone missing but Mr Grimes reckons it's in storage in the attic but the woman isn't so sure, she won't venture up there to check, mind you!' Cook's eyes enlarged.

Lucy sat further forward in her chair with avid interest. 'But why ever not?'

'Well, there's some that work here what reckons as to how it's haunted. Mrs Jeffers used to work as a cleaner here and one day she was sent up there to sort out some stuff but she came out of there howling in fear. She only went and reckoned she heard someone crying! So now all the staff, except for Grimes, reckons it's haunted.'

'So, he's the only person who will go there?'

'Yes, you've got it. Which makes me wonder if he's hiding things there or maybe pilfering from it.' She glanced at the door. 'Now where's that Jenny one got to with our tea? That bloomin' girl!'

An idea was beginning to form in Lucy's mind which both scared and excited her at the same time. She was going to have to take a look in that attic but she'd need to take someone with her for company.

***

'You mean you want me and you to climb into that dusty old attic?' Meg blinked as if she couldn't quite believe Lucy's suggestion. Meg was in Lucy's bedroom after bringing her a glass of milk and a slice of Cook's special yeast cake.

'Yes, we can find out then if Grimes has been robbing Lady Fanshaw of her valuables.'

'Who told you he had?'

'I can't rightly say as I'm sworn to secrecy but I think I'd like to take a look up there.'

Meg narrowed her gaze. 'But you know it's haunted though?'

'I have heard that tale, yes. But isn't that what Grimes would like people to think so they don't venture up there?'

Meg scowled. 'Maybe. I don't much like the man myself but not enough to climb up there meself.'

'Well, you don't have to come in with me, just stay on guard then if anyone comes.'

A look of relief swept over Meg's face. 'Very well then. I'll do that for you. But when would you like to go there?'

'This afternoon when I'm supposed to be resting in my room. How about two o'clock?'

'Yes, that will be all right as it's a quiet time then for me too as I'll have completed most of my duties but need to be back downstairs to help out by half past two.'

Lucy smiled. 'That's settled then,' she smiled. She picked up a knife and sliced the yeast cake in half. 'You can share with me,' she said as Meg nodded eagerly. It was so good to have a new friend who understood her trials and tribulations and Lucy just couldn't wait until they took a peek in that attic.

***

When the rest of the house was quiet, Lucy and Meg climbed the stairway to the top storey of the house, which eventually led to the small winding stone stair case which would take her to the attic. It was cold and draughty on the third floor of the house and Lucy was glad they'd brought candles with them as this floor was rarely used except for two rooms, the one that housed Mrs Tavistock's quarters and the other, belonged to Mr Grimes. Meg had told her that the rest of the rooms were used for storage or else covered in dust cloths to keep the beds and furniture clean, though Lucy reckoned they must be well damp and musty by now through lack of use. Cook had told her how once the rooms were in regular use as frequent balls were held at the house when the Master was alive. But he'd passed away some twenty years since leaving behind a ten-year-old girl and a grieving widow. Though Lady Fanshaw, according to Cook, had got on with her life after a period of mourning until the day her daughter disappeared forever.

The flickering of the candles made the dark corridor look quite spooky as it cast shadows on the wall behind them, and at one point, Lucy felt quite creeped out by it all, but they'd come too far to go back now. She just had to know what was in that attic, so they'd arranged this for when they knew Grimes would be on duty downstairs and Mrs Tavistock busy sorting out laundry with one of the maids.

'Right,' Lucy said, 'you stay put here and let me know if anyone turns up, if someone sees you, say that you'd been sent up here to fetch something for her ladyship from one of the bedrooms. If that doesn't work, start screaming that you've seen a mouse or something, that'll be enough to scare Mrs Tavistock or one of the other maids!' Lucy grinned, then taking on a serious tone she warned, 'Please take care, Meg.'

Meg nodded, then Lucy left the girl to climb the stone stairway. A prickle of fear ran down her spine as she ascended. Slowly she walked up the steps, holding the candle in one hand and scaling the cold uneven wall with the other as she felt her way, until she came to a heavy looking door. But when she tried the door knob, it wouldn't budge. Drat! Someone had locked it and there would be no prizes for guessing who.

'Are you in?' Meg asked.

'No, it's bloomin' well locked. We need a key. I'm just going to have a look through the key hole.'

'All right, but hurry up in case someone shows up.'

Lucy knelt down and peered through the keyhole. It was hard to see at first, but as she focused, she spotted what looked like another painting in the distance. Who was it of? She was going to have to find out and get that key from somewhere soon.

A whistling noise from Meg grabbed her attention, preventing her from seeing anything else, and she rushed back down the stairs to see someone headed towards them and he didn't look best pleased.

Chapter Twenty-One

'What are you both doing here?' Grimes demanded to know.

'We've been sent here by Lady Fanshaw as she thought she could hear mice scampering over her head in her bedroom.' Lucy realised she'd be safe making that up as Lady Fanshaw hardly knew what day it was half the time. She had moments of lucidity, but those were far and few in between.

'I can assure you, there are no mice here!' Grimes's face turned scarlet with fury; he obviously didn't want either of them poking around. 'The handy man lays traps for them, so I doubt it very much.' He stuck his nose in the air as if he were a cut above them which annoyed Lucy.

So as if to torment him further, she added, 'I think you're right, Mr Grimes. I reckon the noise could be coming from the attic, do you have the key?'

Grimes looked as if he was about to burst. 'There is nothing whatsoever to concern you in that attic, young lady!' Then calming down, he added in a gentler tone of voice, 'You can assure Lady Fanshaw there are no rodents whatsoever here.'

Lucy, deciding to play the game for time being added, 'Maybe you're right, Mr Grimes. I'll report what you said back to her ladyship.'

He nodded curtly and forced a smile. For now, she was going to have to bide her time until she could get hold of that key. It was clear that Grimes knew far more about that attic than he was letting on.

***

The following day, Meg accompanied Lucy to the shops in the Village of Crownley to seek out a

Christmas present for Archie. The temperature had dropped so much overnight that the village pond was completely iced over. Crownley was a quaint little village with thatched roofs and lots of smoking chimneys. According to Meg, the old church in the centre of it had been there for around three hundred years.

People they passed by on their way looked blue with the cold, even though they appeared well wrapped up with mufflers, mittens and caps and bonnets.

'It's p...perishing today,' Meg moaned. 'Me feet feel like two blocks of ice. I didn't even feel like getting out of me bed this morning. I had to force meself...'

Lucy looked at her and nodded in sympathy. 'I count myself lucky living at Dunraven House though as at the coaching inn sometimes first thing of a morning, I'd wake up to find the window frame in my bedroom all frosted up from the inside. Once I even found some icicles hanging from them. Apart from that upstairs floor we visited, the rest of the house is kept reasonably warm. What about Mrs Tavistock's room and Grimes's, do they have fire places?'

'Oh yes,' Meg exclaimed. 'I have to light the bleedin' things when Molly, their help, is busy elsewhere in the house.'

Lucy frowned. 'You know it feels to me as if Lady Fanshaw wants to forget about that part of the house.'

'Maybe she does as it reminds her of her daughter.'

'Why? Was her bedroom there?'

'Yes. Cook told me she had a suite of rooms. She even used one as an art studio as she loved painting, but that room is locked up too.'

'I'd love to see those paintings!' Lucy said smiling.

'Me too, but I suppose we never will…'

Lucy's attention was drawn to a little shop with a bay window. The black and white painted sign outside read, "Ye Olde Curiosity Shoppe". Now where had she heard that name before? Then it came to her, there was a Charles Dickens' novel by the same name! The shop keeper was obviously capitalising on that.

'I read the book of the same name once,' Lucy said, pointing to the sign above the door. 'But it was a slightly different name as whoever owns this shop has made the sign look as though the written style is old English.'

'Huh?' Meg wrinkled her pink nose.

'Old English, you know, the sort what they wrote hundreds of years ago. It would be about the same era as that church was built.'

'I think I understand,' she said, letting out a breath that looked like a puff of steam. 'What's the book about anyhow?'

'It's about this man who is ever so kind, he owns a shop and he has a granddaughter called, Nell.' Lucy remembered the story as she could well identify with Nell, who was also an orphan like herself. 'Nell's grandfather ends up with a lot of gambling debt so his greedy landlord takes his shop of treasures away from him. So, he and Nell then end up homeless.'

'Sounds a sad sort of story if you ask me,' Meg said sniffing.

'Yes, it is quite sad. I won't tell you what happens in the end, in case you ever read it.' Taking Meg by the arm, she said, 'Come on, let's go inside and take a look and we can get out of the cold at the same time.'

Meg nodded eagerly, even her vivid green eyes were watering from the cold.

The overhanging roof and Tudor-like gabling gave the shop a unique charm of its own and as they entered, a little bell jangled over head to alert the owner that potential custom had arrived. But if Lucy was expecting Little Nell and her grandfather to make an appearance, then she was to be disappointed because in front of her stood a weedy looking little man who had a pronounced limp as he shuffled towards them. 'Ah, ladies!' he said, rubbing his hands in expectation, 'What can I do for you today?'

It was then as he turned sideways on that Lucy noticed he had a hump on his back, and it wasn't the leg itself that made him limp, but the fact his torso was twisted and out of shape. She immediately felt a surge of empathy towards the man.

'Good morning, sir!' she greeted, while Meg stood behind her as if she was afraid of the man, but Lucy had seen so many sights around the Whitechapel area that the man didn't faze her one little bit. 'I was wondering if you have a gift suitable for a ten-year-old boy, please?'

'We deal with all sorts of customers in this shop and if we take our time, I am sure we can come up with something suitable for him. What kind of things does he like? Is he the sort of boy that likes a bit of rough and tumble of the outdoors or is he more genteel and refined?'

'A bit of both I suppose.'

The man quirked a mystified eyebrow. 'I'm sorry, I'm not quite with you? On one hand this lad sounds like he's a lad of the streets and the next a fine gentleman!'

'Precisely. You see he was an orphan and had a hard life but now he lives with his uncle in a very grand house.'

'I think I understand, miss. Well, we have all sorts here: ships in bottles, tin soldiers, balls, carousels that play music, you name it we sell it!' he smiled as though he were very pleased with himself.

The musty, dusty aroma was beginning to permeate Lucy's nostrils and if she wasn't careful, she was going to sneeze. She sniffed loudly, aware of the tears in her eyes. Then blew her nose quickly into her handkerchief as the man turned his back to check what was on the shelves, as she quickly returned her handkerchief to her skirt pocket.

'To tell the truth, I'm going to have to post his present to him as I won't be seeing him over the Christmas holiday,' she said sadly.

He turned to face her. 'How about a tin soldier then? I can box it up for you, if you like?'

Lucy noticed a soldier that was set a little further away than the others and its clothing painted scarlet and black. 'What's that one over there?' She pointed to the shelf.

The man grinned. 'That's a special one, it's smaller than the others but I'm afraid as it's clockwork, it will cost a little more.'

Lucy blinked. 'Can you show it to me, please?'
The man lifted it from the shelf and wound the key
several times on the back of it, then he set it down on
the wooden counter as the girls watched in awe when
it marched right across it, and was saved from
toppling off the edge as the man caught it in time with
one hand.

'That's the one!' Lucy squealed. 'I've just got to
buy it for Archie!'

'Yes, you really have to,' Meg approved as she
clasped her hands together.

'Sold to the lady in the fur cape!' the man jested.
And she watched as he deftly packed it away in a
tissue-lined cardboard box, then wrapped it in brown
paper adorned in a crisp holly and ivy print.
Considering he had a deformity, he worked with such
dexterity as he secured the package with a piece of
string and tied it in a sharp, well-formed knot. She
was in awe, and she thought he was a good salesman
too.

'I'm Lucy Harper and this 'ere is Megan Wood,'
Lucy introduced.

'I'm so pleased to make your acquaintance, ladies.
I am Mister Elijah Rummage,' he said, taking a
theatrical bow, then he handed over the wrapped
package to Lucy.

'I'm so glad we found this shop,' she enthused as
she slipped some coins into his open palm.

'Call in any time,' Elijah said, as he walked them
to the door. 'Any time at all…'

The doorbell jangled once more as he saw them
outside and closed the door behind them.

'What a curious little man!' Meg exclaimed with wide eyes.

'Yes, he's lovely though. And that name!'

'What? Elijah?'

'No, his surname, Rummage! It seems to fit in well with his shop as customers rummage through the dusty treasures he has for sale! And, as you say, he seems curious, so that name is very apt indeed!'

They were both giggling thinking about it when they noticed Mrs Tavistock walking into a shop ahead of them.

'Where's she off to then?' Lucy looked at Meg.

'I don't know, but that shop sells paintings and framed portraits. Maybe she's Christmas shopping like us.' Meg narrowed her eyes. 'Though she's been acting kind of odd lately.'

'How'd you mean?'

'Her and old Grimes, whispering in corners together. That sort of thing.'

'Maybe there's some sort of romance going on there as isn't she widowed or something?'

'Yes, but I've never noticed any sort of attraction between them before.'

'We shall have to remain alert then!' Lucy chuckled and taking Meg's arm in the crook of her own, they set off to find a tea room.

***

As Lucy waited for Miss Meadows to arrive for her piano lesson, she stared out the French windows of the room. The skies were pewter grey with cumulus clouds. A few snowflakes began to flutter from the sky. Years ago, her aunt often told her snowflakes falling from above was God shaking out his feather quilt. Now when she thought of it, it made her smile. Bessie had some funny sayings indeed. That reminded her, she was going to have to send the presents soon along with Archie's and a couple of Christmas cards too. She'd try to visit between Christmas and the New Year if she was able to. How she missed them all. But at least having a good friend like Meg made it all so bittersweet.

Miss Meadows arrived twenty minutes late. 'I am so sorry, Lucy,' she said as she breezed into the room. My cab driver was forced to take a different route to usual as the roads are so icy. But thankfully he did, as there now appears to have been an accident on our usual road.'

'How do you know that?' Lucy raised a brow.

'A gentleman flagged us down to warn us. He was going that route himself and his cab driver had to turn around and go a different way.' She removed her bonnet and cape and placed them on the table, then went quickly to the fire place to warm her hands.

'I'll send for tea if you like?' Lucy offered. 'You look frozen to the bone.'

'Oh, I am, my teeth were stuck to my top lip when I first arrived,' she chuckled. 'Though I'd rather coffee if any is available?'

'I should think so. I'll ring for a pot now.' She lifted the bell from the mantelpiece.

'And you'll join me in a cup?'

'Yes, please,' she said with enthusiasm. She'd enjoyed that cup of coffee she'd tried the other day.

Lucy rang the bell and Mary turned up. 'Miss?' she said looking at Lucy for instruction.

'A pot of coffee for two please, and if there are any of Cook's cakes, we'd like some of those too!' She asked in a cheeky fashion, causing Miss Meadows to smile at her with approval.

'Very well, miss.' Mary bobbed a curtesy and left the room.

'How are you getting on with your piano practice, Lucy?' Miss Meadows looked into her eyes.

It was no use; she couldn't lie to someone as kind and trusting as Clara Meadows. 'I haven't practiced as much as I should have, miss.'

Clara wagged a finger in mock disapproval and then she laughed. 'All right, I'll forgive you this once as you're such a natural anyhow, but next time I give you homework, you must practice as I know how much it pleases Lady Fanshaw to hear you play.'

This was news to her. 'Really? She hasn't said anything to me.'

'Don't tell her I said so but she told me she was listening to you recently and hearing you play reminded her of Adella so much.'

Lucy took a sharp intake of breath as it felt as though her heart were about to seize up. Was she hearing things? 'Y…you mean Adella was Lady Fanshaw's daughter?'

Clara blinked for a moment. 'Why, yes! Didn't anyone tell you she used to have a daughter?'

'No. I mean, yes. I knew that she had a daughter who went missing and she drowned in the River Thames, but not that her name was Adella!'

'Why, Lucy, my dear, you look as white as a ghost. What's wrong? Come and sit down with me.' She patted the seat beside her.

They both sat together on the chaise lounge as Lucy related the whole story of her birth and the locket with the name Adella on it to Clara. Clara nodded and shook her head throughout but didn't say a thing until Lucy had finished. And at that moment, Mary entered with the tray of coffee.

'We'll discuss this further over coffee,' Clara said. 'You can forget your lesson for today.' Then turning to Mary as Lucy seemed to have lost the power of speech, she said, 'Thank you, Mary. If we need anything else, we'll ring for you.'

If Mary was expecting to eavesdrop then Clara had dealt with her very nicely indeed by dismissing her like that. There was a possibility that walls had ears and Clara had prepared for that. What a shock though to know that Lady Fanshaw might be Lucy's own grandmother! It was now beginning to make sense why the woman had helped Bessie out with her new house and bakery and why she'd taken Lucy on as her companion with a view to turning her into a lady. And then to Lucy's dismay, she found her eyes filling up with tears as Clara took her into her arms and rocked her like a baby as she sobbed her heart out.

Chapter Twenty-Two

When Lucy finally composed herself, Clara poured the coffee into the awaiting cups. By now it was only luke warm.

'Would you like me to send for a fresh pot?' Clara asked.

Lucy took a sip. 'No, it's fine as it is,' Lucy sniffed. 'Not unless you would like it a little hotter?'

Clara shook her head; her eyes held such warmth and compassion that she felt safe in her company. 'Now the question is, what are you do to with the knowledge you've gained? And can you be sure Lady Fanshaw's daughter was your mother?'

'It all fits though,' Lucy said, replacing her cup on its saucer. 'Why would someone get in touch with my auntie and offer her a property with a bake house for a knock down rent otherwise?'

Clara frowned. 'Hmmm who indeed?'

'It was Mr Knight who claimed to be an agent for Lady Fanshaw who made the approach after a letter was initially sent to my aunt. Do you know him? He's often back and forth here.'

Clara nodded in recognition. 'Ah, yes. I was introduced to him the other day and have to say he seems like quite a straightforward, honest sort to me. But you don't feel that way?'

Lucy twisted her handkerchief in her hands. 'I just feel like someone or some people have deceived me and I just don't understand why. But what I do know is this, I am now truly an orphan.'

Clara angled her head to one side in puzzlement. 'I'm sorry, I'm not with you, Lucy?'

'What I mean is, before this I always had some hope in my heart that one day I'd find my mother. My Aunt Bessie was always saying she'd help me to find her. But now I realise my mother died in the River Thames a long time ago. And what if…?'

'What if, what?'

Lucy sniffed loudly. 'W…what if giving birth to a baby and having the responsibility of looking after that young infant was enough to make her throw herself in the river and drown herself? I'll never live with myself if I find that to be the truth—that I was the cause of her death.'

'Oh, you poor girl. Then you have to speak to someone. I don't know if Lady Fanshaw will be the best person to speak to though if what you've been telling me lately about her mental state is true.'

'Then who?'

'Maybe Mr Knight himself would be a good start.'

'That might be a good idea.' Lucy brightened up a little.

'Now,' said Clara in a kindly fashion, 'when is he due here next?'

'I heard Lady Fanshaw inviting him here for Christmas Eve.'

'Then you must take your chance to ask him then,' Clara said softly. 'See if you can manage to get him on his own for a private chat. That's the best.'

Lucy nodded. 'I will, I just have to. And I have to try somehow to take a peek in that attic room, I told you about.'

No matter how hard the truth, she was going to have to know what that was, even if it broke her heart even more than it already was.

***

The following day it would be Christmas Eve and the kitchen was bustling in preparation for it. A large ham was being removed from a pan of brine ready for roasting by Sylvia, Jenny was busy icing a Christmas cake, and Cook was in the middle of rolling out some pastry to make lots of mince pies, but she was in a good mood, nevertheless.

'Come to join us, 'ave you, gal?' she asked, looking up from the well-floured counter.

'Er, no,' Lucy smiled. 'I'm looking for Meg, and wondered if she was in here with you?'

Cook laid down her rolling pin. 'Can't say I've seen her for the past hour. Last time I did, Mrs Tavistock had sent her to clean the dining room in preparation for tomorrow.'

'I'll check there then, thank you, Mrs Farley.'

Cook smiled. 'Come back later and I'll have a nice mince pie and a glass of sherry ready for both of you, if you find her that is.' She winked and then went back to her work.

There was a real feeling of festivity in the house and Lucy wished she could join in with it all, but needing to know the truth about Adella was piercing her heart. She entered the dining room and was disappointed thinking it was empty, but then she spotted Meg on her hands and knees clearing the grate. She had to smile when she saw the sooty marks on the girl's face and white pinafore where she'd obviously rubbed her fingers.

'Meg, I have something to tell you!' she exclaimed.

Lucy grinned. 'And I have something exciting to tell you too! But you first, and if you can, please can you 'elp me light this bleedin' fire, I been trying for ages. I know you are good at that sort of thing as you told me about what you did at the inn.'

Lucy nodded. 'Of course, but come here I don't want anyone to overhear us.'

Meg rose to her feet and brushed down her pinafore as if it would magically make it clean again, but of course, it did not, it made it dirtier than it already was.

She drew nearer to Lucy and adjusted her mobcap on her head. 'What did you want to tell me? 'Ere you look as if you've been crying. Who's upset you?'

'No one really, just something I found out by accident. Clara told me that Lady Fanshaw's daughter's name was Adella.'

'So? Why would it upset you?'

'Because when I was born me mother left a silver locket behind with a lock of my hair inside and there was the name Adella engraved on the back of it.'

Meg drew a breath. 'Maybe there are a few people with that name though?'

'I don't think it's that common a name or spelling in these parts. Adele, yes, even Adela, maybe, but not,' she spelled out the name for her: 'A..D…E…L…L…A.'

'But still, it all sounds unlikely to me going by your background which you said was quite poor, compared to how the lady lives.'

'Yes, I know, but it all makes sense. Why would my aunt have been approached by Mr Knight to rent that house so cheaply? Why am I working here?'

'Do you think Lady Fanshaw knows that you might be her granddaughter?'

'I've no idea, but I intend finding out. Mr Knight is due to dine here for Christmas Eve and I'll ask him outright then…' Meg's eyes widened with surprise. Lucy suddenly remembered what Meg had said to her a little earlier. 'What did you have to tell me?'

Meg dipped her hand into her pinafore pocket. 'I found this earlier!' she exclaimed proudly as opened the palm of her hand.

'What is it?'

'A key, silly!'

'I can see that, but a key to what?' Then it dawned on her. 'It's never a key to the attic, is it?'

Megan's eyes grew large. 'Yes!'

Lucy's hands flew to her face. 'Oh, my goodness! However did you manage to get it?'

'I sneaked into that little room beneath the back stairs where Grimes keeps all the keys to this house, you know the one where he often has a kip when he's not busy?' Lucy nodded. 'So, when he was fast asleep I snuck in there. He was out for the count snoring like a good 'un, you should have heard him. All the keys are hanging on labelled hooks except one, which isn't labelled, so I reckon this has got to be the one!' She dangled the key in front of Lucy's face. 'He wouldn't want anyone to know which key belongs to the attic, and he can't want anyone to know he's thieving and hiding the stuff he's pilfering from the lady there, either. '

***

'Meg, I could kiss you!' Lucy laughed, 'but first I'd better 'elp you start that fire. From what I can see, you've not used enough kindling, that's mainly coal there, not enough stick and newspaper. Take everything out of the grate and we'll begin again. Then when we've got the fire going, we're going to see Cook in the kitchen.'

Meg raised her brows. 'What for?'

'She's promised us a mince pie and a glass of sherry each!'

'Oh, lovely! We'd better crack on with it then,' Meg said as she knelt down to clear the grate.

Lucy's eyes widened. 'And then, when everyone in the house is asleep tonight, come to my room and we'll try to get into the attic.'

Meg turned, her mouth open wide. 'Oh heck, I thought you'd want to try it during daylight hours. It will be right spooky at night…'

Lucy shook her head. 'No, that's no good, we almost got caught red-handed last time. This time we do it when the enemy least suspects.'

'You mean old Grimes?' Meg giggled.

'Yes, and Mrs Tavistock, I reckon they're in this together.'

***

When they'd finally got the fire underway, the girls made their way to the kitchen where there was a lot of merriment ensuing. Cook was seated red-cheeked in the armchair near the fire place raising a glass of sherry to her lips; by the look of the crumbs around them, she'd already been into the mince pies. A wonderful aroma of roast ham filled the air, making Lucy's mouth water.

'Come in, girls!' Cook invited. 'Sylvia, fetch that plate of mince pies near the hob and pour them a glass of sherry each...'

Sylvia muttered under her breath; she was already in the process of draining something through a colander into the stone sink. Strands of hair clung to her face outside of her mobcap as if she was too hot and perspiring profusely in the steamy kitchen. No doubt she had been run ragged by Cook all day. Lucy felt a pang of empathy for the girl. 'It's all right, Mrs Farley. I'll fetch them,' she suggested.

Sylvia smiled at her and mouthed, 'Thank you,' as she finished draining the saucepan in the sink. It was probably something for the evening meal.

Lucy took the arm chair opposite Cook, while Meg sat on a footstool as they sipped their glasses of sherry with the plate of mince pies in between them. Staring into the crackling flames of the fire, Lucy could think of nothing other than what they were going to do later that night, as Cook began to doze in her chair. The woman had been up since five o'clock and was exhausted, but probably no more so than Sylvia and Jenny were and they were still on their feet. But still, Cook was a lot older than them and needed to rest more at her age.

As all was quiet for a moment, Lucy heard a faint sound in the distance. A melodious one that was sweet to the ears. 'Carol singers!' she exclaimed, placing her glass of sherry on a nearby occasional table as she ran to the window to see.

Cook stirred in her chair. 'Aye, they always come to the back door here, that's why I prepared so many mince pies. Go and open the door, Jenny.'

Jenny set down a baking tray of roast potatoes on the counter and wiped her hands on her pinafore. Then she walked over to the back door and opened it. Snow was beginning to fall and the group looked a festive sight. The men wore top hats, mufflers and long black frock coats through which Lucy noticed they sported red and gold brocade waistcoats and red silk cravats, whilst the ladies wore green velvet dresses, matching bonnets and fur capes as they held lanterns before them. Snowflakes had settled on their clothing, but they carried on singing, *The Holly and the Ivy* until the end.

Miss Meadow's favourite carol! Lucy wished she were here right now to hear it.

Then Mrs Farley stood and walking towards the door, began to clap as everyone else stopped what they were doing and joined in with a collective ripple of appreciation. It was then Lucy noticed a familiar looking face at the back of the group, he was a lot shorter than the other men so she hadn't noticed him initially. He tipped his hat and smiled at her. Elijah Rummage! She nudged Meg, who waved in excitement to see the man again.

'Wonderful. Thank you so much!' Cook greeted them. 'Come inside out of the cold. Lady Fanshaw has left money for your charitable cause and there are some warm mince pies and glasses of sherry here for you too.'

The troupe of singers smiled and appeared grateful for the generosity shown towards them. As they entered the kitchen, they brought a flurry of snowflakes with them. 'I hope yer not all walkin' home tonight?' Cook questioned.

'No, thankfully,' a young smart looking man said as he removed his top hat and placed it on the counter beside the tray of mince pies. 'We've a couple of carriages outside, but we won't stop too long as it's blowing a gale outside, and there might be snowdrifts tonight. We don't want to get stranded on Christmas Eve!'

Cook nodded. 'Very sensible indeed! Well, yer all welcome to the refreshments provided and a warm by me fire before you head off home.'

The man thanked her and joined his colleagues to partake of the festive feast Cook had arranged for them.

Lucy chatted with Elijah as he warmed himself by the fire, and Meg passed him a mince pie and a glass of sherry. It was like chatting to an old friend as he explained that the Carol singing troupe were a group of shopkeepers from the village who liked to sing for charitable causes.

Later the group sang a couple more songs inside the kitchen, finishing with *Silent Night*, which brought a tear to everyone's eye and then they were gone out into the night. But they'd brought a little of the Christmas spirit with them, which had warmed everyone's heart that cold winter night. And Lucy thought to herself that maybe Lady Fanshaw wasn't all that unhinged after all if she'd remembered to leave out an envelope of money for them for their charitable cause.

Chapter Twenty-Three

When everyone was fast asleep, Lucy and Meg crept across the landing on the third floor with a single candle between them. It was far scarier at night than during the day as their flickering shadows reflected like huge ghastly ghouls on the walls surrounding them.

'I'm frightened. I don't think this was such a good idea!' Meg wailed.

'Sssh,' Lucy scolded. 'This might be our only chance.' She fumbled for the key in her dressing gown pocket to ensure it was still there. 'Now you can stay watch at the bottom of the steps and if you hear anyone coming, warn me. Right?'

'But what about me? I'm going to be in total darkness. We only have the one candle between us.'

'I know, and it was a bit silly that I could only find this one, but it's too late now. You'll have to rely on the moonlight streaming in through the windows for you to see any approaching shadows. I won't be long.'

Meg nodded as her lips quivered. Lucy realised how frightened the girl was, so to reassure her she said as she patted her shoulder, 'I won't be long, I promise.'

Lucy turned. Each step she took up the winding stone steps made her heart lurch with fear and trepidation. She fiddled for the key in her pocket and held her breath as she inserted it into the lock. Then she tried to turn it. 'Blast! I think it's the wrong key! So annoying!' She hissed to Meg down below.

'Try it again, maybe the lock is a bit stiff.'

Lucy tried again and this time it turned a fraction and then a little more and a little more, until the door creaked open wide. What Lucy saw inside the room made her heart beat even faster than it already was.

She held up the candle, and in the barely illuminated darkness, she made out a baby's crib and a rocking chair beside it. On the chair, was a baby china doll and a large teddy bear. The hairs on the back of her neck prickled. She turned her head slightly and on the wall behind those was that painting she'd spied through the keyhole. She gulped when she saw who it was: the same young woman from the painting with the sad eyes, but this time there was no sadness as she cradled her baby to her chest.

'This room was for me...' Lucy whispered, and then she swallowed as instinctively, she realised this was the case. As she drew even closer, she set down the candle in its holder on a low wooden ledge and lifted the baby doll to her chest. It wore a bonnet and was wrapped in a similar knitted blanket that Bessie had found her wrapped in that night when she was abandoned.

This is all so strange.

Mesmerised, she wondered why such a room even existed, and then, she heard footsteps ascending the stairs. She turned to find Meg stood behind her.

'I couldn't stay down there on my own in the dark any longer, it was scary. What have you found?'

'I really don't know. It seems to be some sort of nursery and I think it was supposed to be mine.'

Both girls stood in silence for a moment as Meg stared at the sight before her, and she broke it by touching Lucy on the shoulder. 'Oh, Lucy, this seems so creepy to me. Let's lock up and get that key back where it belongs, before we're discovered. We were wrong about Grimes and Mrs Tavistock, there's no sign of any of Lady Fanshaw's stolen silver here, only this baby stuff.'

Lucy nodded. 'You're right, but whatever has been going on they are some sort of accomplices, I'm sure of it!'

'By saying that you make them sound like they're in on some sort of crime anyhow.'

'Maybe they are, and I'd like to get to the bottom of this as it seems to involve me.'

'Do you think the lady knows?'

'I've no idea, I'm afraid to say anything to her as you know what her state of mind has been like lately.'

A tear coursed Lucy's cheek as she lifted the candle and handed it Meg, then she locked the attic door, leaving the secret where it was for time being.

***

The following morning, Lucy was awoken by a fresh fall of snow slipping off the roof. She jumped out of bed and drew back the curtains to reveal a winter wonderland outside. She could no longer see the fountain or flowerbeds as now they were completely covered over. This would entirely scupper her chances of speaking to Mr Knight as surely he wouldn't be able to get here today for the Christmas Eve dinner? She didn't know how far away he lived and even if he lived nearby, he'd have to trudge through all that ice-cold snow to get to the house.

There was a tap at the door and Lucy grabbed her dressing gown to put on over her nightdress, then shouted, 'Please enter!'

Meg walked into the room carrying a tray with a silver salver on top of it. 'I've brought you some breakfast, miss!' She didn't use Lucy's name probably because Mrs Tavistock was hovering about somewhere on the landing.

Lucy frowned. 'But aren't I dining with the lady this morning as usual?'

'No, miss. That's why I've brought your breakfast to you. There's some sort of meeting going on downstairs.' She set the tray down on the escritoire and closed the door behind her. Then she spoke in barely a whisper so that Lucy had to strain to hear what was being said. 'It seems that Mr Knight arrived late last night before this heavy fall of snow and he's brought some people with him. They were all put up in bedrooms down the corridor.'

'That's most odd,' Lucy blinked. 'This is the first I've heard of any guests staying here, Meg!'

Meg shrugged her shoulders. 'I know, but then again the Lady might have invited some guests we don't know about. I've spoken to Mrs Farley but she's not giving anything away, she just tutted that she has a few more to cater for now.'

'I see. Well whoever they are, I hope they're nice. I don't much fancy being stuck here for the holiday with people who are difficult to get along with. It'll mean more work for you too, Meg.'

Meg smiled. 'I don't mind too much. Now eat up your scrambled eggs and kipper before they get cold. I've brought you a glass of warm milk as well.'

'Thank you.'

'How do you feel after what you discovered last night?'

Lucy shrugged her shoulders. 'It kept me awake for a couple of hours but after that I fell into a sound sleep where I dreamt my mother was stroking my head.' A tear ran down her cheek as she realised that was never, ever going to happen.

'Aw Lucy, I don't know what to say. I feel for you, I really do.' Meg gave her friend a big hug.

'It's all right, Meg. I'll be all right. I've never had a mother all my life so it's not going to make much of a difference right now.'

Meg nodded. 'I do know what you mean as I haven't had a mother to call me own for years, but I still remember her soft touch as she tucked me into bed at night. I'd give anything to feel that touch and smell her lovely lavender perfume just one more time.'

They were kindred spirits that was for certain. 'At least we have this evening to look forward to and all day on Christmas day!' Lucy enthused. 'Cook told me the Christmas Eve dinner is the one day of the year when all the staff at the house are allowed to join in the festivities.'

'Oh yes!' Meg tossed back her blonde curls and her eyes shone with expectation. 'It was great last year; we had such fine food and there were parlour games afterwards. Now you'd better eat your food before it gets cold.'

The truth was Lucy didn't have much of an appetite but she was going to force herself to eat it anyhow. Then if she did get the opportunity to speak to Mr Knight, she would. But maybe he wouldn't have much of a chance to speak or tell her anything for that matter. Maybe the lady she'd seen him with in the market just looked like her mother. After all, her mother had met with a horrible watery death.

After breakfast she got herself togged up in some warm undergarments beneath her dress as she and Meg went outside to play in the snow. Her hooded fur lined cape was quite cosy and she loaned her old cape to the girl as her shawl was so thin. Their mitten-covered hands pelted one another with snow balls. Then they created snow angels by lying on their backs in the fresh fall of snow and moving their arms and legs up and down. How they laughed until they could laugh no more. Their cheeks and noses red and pinched from the cold and their eyes misted up from the merriment of it all.

The afternoon was spent quietly in Lucy's bedroom, where Meg dried their clothing in front of the fire on the wire guard. She wore one of Lucy's old dresses, whilst she filled the bath with hot water for Lucy to bathe in, in readiness for the Christmas Eve dinner.

'Cor, Lucy!' Meg exclaimed, 'Yer look like a right lady in that dress!' Meg had helped Lucy pick out a red velvet dress that was nipped in at the waist and had leg o' mutton sleeves. She did feel very Christmassy in it and grown up too.

Then Meg helped Lucy to pin up her hair in an elegant fashion, secured with hairpins. 'Oh Lucy, I almost forgot. Something arrived for you earlier. I'll just go and fetch it.'

Baffled, Lucy waited patiently for the girl to return and moments later, she handed Lucy a small white wooden box, which was nicely presented with a red ribbon and piece of holly on top.

'What's this?'

'There's a note with it!' Meg said enthusiastically. 'It's just beneath the ribbon, watch you don't prickle yourself on the holly though!'

Lucy looked down to see indeed there was a small gold embossed card hidden there. She removed it carefully from beneath the red ribbon which adorned the box. It read:

Best wishes for Christmas and the New Year from your friend, Archie.

Lucy opened the box and then let out a little gasp as she saw the beautiful white Christmas rose inside. 'How lovely!' She gazed at it in awe. 'No one's ever given me a rose before!'

'That rose would look lovely in your hair,' Meg enthused as she peered over Lucy's shoulder.

'Oh, would you fix it in my hair with a comb slide, please?'

'I think I can manage that.' Meg nodded and smiled, as she removed the white rose from its box and then affixed it in Lucy's hair.

'Thank you, Meg!' Lucy's eyes shone as she gazed into the mirror, liking what she saw before her. She wondered if she looked like her mother at the same age and thought of how excited she would be at Christmas time, but what had possessed her to leave her baby behind on a park bench that particular Christmas, she just could not fathom.

'You look a picture, Lucy!' Meg beamed, satisfied with her handywork. 'That rose really sets off your hair style.'

'I've got a dress you can borrow if you're allowed, Meg?' Lucy walked towards the wardrobe and opened the door. 'It's one my auntie had made for me before I came here, I ain't had chance to wear it yet as Lady Fanshaw wants to see me in the gowns she has provided for me.'

Meg's eyes enlarged as she saw the pretty blue dress edged with lace and matching ribbon. 'Cor, thank you, Lucy!' she hugged her, and then stepping back said, 'Sorry, maids shouldn't do that sort of thing.'

'Well I don't care,' Lucy looked into Meg's eyes. 'To me, you are my friend as well as my maid.' Meg's eyes filled with tears. 'Please don't cry, Meg. Today should be a happy occasion...'

'I'm crying as I'm so happy, Lucy, and you're so kind to me.'

Lucy smiled. 'That's all right then. I'm glad they're tears of happiness, not of despair,' she said. 'You'd better go now to get ready, I'll see you downstairs shortly...'

Chapter Twenty-Four

The first thing Lucy noticed when she descended the staircase towards the entrance hall at Dunraven House was the large Christmas tree stood near the foot of the stairs. It was a beautiful pine green and the mass of colourful glass baubles shone and sparkled, reflecting the lights from its candles which were ablaze. A feeling of excitement made her stomach flip over. As she reached the bottom step, she paused to inhale the smell of beeswax and lemon, indicating the servants had been busy cleaning and polishing the place. The eaves of the various doorways were adorned with garlands of mistletoe and ivy, interwoven with holly and red berries. There was a real spirit of Christmas in the air and as she turned, she noticed a familiar figure who had his back to her, striding towards the dining room.

Mr Knight!

She hurried to catch up with him. 'Mr Knight, please stop, I need a word with you! Mr Knight!' She called after him.

He paused with his hand on the dining room door, then he turned to face her with an amused grin on his face. 'And what can I do for you, young lady? Shouldn't we both be in the dining room?'

'I'll only take a moment of your time, I promise...' she said breathlessly. Meg was walking towards them carrying a tray of pastries, looking very smart in the dress Lucy had loaned her. She paused out of respect, instead of passing them to enter the dining room.

There appeared to be a flicker of merriment in his eyes. 'Not now, Lucy. It's a most inopportune time for me to stop and speak to you, I do not wish to keep her ladyship and the rest of the guests waiting. We shall have time later to speak to one another.'

Lucy felt her heart slump. 'After you...' he said, with a flourishing gesture of his hand.

She nodded and walked into the room with Meg following up behind her.

Lady Fanshaw was already seated at the table and for once, appeared quite sober. 'What on earth is going on, Nathaniel?' She asked, glaring at Mr Knight.

'All will be revealed soon enough, Conchetta.'

Conchetta?

Lucy had never heard anyone use the woman's Christian name before and this was the first time she even knew of it. To be on such casual terms with one another, they must be pretty close, she assumed. And it was the first time she'd ever heard Mr Knight referred to as Nathaniel, too.

Lady Fanshaw sniffed loudly. 'But why are we the only ones here? And who are these special guests you've been teasing me about? Do I know any of them?'

'Of course you do.' He cocked a cheeky grin.

'All I know is, they were brought here under the cover of darkness last night and have been put up in three of my bedrooms upstairs.' She rolled her eyes at him.

'And they rested very well over night, Conchetta. You shall be meeting them shortly, and you too, Lucy.'

Lucy didn't much fancy meeting the guests at all. She'd have far preferred it if they weren't strangers to her, but then a side door opened unexpectedly and a lady with a beaming face began walking towards her. Each step the woman took made Lucy's heart thud a little faster.

Bessie! Dearest Aunt Bessie!

She looked so well that it even appeared as though she'd put on a little weight. Her cheeks were rosy and plump. Her appearance contrasted sharply with the last time Lucy had encountered her where she'd looked a shadow of her former self. Back then, she'd appeared a little gaunt and tired.

'Auntie!' she exclaimed with such happiness inside her she feared she'd burst as it bubbled over. This was the best Christmas present anyone could possibly have given her. And within seconds she was in her aunt's embrace, feeling reassured and comforted once more.

'But how? Why?' Lucy blinked.

Bessie's eyes were brimming with unshed tears. 'We were sent an invitation to spend the Christmas holiday at Dunraven House...' she explained, breathless with excitement.

Lucy angled her head to one side with curiosity. 'You said, "we"?'

'Yes, Harry and Jacob are here, too. They're out in the grounds having a snowball fight.'

'Some things never change!' Lucy chuckled. Then glancing at Lady Fanshaw, she said, 'Thank you, ma'am.'

The lady shook her head. 'Please do not thank me, I am not behind this. I am as mystified as you are, Lucy. But I am pleased at last to make your acquaintance, Mrs Harper.'

Lucy frowned. Then looked at Mr Knight. 'Then who? Who is behind this, Mr Knight?'

Mr Knight smiled, 'All shall become clear...' Then he walked towards the door where Bessie had entered the room as Lady Fanshaw rose from her chair in astonishment. All eyes were on the door as it slowly opened wide.

'Oh, my giddy aunt!' Lady Fanshaw's face paled a deadly shade of white as she slumped heavily to the floor.

'I'll get some smellin' salts!' Meg shouted, but Lucy couldn't reply as there, framed in the doorway, was Adella. Her Adella, her mother, looking a vision in a dark blue dress, trimmed in white ermine.

Lucy swallowed hard as the woman stepped towards her. There appeared to be a glowing radiance all around her just like an angel.

Am I dreaming? Or am I seeing a ghost?

'My darling daughter,' she said, stepping forward with tears in her eyes. 'Seeing you once again and having you back in my life, is the best Christmas present I could ever have hoped for...'

Somewhere behind her, in a haze of confusion, Lucy was aware of people in attendance to Lady Fanshaw and she could have sworn she heard Cook say, 'Tap her ladyship's face, Megan, to help bring her around and I'll hold the smelling salts beneath her nose.'

Lucy began to sob, huge wracking tears to be reunited with her mother after believing she had died all those years ago.

'I think you two need to talk away from here,' Nathaniel Knight advised as he led both of them in the direction of the drawing room.

Chapter Twenty-Five

Lucy and her mother were seated on the chaise lounge whilst Mr Knight remained near the door to ensure they were not disturbed, as not just Lady Fanshaw, but all the staff appeared to be in a state of disbelief.

Adella took her daughter's hand. 'I know everything has come as a shock to you, Lucy, and for Mama in particular. You see, I need to explain to you that when I was only three years older than you are right now, I did a foolish thing…'

Lucy looked deep into her mother's chocolate brown eyes and saw a sadness within, just like in the portrait hanging on the wall. Even though her eyes looked sad, now they had life behind them, which back then when it was painted, they didn't appear to have. 'Go on,' she urged, squeezing her mother's hand in reassurance.

'I became involved with a married man who was an advisor to my mother. It was exciting at first as he paid me a lot of attention, there were long walks in the grounds all with Mama's approval, as he was a trusted family friend. We even went horse riding together. But then one day, when we were both out riding there was a severe thunderstorm and my horse bolted. I was thrown from him and he ran off. I wasn't injured though and I ended up sheltering with the man in an old barn at a neighbouring property. We had to stay there for a couple of hours and all my feelings for him came to the fore. I suppose I was attracted to him as he was a sort of father figure to me, which sounds crazy now.'

'No, it doesn't at all,' Lucy reassured. 'Particularly as your father had passed away.'

Adella dabbed at her eyes with a lace edged cotton handkerchief. 'Anyhow, the inevitable happened. I wanted to see him again and again as my heart yearned for him, but he put a stop to it as he had a wife and young children. Please don't think badly of me, but his wife was expecting another baby. I broke my heart of course when I discovered that…' she bit her knuckle as she remembered the pain of it all.

'How awful for you.'

Adella nodded. 'Yes. I realised I had just been a distraction for him and what was important to me was trivial to him. I started to get on with my life, but then the sickness began. Initially, I thought I was ill, but then when it happened every morning, it was obvious I was pregnant. Mrs Tavistock had noticed something amiss and she urged me to confide in her. When she discovered what it was making me so ill, she warned me to keep it from Mama as she said I'd be banished from the house for bringing shame on the family name. She told me she knew a childless couple who would gladly take the baby from me when it was born. I'm sorry, I mean *you*. Though at that time I had no idea if I was having a boy or a girl, of course. I agreed to her plan and did everything I could to stop myself from looking pregnant. I wore dresses that made me look slimmer and even, foolishly, bound my breasts and stomach to keep them as flat as possible. Then when the pregnancy became more evident, Mrs Tavistock suggested I go away somewhere so my mother wouldn't find out. So I ended up staying at the house we owned in Court Terrace, but I tried to hide away from the neighbours. Nathaniel…Mr Knight, didn't like the idea of me being there all alone so he used to kindly call to see me and bring me provisions from time to time. He felt like the only friend I had in the whole world…' She stared into space as if she was all alone at that point before jolting herself back to reality.

'That was so wrong what Mrs Tavistock did!' Lucy could hardly believe her ears. 'It all makes sense now then why my Aunt Bessie's neighbours told her they had heard strange things at the house and thought a young woman was staying there as she was seen at the window, or else it was some sort of ghost.'

She nodded. 'Yes, that was me, I was so out of my mind at the time that I barely remember it. When it came to the time when I was due to give birth, I ended up going to stay at the couple's home whilst Mama thought all the while I was away that I was at finishing school in Scotland…' She sobbed at the memory of it, before composing herself.

'How awful for you,' Lucy rubbed her mother's shoulder and then gave her a hug. 'What happened then?'

'I could hear the couple discussing things at night when they thought I was asleep. They were plotting to flee with you and to get rid of me at the earliest opportunity so I'd never see you again. I started to become mentally unwell and I missed my mother so much but they wouldn't allow me to leave the house even to visit her whilst I was pregnant. I felt like a prisoner. Then I started to bleed in the middle of the night and you were born by the morning. As I suspected, I was sent back to Dunraven House afterwards and used to spend a lot of time in the attic making up that nursery for you. I'd sit holding one of my old childhood baby dolls, imagining it was you and hoping they'd return you to me.'

Lucy could have wept for her mother, the pain she must have gone through. 'But how did you end up with me the night you left me on the park bench?'

'Oh Lucy,' Adella's eyes filled with tears. 'I broke into the couple's house one night and stole you from the crib when you were just nine or ten months old. I ended up taking a cab to Whitechapel and I'd already informed Mr Knight of what I was about to do as he used to call to their house to check on me, but the couple had warned me not to say anything but I finally defied them. He had said he'd help me bring the baby back to Dunraven House and he'd speak to Mama with a view to keeping you when he realised how miserable I really was.'

'So, he was the gentleman that you were seen with in the chop house at Spitalfields that night when Bessie made enquiries?' She glanced at Mr Knight but he didn't make any eye contact with her, though he must have heard what they were saying.

'Yes, he gave me money to get something to eat and while he was arranging to find a cab to pick us up, I ran away fearing he wouldn't really help as it was all a trap. You see after you were born, my mind started to play tricks on me. I became suspicious of everyone, yet, Nathaniel was the only one who was looking out for me, but I didn't realise that. In my poor mental state, I ended up leaving you on that bench with the locket in the palm of your hand. But I didn't just leave you there, Lucy, honest I didn't. I hid behind a tree and saw your Aunt Bessie pick you up and I just knew that you would be safe with her. I even followed you both to the chop house and watched through the window. If I had seen anyone who I thought was bad approaching, I planned to grab hold of you before they found you. My mind was so mixed up that I felt everyone from my own world was the enemy.'

Lucy nodded with understanding. 'What happened then?'

'Nathaniel returned and found me in a terrible state. I told him what I had done and then, feeling horrified at myself, I ran all through the night until eventually I reached the river and tried to throw myself off the bridge. But someone must have been looking after me that night, as further down the river, I was picked up by a boat and taken to safety. I think if I'd been in the river for a minute or two longer, I would have died from the cold if I hadn't drowned. I've no idea what happened after that but I ended up in a mental institution. It's all a haze now to be honest with you...'

'But why did you mother then believe you had drowned?'

'Because that's what Nathaniel told her as he believed it himself. He'd searched the streets for me that night and came to that conclusion when someone told him a woman fitting my description had tried to take her own life. The person didn't know I'd been hauled to safety further down the river though.'

Lucy nodded. 'There's something I don't understand?'

'Go on?'

'Why then did Lady Fanshaw arrange to help my aunt by finding her premises to rent cheaply? And then to ask me to become a companion to her at the house if she knew nothing for all those years?'

'Ah, that's easy to explain. When Nathaniel made enquiries at the chop house that night I went missing, he found out from the waitress where your aunt lived. For many years he would secretly watch what was going on with you. My mother was in a bad way as she, as did Nathaniel, believed I was dead, so he felt he couldn't tell her about the baby to save her feelings. But a few months ago, when a local newspaper ran an article asking who the mystery woman was at the asylum, it all fitted into place. He needed to check it was me, so came to visit. He employed one of the finest teams of psychiatrists in London and they sorted my mental state out with the correct therapy and medication. You see, I'd been sedated for many years at that place—I had no idea what time of day it was, never mind where I was. Mr Knight finally plucked up courage to tell my mother about you and she kindly offered to help you and your aunt. Though she didn't know I was alive then.'

Lucy was outraged. 'But why didn't Mr Knight tell her there and then?' She glared at him but he was gazing in the other direction.

'Please don't look so annoyed, Lucy. He had his reasons. The main one being, he wanted to make sure I was well enough first before we told her. You can see what she's been like through grief, believing I had died and then she took to the bottle. It was a great shock to her to see me like that just now and when she comes around, I am going to speak with her.'

'Yes, I do understand. I hope it won't be too much for her to bear.'

At that point, Nathaniel walked towards them and he pulled out the piano stool to sit on. 'I'm sorry you've been in the dark like this, Lucy. But I feel it was for the best. Adella,' his eyes lit up when he mentioned her name, 'wanted to keep it as a Christmas surprise for you and her mother. She's aware that things won't go back to normal overnight.'

Adella nodded. 'I hope you don't hate me, Lucy?' Her mother looked at her with expectant eyes.

'I could never hate you, Mama...'

Mr Knight stood and placed his hand on Adella's shoulder and she too lifted her hand to hold his. 'Nathaniel has been my rock through all of this and I have something to tell you.'

'Yes?' Lucy blinked.

'We were married yesterday, I want you to be the first to know.' A tear slipped down Lucy's cheek. 'I hope I haven't upset you?'

'No, it's not that but I thought I saw him walking with a lady at the Christmas market one afternoon. The lady looked so much like the young lady painted on the portrait upstairs and I thought I must have imagined things, now it all makes so much sense to me.'

'Yes, that would have been me. I've been in love since he found me again,' she said softly, then she gazed up at him.

'And I've loved your mother for as long as I can remember, Lucy...' he made eye contact with her and smiled. That wonderful man who had arranged for her aunt to have that new house and business premises, and for she, herself, to move here had it planned all along.

'Thank you for everything you've done for us all,' Lucy said through glassy eyes. Then she looked at her mother. 'This past few months, I've had this to remind me of you.' She brought out the silver locket from her pocket and handed it to her mother. 'Please put it on where it rightfully belongs...'

Lucy's mother gasped in awe as she took the silver locket from the palm of her daughter's hand and they both wept tears of joy.

Epilogue
New Year's Eve 1873

They were all seated around the dining table for a special meal to see in the New Year in fine style. Mama and Nathaniel were side by side, then Bessie and the boys and Lucy herself, and head of the table was Lady Fanshaw.

The lady, although having a shock to see her daughter again, was beginning to settle down and she seemed more normal. Much to Lucy's relief, she'd given up drinking copious amounts of alcohol. It was good to see her sober and steady, and she looked so proud of Nathaniel as her son in law.

Lucy fumbled in her dress pocket. It was still there. The invitation from her friend, Archie, inviting her to a special tea at Huntingdon Hall. It would be good to see him again. It had arrived that morning and she'd shook with excitement as she'd opened it. And she still had the white Christmas rose he'd given her. She'd kept it for a week and then she'd pressed it inside the covers of a book so she could keep it forever.

'I'd like to propose a toast to us all,' said Lady Fanshaw, breaking into her thoughts. She'd kept to her word and wasn't drinking wine like the rest of them. Lucy had noticed Grimes fill her glass with lemonade and she'd winked at him to put him in his place for once. Maybe she'd suggest to her grandmother that she replace him with a new butler in the New Year as she didn't feel he had her grandmother's best interests at heart. And old Tavistock might just as well leave at the same time for her part in the deceit, but for now, she said nothing, just joined in the toast, realising this wasn't the appropriate time to voice her concerns.

Meg was stood behind Grimes with a tray of pastries especially made for the occasion. She smiled at Lucy.

They all looked at Lady Fanshaw as they raised their glasses. 'To my daughter and her new husband, might they have health, wealth and prosperity!' the lady said, 'To my granddaughter, Lucy, who gave me a reason to live again and watched out for my welfare, I wish you a wonderful year to come, young lady! And to everyone else in this room, bless us everyone! May 1874 be a good year for us all!'

Everyone took a sip from their glasses and cheered. Lucy glanced across the table at her mother who still wore the silver locket around her neck as she smiled back at her. The clock began to chime the midnight hour, heralding the start of a new year which would provide her with the chance to get to know the woman who had given birth to her and left her with that precious locket one winter night in Whitechapel, so many years ago.

The Rags to Riches Series

1.The Ragged Urchin

2.The Christmas Locket

3.The Lily and the Flame

Coming soon: The Lily and the Flame

Archie and Lucy carry on their blossoming friendship into their adult years and they eventually fall in love, but something happens to challenge their relationship, threatening their future together. Will the pair be able to get back on course or will love's labour be lost forever?

Other books by Lynette Rees

[The Seasons of Change Series]

Black Diamonds

White Roses

Blue Skies

Red Poppies

[Books published by Quercus]

The Workhouse Waif

The Matchgirl

A Daughter's Promise

The Cobbler's Wife

Manufactured by Amazon.ca
Bolton, ON